"Jane, stop. Just tell me what's going on in your heart. I need to know. I'm not asking for anything else."

Jane's eyelids slid shut. She could not look at Alex. Another second, and she would absolutely melt into that raw vulnerability of Alex's. Her defenses were nearly shattered. She would not do that, she told herself. There was not another soul on this earth with whom she shared absolutely every facet of her life, her thoughts, her feelings. And she was not about to completely open herself up now. Especially not in the middle of a campaign. She had to stay strong, focused. "No," she said.

"I can't do this alone, Jane."

"Do what, Alex?"

"This."

Jane suddenly felt soft lips pressing lightly against hers. She flinched in surprise. Her eyes flew open. *My God, she's kissing me!* Indisputably, irrevocably, Alex was slowly but soundly kissing her into heavenly oblivion. Jane's eyelids fluttered closed again. She hardly knew if she was even breathing anymore. Alex's lips were so soft, so agonizingly tender against her own, that Jane felt herself gasp in surprise and delight. It felt so damned good, so perfect. The kiss persisted and deepened in sweet exploration. It was like nothing she'd ever experienced before, and Jane found herself happily surrendering to it. Fire swept through her veins, the warmth lodging deep in her belly as Alex's tongue parted her lips. *My God, Alex, I am physically powerless against you.*

Visit

Bella Books

at

BellaBooks.com

or call our toll-free number

1-800-729-4992

The
CANDIDATE

Tracey Richardson

Bella
BOOKS
2008

Bella Books, Inc.
P.O. Box 10543
Tallahassee, FL 32302

Printed in the United States of America on acid-free paper
First Edition

Editor: Cindy Cresap
Cover designer: LA Callaghan

ISBN-10: 1-59493-133-X
ISBN-13: 978-1-59493-133-8

To Sandra

Acknowledgments

As always, my first thanks goes to my wife, Sandra, who gives me endless love and support, without which I would not have the time, energy or imagination to do what I do. I thank my friends Brenda and Stacey for reading my work and making helpful suggestions. My other friends also deserve my appreciation for their support and inspiration, and for bringing joy to my life. My editor, Cindy Cresap, pushed me further than I thought possible. Her suggestions were a tremendous help, and I am deeply grateful. Thank you, Bella, for giving me this wonderful opportunity, and for Becky and Linda for believing in me.

About the Author

Tracey sometimes finds inspiration with a glass of wine and a fine cigar on her back deck, just a stone's throw from Ontario's Georgian Bay. When not writing fiction, she works as an editor at a daily newspaper.

She and her partner of 17 years, Sandra, were legally married in Toronto, Ontario, in October, 2003. Besides writing, in her spare time Tracey enjoys the great Canadian pastime of playing hockey (with a wonderful group of women!), skiing, golfing, playing tennis and spending time with the couple's chocolate Labrador retriever and golden retriever.

Chapter 1

"Are you scared, Al?"

"Outta my wits."

"Good." Kim Stewart laughed and amiably slapped her long-time friend on the back. "That means you'll do great."

Alex Warner cradled the frosty mug of beer in her large, sweaty hands. She could never show fear like this to anyone but her former colleague and best friend. "I wish I could be as confident as you, Kim. This isn't exactly routine traffic detail on the I-75. Or guarding little old ladies while they get their hair done."

Kim drained the last of her beer, momentarily distracted by the latest boarding announcement on the airport intercom. "Hey, I've seen you up against it. You've got more confidence than anyone I've ever seen, Alex."

Alex wasn't so sure. She'd felt these same seeds of doubt many times during her career as a state trooper and in her first protection detail. But this. This assignment was different. This was the big time. There would be a hell of a lot riding on her abilities, on that so-called confidence Kim seemed to think she had an abundance of. "I'll let you in on something, Kimmy. That confidence thing is just a healthy dose of fear and some shit-ass luck."

Kim laughed. "Nice try, my friend. It's just good ol' fashioned guts. Like the time you ran into that burning house and carried those two kids out." Her eyes shone with the memory. "I was there, remember? I was the one shitting myself, trying to decide what to do while we waited for backup. But not you. You just took off and went in there without thinking."

Alex stared blankly into her beer. "I always reckoned you were the better cop, Kim. The way you talked to people, the way you went by the book, the way you always kept your cool."

"Yeah, but you're special, Alex." She tipped her empty glass in salute. "Following all the rules doesn't work for people like you. It's all guts and instinct. It's who you are." Kim frowned a little. "It's why you're doing what you're doing and I'm still . . . doing what I'm doing."

Alex shrugged lightly, queasiness still in her gut. "I feel like I'm about to dive into the deep end of a pool without knowing how to swim. Jesus. Can you believe it? Putting a presidential candidate's life into *my* hands!"

"Honey, Jane Kincaid is damned lucky to be getting you."

Alex knew Kim meant it because there was real pride when she looked at Alex.

"Listen, that's my plane." Kim hopped off the bar stool, slinging a carry bag over her shoulder. "I'm sure the Kincaid campaign will be stopping in Detroit. When it does, come see us, okay?"

"Of course I will," Alex said, and the two women hugged for a long moment. "Thanks for the visit. And the pep talk."

"Hey. Just returning the favor."

"Give my love to Linny."

"Speaking of my dear love, she insisted I ask you to get Jane Kincaid's autograph for her." Kim gave a sly wink. "I think she has a crush on the good Senator from Michigan."

"A crush is one thing. But an autograph?" Alex made a face. "Remind Linny the woman's just a politician, not God." She didn't really get the whole celebrity adoration thing. These people were real to Alex. Special, for sure, but real, with all their quirks and faults and bad days, just like everyone else.

Kim laughed. "*You* can tell her that next time you see her. And listen, Al, please be careful, okay? I don't want to see you on CNN."

Jane Kincaid studied the color photograph in her hands.

She was immediately struck by how handsome the woman was, though it was in an austere way: Short, blond hair with sunny highlights, wide-set green eyes, serious and resolute with just the hint of a question in them, good bone structure, straight nose. Firm but expressionless mouth, nice jawline. A strong face. Capable and intelligent looking, but no trace of joy, no smile. And that caused Jane concern.

Nothing in the six-page dossier on Alexandria Warner—or Alex, as she apparently preferred—indicated a sense of humor existed in this Secret Service agent. And if, *if*, she were going to be assigned to Jane's security detail, a sense of humor was vital. Jane didn't want a bunch of grim-looking creatures in dark glasses and starched suits shadowing her as she campaigned her way across America. A bit of fun now and again was as necessary as breathing. She thought she'd made that abundantly clear to Commanding Agent Harry Johnson.

Jane dropped the eight-by-ten on her desk just as her secretary buzzed to tell her the Secret Service commander was waiting for her in her outer office. She frowned. She'd obviously need to remind him again. No Terminator types.

"You ready to meet your newest bodyguard, Dr. Kincaid?"

Commander Johnson was grinning like a Cheshire cat. Jane's reply was a groan of annoyance.

They left her cramped office, striding side-by-side down the wide, carpeted hallway of the Dirksen Senate Office Building.

"Harry, is this really necessary?"

"For the hundredth time, yes. You have no choice, Dr. Kincaid." His tone was reserved, but Jane knew he was enjoying every second of it. She always protested any extra protection, and he always needled her about it, knowing and perversely enjoying that it was beyond her control. Their cat-and-mouse game had escalated over the last two weeks, ever since he'd told her the Secret Service was adding another personal bodyguard to her detail—this time a female who would be her shadow on the campaign trail.

To Jane, this ever-increasing army around her was making her job a lot harder. Since her campaign had begun to pick up steam after the New Hampshire, Wisconsin and Illinois primaries, and as the voters and the media began to take her more seriously, so had the Secret Service. Every month it seemed like they were adding another bodyguard to her detail, and every new agent felt like another brick in the wall that kept her from her public. The bigger the army around her, the harder it was for her to show the voters who she was, and just as importantly, for her to get to know the voters. The fact that the newest addition was going to be in her pocket all the time just down right pissed her off because it would make her that much more removed from the people.

As usual, Jane skipped the elevator and headed for the stairs. "Harry, there have been no threats, or at least none you've told me about. So why do I suddenly need someone permanently affixed to my hip, for God's sake? There's enough of you people as it is making my life difficult." She still held out faint hope that she could talk him out of this if she just complained loudly and long enough.

Harry Johnson sighed in exasperation. They'd fought many rounds over this and much to Jane's satisfaction, he still got sucked into it. "We're not trying to make it difficult for you. We're trying to keep your ass safe, remember?" Jane scurried down the marble steps, the older agent a step behind and still trying his best to reassure her. "It won't change anything, Dr. Kincaid. We're just ratcheting up the security as the national convention gets closer. It's policy. You know that. And besides, if you weren't so damned popular, maybe you'd just be stuck with little old me instead of all this extra attention."

Jane finally chuckled, if grudgingly. "Don't worry. After next week's speech to the Southern Christian Fellowship, I may not need any of you!"

Jane halted before they reached the basement cafeteria. She grabbed the commander's forearm. "Please tell me this Alex Warner has a sense of humor. That she's cool, you know? Because I hate those Arnold types."

Harry Johnson fixed Jane with a well-practiced glare. "Don't you give my agent a hard time in here. This is just a little meet-and-greet over coffee before she starts her duties tomorrow. It's not an interrogation or a job interview."

"I thought this was to see if I approved her?" Jane gave her own version of a glare. She knew without doubt that there was no getting around adding another agent to her detail, but she figured the commander would at least give her veto rights if she didn't like the character. Kind of like picking out a pair of shoes off the rack; if she didn't like one pair, there were hundreds more to choose from.

Harry was shaking his head, exasperation sagging his shoulders as he seemingly read her mind. "You've got to trust me on this, Dr. Kincaid. Alex Warner is a good young agent and she's going to get even better. She'll be a nice addition to your detail."

They were moving quickly through the cafeteria, Jane casting off her annoyance as effortlessly as if she were removing a hat. She slid seamlessly into her public persona—her smile cheerful and automatic. Her public face had become as instinctive as breathing or walking.

Agent Alex Warner stood as they approached the table. She was as tall as Jane, which was considerable at just under six feet. But where Jane was slender and lithe, Alex was muscular, with the poise and carriage of an athlete. They shook hands, each woman's grip firm. Those river green eyes, flecks of gold in them, gave away nothing in their cool appraisal.

Smile, dammit, thought Jane. *It won't kill you, honest.* But all she got from Alex Warner was a closed-lip, near-wince.

They sat down. Harry Johnson ordered coffee all around, and each woman waited for the other to speak first.

Jane looked intently and unblinkingly at Alex Warner, finally ending the stalemate with a cool observation. "You've never covered a presidential candidate before."

Alex's chin rose slightly in a sign of quiet defiance. "You're my first, ma'am."

"Well." Jane nodded slowly, a little detached, then softened. She smiled and meant it. She would not truly give Alex a hard time. *At least not today.* She leaned in close and hesitated for just a moment. "That makes us even. I've never been a presidential candidate before. Think we can figure this thing out together?"

Ah, finally, a smile! Jane inwardly marveled at the flash of raw openness and innocence and trust in that spontaneous smile. It was a beautiful smile, angelic almost, and totally incongruous to Alex's veiled demeanor. It was gone too quickly.

Alex looked, almost shy, as she said, "Looks like you've mastered your part, ma'am. I'll try to do the same."

Jane felt herself involuntarily yielding to the southern charm, the smooth drawl, the honeyed wholesomeness, even though she knew it was probably a well-polished tactic of Alex's. It was like melting sweetness, and she felt a little tingly, probably like every other woman who'd been subjected to it, she mused. She smiled in appreciation. Obviously, she wasn't the only one who knew how to charm people into capitulation.

"Flattery," Jane responded genially, "won't necessarily make me do what you want. Though it certainly can't hurt."

"Alex, you'll have your hands full with Dr. Kincaid." The commander was grinning, clearly enjoying the little game.

Alex shrugged, nonplussed, looking squarely at Jane. "I like a challenge."

Jane liked Alex Warner's cool confidence, her courage. Perhaps she had initially underestimated her.

"By the way, ma'am," Alex said as the coffee arrived. "Do you prefer to be called Dr. Kincaid, or Senator, or—"

"Please. Just Jane." Jane stirred her coffee with automatic precision. "I think Harry has a thing for doctors." She winked across the table at the suddenly blushing agent. "That's the only reason I figure he calls me doctor all the time. I mean, I haven't practiced medicine in a decade." She waggled a finger teasingly at Harry. "Harry, you're way out of date. You really must ask your boss for a new dossier on me one of these days . . . one that skips ahead to the part where I'm a member of the Senate and a candidate for the presidency."

Harry gave her a lopsided smile. "Jeez. You people with fourteen titles and degrees. How am I supposed to know which one to call you?"

Jane felt herself grow wistful as she thought of her ultimate goal. She never really lost sight of it, but there were moments, like this, when thoughts of the presidency absolutely awed and overwhelmed her. "Hopefully in a few months, Harry, you'll only have to remember one title."

Harry noisily cleared his throat, looking less like a Secret Service agent and more like a friend. He looked like he could almost cry. "It would be my honor to call you Madam President."

Jane smiled and touched his arm briefly. "Thank you, Harry." Then with a sigh that signaled there was no more time for daydreaming, Jane wrested her attention back to Alex, leaned in and laid her hand gently on Alex's sleeve. Her gesture was meant to drive home the seriousness of her message. "I don't mean to be a pain, Alex. But you need to know that I have to be accessible to the public. It's imperative that I have some space." Jane ignored the stony glare she felt from Harry. "I won't get elected to dog catcher if I can't get close to people—talk to them, touch them, listen to them. I need to feel their energy and I don't want to hide behind a bunch of suits with sunglasses and guns." She would do little negotiating on this point, and the sooner Alex understood that, the better. "You understand."

Alex nodded slowly, patiently. She was intrinsically polite. And unflappable. "I do understand, ma'am. But my job from here on is to cover you like a flea on a dog. So any space you need will have to be planned well in advance."

Jane silently chuckled at Alex's pronunciation of "dawg" and the amusing analogy, though she remained resolute. "Well, Agent Warner, we both have our jobs to do. I will try not to shake off my fleas, but you must indulge me the occasional itch, if we're to get along."

Alex nodded—barely. Her mouth was a hard line.

Well, well. Cool and confident was one thing, but this woman was bordering on imperious. Alex Warner would not be an easy one. *Damn.* She should have known Harry wouldn't throw some quaking rookie at her, someone who couldn't stand up to her. For her own safety and well-being, she knew the commander was right to put someone like Alex on her detail. But it was another obstacle, another person in authority to tell her no, to say things couldn't be done the way she wanted. It would make campaigning that much more difficult.

"Alex." Jane had a habit of switching subjects and salutations quickly. "It's still a long campaign ahead. The national

Democratic convention is still a few months away, and after that, well, who knows."

Alex nodded. "I understand this isn't a short-term assignment."

"It's a lot of traveling, Alex. Away from home, away from friends. Do you have a girlfriend?"

Alex fidgeted just enough to expose a sudden and unexpected chink in her cool composure. She flashed a hot, incredulous glare at Harry Johnson. "*That* was in my dossier?"

Jane held up a placating hand. "No, no, of course not. I didn't mean to alarm you, Alex. I do my homework, that's all."

And she had. She knew Alex Warner was thirty-six years old, a North Carolinian who'd graduated from the University of Minnesota, a Michigan state trooper for eight years before joining the United States Secret Service four years ago. She'd already served a year protecting dear, old Betty Ford. She had exemplary academic and work records. A state commendation, and she was an athlete of some repute. Jane couldn't help but be impressed. There was certainly nothing on paper to give her pause about having Alex on her detail.

Alex looked unapologetic and Jane immediately thought, *good for you, Alex*. "Is it a problem?"

Jane smiled reassuringly. "That you're gay?" She dismissed the idea with a quick wave of her hand. "Please. But if you're in a serious relationship . . ." Jane didn't want to make it sound like protecting her was a jail sentence. But she understood it was a sacrifice for her staff and the agents, and she had to be sure Alex understood that there would not be a lot of down time. "Let's just say the campaign trail isn't exactly ideal for relationships."

"Don't worry, I'm not," Alex snapped, a little too abruptly. "In a serious relationship, I mean. Or any . . . I mean, not . . ." Her face was slowly flushing, her knuckles white from clutching her coffee cup like a lifeline. There was a look of mortification on her face, and it struck Jane as extremely charming. Even touching. They could have shared a good laugh over it if only they knew each other better.

But Alex was clearly embarrassed and it was Jane's fault, after all. She didn't enjoy making people uncomfortable. Well, unless they deserved it. Like most of her fellow senators on the health and education committee who kept trying to water down her proposals.

She touched Alex's arm by way of apology. "Sorry. I didn't mean to throw you a curve ball." Her smile was conciliatory. "I can see you're at a bit of a disadvantage here. So, to even things up, I can tell you that I'm not involved with anyone either. And if I was, I'm afraid it would be with a man, since that's the only team I've ever played for." She shot a mischievous wink at Alex, then looked questioningly across the table at Harry. "Harry, have you ever batted for the other team?"

Harry Johnson choked on his coffee while the two women laughed in an easy alliance.

Jane glanced at her watch, silently berating herself for being so obvious about it. She didn't like people to think they were on the clock, even though they always were these days. A schedule that had to run like a Swiss watch was one of the more unpleasant realities of her situation. "You know what, Alex? I think we're going to get to know each other really well. But all in good time, okay? But right now there is one thing we need to clear up right away."

"Yes?"

"You've really got to stop calling me ma'am. You're not still covering Betty Ford, you know." She gave a little laugh. "Don't get me wrong. I love Betty. She's a sweet, old woman. But that's just it. She's *old* and I'm, well . . . not."

Alex smiled widely, small dimples forming at the corners of her mouth. "I'll remember that. I mean, about not calling you ma'am."

Jane wanted to laugh but didn't. "Well, you'll be one up on Harry. It's been three months since he's been on my detail, and

I'm still trying to get him to call me Jane."

"I told you," Harry said. "My dog's name is Jane. It just doesn't feel right."

Jane still couldn't figure out if the commander was joshing her about his dog. "What's all this talk about dogs today, anyway? Is it some kind of Secret Service code?"

"You started it when you said you couldn't get elected to dog catcher," Harry reminded her.

Jane sighed loudly in mock irritation, secretly enjoying the banter. "You're right, I did. But you." She looked at Alex. "If you're going to have a tight leash on me, I'll only answer to Jane. Just like Agent Johnson's loyal, old dog."

Alex's smile came easily now.

Satisfied and feeling a little cocky, Jane stood up to take her leave. She couldn't resist another barb and leaned close to Alex. "If I'm the dog and you're a flea, as you put it, may I remind you that fleas are almost invisible to the naked eye?"

Alex was looking smug. "Not if you know where to look."

They shook hands in silent understanding, and Jane watched Alex depart in sure strides.

She winked at Harry. "She's good, you son of a bitch." More than that, Jane liked her.

The commander smiled.

Alex liked her all right. She had been prepared not to, or at least not so quickly. She'd expected Jane Kincaid to barely give her the time of day—to be self-absorbed, preoccupied, dismissive. After all, Alex was a stranger and another agent she clearly didn't want. But Jane's warmth and easy inclusion had surprised Alex.

Professional objectivity aside, Alex now understood why this candidate for the Democratic presidential nomination, virtually unheard of a couple of years ago, was steamrolling the nation with her charm, sharp wit, and no-nonsense social liberalism.

Alex could see that the woman was incisive, stubborn, demand-ing, even shrewd. Probably ruthless when she wanted to be. She had a commanding presence, and yet there was clearly a very human side to her—an easy intimacy and a spirited vitality.

She wiped the sweat from her face again and took a swig of beer, still half-dressed in her hockey gear. She might not get to play again for a few months and she didn't want to leave the game behind just yet.

"You haven't stopped smiling all night, Warns," bellowed one of Alex's teammates from across the locker room. "And don't tell me it's the hockey."

"I'd have a shit-eating grin too, if I were her." Donna was the relentless teaser on the team, the one with the laser tongue. "Hey, Alex. Is Jane Kincaid as hot in person?"

Alex took another drink, wiping her mouth with the back of her sweaty hand. It was a pleasure recalling the shoulder-length, wavy brown hair, the piercing dark eyes, high, wide cheekbones and sensual mouth, the strong jawline. Not a delicate, dark beauty like a Jackie Kennedy. No. Much stronger and pluckier than that. Jane Kincaid was beautiful, to be sure. Stunning, actu-ally. But it was that strong personality that could almost make you forget the package it was in. Almost. Alex certainly didn't want to disappoint her eager audience.

She winked at Donna and blushed a little for good measure. "Hotter."

That drew a roar from the women, even the straight ones.

"Better be careful, Alex. The hotter they are, the more they scorch." It was Sue, the mother figure on the team.

"Don't worry. There won't be any of *that*. It'll be all business, believe me. Besides, she's straight anyway."

"That's never stopped you before." It was Donna again. She was just warming up, Alex could tell.

Alex shook her head. "The only 'covering' I'll be doing, girls, will be from about six feet away."

"Yeah, until she calls you to her room one night to help her unzip her slinky dress." Donna laughed, the pitch of her voice rising. "'Oh please, Agent Warner, this zipper's trying to attack me. You must rescue me from it.'"

Alex laughed along with the rest of them, stood and began to unhitch her hockey pants. She tossed a full water bottle at the unsuspecting Donna, clipping her nicely on the shoulder.

It was Alex's last night of real freedom for a few months, other than the occasional days off when Jane Kincaid was back in Washington. On the road, which would be often, Alex would easily be working twelve-hour shifts, seven days a week. Her stamina would be taxed, both mentally and physically. Not many agents could hack the strain of a campaign, she'd been told. She knew it would be like night and day compared to the year she'd had protecting Betty Ford. That had been a piece of cake. But this . . . Alex cast off the doubts she'd shared just days ago with her friend Kim. Kim was right. She *was* up to the job. Her training was superb. She'd talked at length with agents who had covered other candidates and with those already on Jane's detail. She'd read everything she could about the forty-three-year-old, second-term Senator from Michigan.

Jane Kincaid, by all accounts, was an intense candidate with boundless energy. She liked crowds, liked to meet people, was an excellent speaker, was quick on her feet, and she drove herself even harder than those around her. It was the spontaneous interactions, which Jane apparently thrived on, that would undoubtedly drive Alex and the other agents nuts.

Alex stretched languidly, twirling the cotton sheet between her toes. An evening of hockey, a couple of beers . . . all to keep her mind off what lay ahead, starting tomorrow. Well, there was one last distraction.

She rolled over to the young woman beside her.

13

Chapter 2

An unmistakable pall had settled over Jane Kincaid's campaign following the dismal results of the Florida primary two days before. Alex surmised that Team Kincaid had expected much better results than a third-place finish for their candidate, who, after a handful of primaries, was still overall a close second to the Democratic frontrunner, Dennis Collins. But she was losing steam, and Jane Kincaid desperately needed to pull out a primary win in Pennsylvania to get some momentum going into Super Tuesday, when more than a dozen states would choose their candidate. Alex was a political novice, but she knew Jane had to firmly establish that it was still very much a two-horse race.

Alex, sitting a couple of rows back in the chartered plane, heard the quiet desperation in the voices of Jane and her closest staffers. The foursome had their heads together in facing seats, hunched over thick pads of yellow legal paper. They looked tense as hell and sounded it, too.

Alex could hear Jane arguing to return to her liberal perch, to sound the battle cry to fight poverty, stanch the bloodletting in health care and education, increase foreign aid to the world's poorest countries and strengthen environmental legislation—all issues that formed the meat of her campaign platform.

"This is killing us," Jane said wearily. "I can't keep pretending to be some moderate—a bloody fence-sitter who's trying to pander to both sides. Hell, that's Collins's job." She pulled a copy of the *New York Times* from her briefcase and pointed to a headline that screamed: "Will the real Jane Kincaid please stand up?" The subhead read: "Would daddy be ashamed?" Alex had already seen the paper and knew what the article said. It had not been kind to Jane.

Jane threw the paper down in disgust. "We're not going to fool anyone by pretending to be moderate. America knows perfectly well where I stand on things. My father was probably the most socialist governor this country ever saw. And they're right—he would be ashamed." She angrily flicked away a stray lock of hair.

"But your father was governor of Michigan almost forty years ago," said Steph Cameron, Jane's old college friend and a trusted advisor. "Roles were so much more defined back then. Today it's all shades of gray. Democrats can no longer ignore the right-wing agenda. Not if they want to go anywhere."

"She's right, Jane." It was the baritone voice of Jack Wilson, Jane's campaign manager and chief of staff. Alex's research told her he'd been a trusted aide to her father, a close family friend for decades and almost a surrogate father to Jane in more recent years. "The candidates all just want to blend in," he continued. "They don't dare want to offend anyone by coming out too strongly for or against anything. It's ridiculous, but what's even more ridiculous is that it's become necessary."

"I know, Jack. But I don't want to be like that. I want to stand out, with all my faults and all my loud-mouthed, unpopular beliefs. That's how I started this campaign before I tried playing it safe. And if I lose because of it . . ." Jane's voice trailed off as she gazed out the tiny window. "Well, let's just say it's not worth winning if I lose myself in the process," she said quietly.

Jack was nodding his agreement, but Steph was looking far more cautious.

"Carter?" Jane prodded.

Will Carter, a young Harvard graduate with a photographic memory and mathematical mind who served as Jane's press secretary, pollster, spin doctor and general gopher, looked up from his yellow legal pad. "Well, support *is* dropping, and rather quickly. Yesterday's media darling is quickly becoming just plain yesterday. Columnists in the major newspapers aren't taking us as seriously anymore. We're losing ground in polls—"

"All right," Jane snapped. "Like I said, we already have one fence-sitter in this campaign. It's a little redundant for me to do the same, don't you think?"

There were audible sighs, then silence. Jack Wilson finally spoke up. "If we're losing ground, and we are, then there's nothing to lose but more ground. We've got to turn it around. There's no question about that."

Alex watched Jane gnaw on a pencil, consumed by her thoughts, then stare out the tiny airplane window again. She was smiling when she finally turned her attention back to her staff, her hand curled into a fist by her side. "People are either going to love me or hate me, but at least they'll feel *something* for me. Let's give them that, shall we?"

Steph was smiling in agreement. "That's more like it, Jane." She reached across and lightly tapped Jane's knee. "We've got a lot of work to do before we hit the trail again."

"That's true, but in the meantime, I think a little celebration is in order." Jane winked indulgently at her associates. Alex could hear good-natured groaning. She knew they would do anything for Jane, and any protests were just superficial.

The plane taxied to the terminal. They were in Washington, where they would stay for a few days, and that meant a much-needed breather for Alex. Secret Service agents from the Washington bureau would be waiting inside, ready to take the reins. Her first couple of weeks on Jane Kincaid's detail had been educational, challenging, even thrilling at times. But mostly they had been just bone-weary exhausting, and Alex planned on catching up on her sleep and spending some quiet time to herself.

Thinking longingly of the bed and the drink that awaited her, Alex was one of the last to exit the plane. She was surprised to find Will Carter waiting for her just inside the terminal. He was tall and striking—skin the color of latte, slicked jet black hair, eyes like black olives. He and Alex had exchanged little more than pleasantries over the last couple of weeks, their acquaintanceship veneer thin so far.

Will Carter's smile was bashful and in direct contrast to his bold, good looks. "Alex. I have a special invitation for you."

Alex was immediately suspicious but silently waited him out.

"Dancing and drinks tonight, at Glitters. Your presence would be most desirable."

Alex picked up the pace toward the baggage claim area, Will falling into perfect step beside her. *Oh, Lord, I hope he's not fixin' to ask me out on a date.* She sighed to herself, annoyed. It didn't happen very often, but occasionally some clueless guy would ask her out in tremendously awkward fashion, and after a few tactful but unheeded hints, she would be forced to be blunt and even rude.

"Will, I'm real sorry, but it's been a long first couple of weeks on the job. I'm really just looking forward to a few days to myself."

"I understand, Alex," he said cheerily in his well-heeled eastern seaboard accent. "But I really think you should come."

Jesus. This guy isn't taking no for an answer. She halted to face him and made no attempt to disguise her irritation. "Look, Will, I can't go out with you tonight or any other time."

He looked startled. "But, I—"

"Look, I'm gay, all right?" she said impatiently. "I only go out with women."

Will suddenly collapsed into peals of laughter, which instantly and thoroughly pissed Alex off. She felt her face flushing. "What's so damned funny?"

The young aide struggled and failed to smother a new round of laughter. His voice, still strangled with laughter, squealed in astonishment. "You thought I was asking you out?"

"Well, duh, what else am I supposed to think?" Alex felt the heat of anger.

His mirth having finally settled into a friendly smile, Will said, "Oh, Alex. I'm gay too. Didn't you know that?"

The astonishment was all Alex's now. And feeling as though she'd been a complete fool. *Shit!* She slowly smiled and punched Will in the arm. "How the hell am I supposed to know you're a card-carrying queer?"

He winked. "Where's your gaydar, woman? Out for repairs?"

"Jesus. This campaigning is so unreal. I've been so focused on the job, I don't even know who I am anymore. Or who anyone else is."

"No, never forget you're gay, Alex," he lightly admonished, then took her elbow and guided them toward the baggage claim area. "You'll get used to this crazy pace, I promise. And listen, about tonight. I was going for the whole understated thing, but your presence at Glitters is kind of a command performance. Jane's rented the place for a private party."

Alex frowned. "So that's how it is? I'm being ordered to go dancing."

Will shrugged. "Well, that's a bit strong. Let's just say you're being urged to go."

"By Jane?"

"Of course. Who else?"

Alex stopped at the first carousel. "Look, I'm off duty now." She knew she sounded like a whiney kid, but she didn't care. She was tired and just wanted to go home.

"I know, and so does Jane, but she wants all of us to party with her tonight. Staff, volunteers, supporters, some of the agents."

"But I'm not one of you all." She knew she wasn't sounding particularly persuasive.

"Meaning you don't take orders from her, right?"

Alex kept her eyes on the luggage being spit out on the carousel. "Well, no, not for something like this, on my own time and all. I'm a public servant just doing my job. And right now I'm off the clock."

Will sighed heavily, as though Alex were being ridiculously difficult. "She won't be happy with that kind of talk."

"Sorry." Alex's apology rang hollow, but at this point, she didn't really care.

"Your funeral," Will quipped in pissed-off queen fashion. He waved good-bye and melted into the crowd.

Alex pulled her bags off the carousel and made her way up the escalator to the front doors of the terminal. She spotted an empty cab in the distance, waiting in a smoggy queue behind assorted limos, vans and buses and waved at it. *Just a few more minutes of this, and then I'll be home with a cold beer in my hands.*

A hand lightly touched her shoulder. She spun around, stunned to find Jane Kincaid standing behind her. In the airport chaos, Jane looked perfectly at ease. Totally composed. Exceptionally beautiful. Alex felt her pulse automatically quicken.

"I understand you're not in the mood for a little dancing tonight, Agent Warner?"

Alex was still shocked by Jane's surprise appearance. Why

would Jane care one way or the other whether she went to this private party? Did she really hate rejection that badly? Alex still didn't know her well, despite Jane's earlier promise that they would have time to get to know each other. Now she considered the possibility that Jane was some kind of ego-maniac or control freak, unwilling to accept no for an answer. *Well, I'm not her puppet . . . her slave!*

Alex swallowed her haughtiness, too polite and too professional to say what she felt. "That's right, ma'am—Jane."

"Big plans?" Jane smiled, her tone light, but her eyes were like gunsights on Alex.

Alex tried hard not to squirm, then summoned confidence she wasn't sure she really felt. It didn't feel particularly easy saying no to Jane in the first personal conversation they'd had since Alex joined the detail. "I thought I'd take it easy tonight and hit the gym early tomorrow."

"All work and no play make Alex a dull agent." Jane leaned closer until Alex could smell her subtle and very pleasant perfume. Her look had turned convivial and her voice was low and intimate, sending a small and surprising shiver through Alex. "You should come. I'd really like it if you did, Alex."

Beads of sweat had begun rolling down Alex's sides. She felt ridiculously helpless under Jane's very direct attention, unsure whether she was nervous because of Jane's position and stature, or simply because this very attractive and intelligent woman was asking *her* to go dancing. Thinking—hoping—it was the latter, Alex was nearly ready to trip over herself to accept the invitation before she mentally regained her balance. She felt the lure of mischief and couldn't help but give in to it a little. "So I'm dull, is that what you're saying?"

Jane paused, giving Alex the once-over. "Yes." Then she let loose one of her blinding, scorching smiles that could melt a glacier. "But we have a remedy for that. And the cure is very quick and painless."

"Ah, so now you're talking to me as a doctor."

"Of course. I'm prescribing some dancing, a few drinks. Glitters, tonight, at nine. And tomorrow, you will wake up feeling much better, I promise."

"And if I don't, can I sue for malpractice?"

Jane threw her head back and laughed. "Now, *that* is so not funny!"

Alex had never been to Glitters before, not surprising since only the wealthy, beautiful and connected people could gain entry into one of Washington, D.C.'s hippest nightclubs.

The place was packed, all with screened and invited guests that mercifully did not include the press. Alex quickly spotted the long table in a dark corner that belonged to Jane and her group. She took an empty chair beside Will Carter, at the extreme opposite end of where Jane was jovially holding court.

"Who are *they*?" Alex nodded cynically at the knot of twenty-somethings in animated conversation with Jane.

"Relax." Will patted her knee. "You're not on duty tonight, remember? Some of them are campaign volunteers, some are just plain groupies."

Alex looked around the club, quickly spotting the four agents on duty. They were without dark glasses and ties, but to her, they still stood out with their mocktails and polished shoes and their straight backs. It felt foreign to be around Jane without being on duty, and it made Alex feel edgy, as though she should be doing something. She drummed her fingers on the table and looked around until she spotted all the exits.

"You look like you could use a drink, Alex. And it's all on Jane, by the way."

Alex grudgingly relented. She still wasn't thrilled to be here, two weeks worth of exhaustion having practically numbed her into a coma. *But what the hell.* She could certainly use a drink while she put in an obligatory appearance. "In that case, Scotch. Rocks."

Will went off in search of a waiter. Despite the human obstacles between them, Jane shot a wink at Alex and tipped her glass in salute. Her smile told Alex that she was pleased, maybe even a little surprised by her appearance at the club. Alex offered a good, stiff, military salute in response, which had the desired effect of making Jane laugh.

"Here you go, Alex." Will set the glass of Scotch in front of her. It looked like a triple.

"Jesus, Will. My first drink in two weeks. I'm going to be under this table in no time."

"No hiding under tables. Not before you make a crazy fool of yourself on the dance floor like the rest of us."

"Trust me, it'll take considerably more than this Scotch to get me out on the floor tonight."

Carter laughed, mischief lacing his voice. "Okay, how about two of those Scotches and one fine looking babe?"

Alex took a healthy sip and considered. "You've got a point there, Carter. Mind if I call you Carter? You look more like a Carter than a Will to me."

"Fine by me. Everyone calls me Carter. Actually, the only people who call me Will are my mom and my garçon du jour."

Alex took another drink. The Scotch was cool in her mouth but like fire on her insides. She felt two weeks of stress quickly turning to liquid. "Do you have many of those?"

"What, mothers or boyfriends?"

Alex laughed, enjoying her new friend's company. The campaign trail could be awfully straight. And lonely.

Carter sipped his fancy cocktail through a delicate straw. "Mothers, one, boyfriends, a few. But no one special. No damned time. You?"

Alex shook her head, deadly serious. "No, no boyfriends."

Carter swatted her arm. "I'm serious, silly."

Alex took another sip, leaned back in her chair and stretched her legs out in front of her. She was enjoying this night more than she had expected. "No girlfriend to speak of. I like being single."

Carter frowned. "A good-looking butch like you, you must have to beat the girls off."

Alex laughed. "Well, not exactly." She drank more Scotch and felt more effusive by the minute. "That's not to say I'm celibate. Just nothing serious."

Carter raised his glass in a toast. "Well, I hope you don't become a nun on this campaign, but it happens to the best of us."

Alex was puzzled. "Don't tell me y'all behave yourselves the whole time. Jane doesn't approve of any hanky-panky?"

"It's not that she's Mother Superior with us or anything like that. She just keeps us so frigging busy, you know? And when I have a minute to myself, I'm so tired, I just collapse." He stood and swooned into his chair, producing a giggle from Alex. "Tonight is the first time in months we've cut loose like this."

Jane did keep everyone hopping, most of all herself, Alex knew. She kept long hours, and even when she wasn't making speeches or in meetings with people, there always seemed to be a phone stuck to her ear or a laptop computer at the end of her fingertips.

"Is Jane a nun, too?" Alex surprised herself with the brazen question. She had not seen Jane even flirt with anyone over the last two weeks.

Carter sipped his drink, then toyed with the little umbrella. "I dunno. She doesn't sleep around, if that's what you mean. She's very private, but she certainly could have her pick. She's sexy as hell . . . I mean, if you were a straight guy."

"Hey, that's not fair, Carter. What about if you're a gay woman?"

Carter laughed. "Okay, you got me there. To a lesbian or a straight man, Jane Kincaid sizzles." He gestured in frustration.

"She's so naïve about it though . . . like she has no idea. Or she doesn't care."

Another Scotch appeared beside Alex's empty glass. "Too busy for a boyfriend would be my guess."

Carter shrugged, drained his drink and then signaled for another. "If you ask me, I think she still carries a torch for her dead husband."

Alex had read about Dan Olson. Killed in a plane crash ten or eleven years ago. The two had met in medical school and then got married after graduation. They had no kids in their short time together.

"They were madly in love?"

Carter shrugged. "You'd have to ask someone who knew them back then. She doesn't talk much about that part of her life, but I mean, why else would she never even look at anyone, let alone go on a date? Shit. Everyone needs a good lay at least once in a while."

Alex certainly couldn't disagree with that. She took another drink and felt the faint but welcome cloud of intoxication descending. "Maybe she just doesn't want to get hurt again. Doesn't want to get that close to anyone."

Carter looked challengingly at Alex. "Is this the voice of experience talking?"

Alex mentally retreated. "Heck, I'm no expert. I just mean, she's a complicated woman, right?"

Carter's cocktail arrived and he took a healthy sip. "Got that right. I bet you dollars to donuts you've never met anyone like her before."

Alex chuckled into her drink. "Dollars to donuts? I thought us southerners were the only ones with funny sayings."

Carter ignored her. He was looking contemplative and serious. "I first met her when I was doing an internship on Capitol Hill a few years ago. I never met anyone like her before or since, you know? It's hard to explain." His words were beginning to slur. "She just rocked my world, Alex. She still does. And I'll stay loyal to her for as long as she needs me."

Alex concentrated on her drink and felt a surprising twinge of jealousy that Carter and Jane's other aides had such an intense bond with the senator. The trust, loyalty and genuine love between them was obvious, and Alex very much felt like the outsider she was. She was a civil servant who, unlike them, did not come from the Ivy League, old money or politics. Alex had a job to do, just like Carter and Steph and Jack, but it was out of duty to the position, not the person. For just a moment—a very inappropriate moment, Alex knew—she found herself wishing she were doing this because she shared Jane's vision. And because Jane was the most important person in her life.

"What are you two looking so serious about?"

It was Jane, suddenly hovering over them, an arm lightly around each of them as though she were corralling her children. "We're not here to drown any sorrows, you know."

Alex smiled bashfully, silently cursing Jane's uncanny and timely perceptiveness. "Sorry. I don't mean to look like a party pooper."

"Oh, no you don't, Agent Warner."

"Huh?"

"Somewhere in there lurks a party girl. I'm sure of it." She looked Alex up and down, then nodded playfully. "And you can show me right now, both of you, by getting up on the dance floor with me."

Carter looked at Alex with a knowing grin. He winked at her diminishing glass of Scotch, then jerked his head toward Jane. "You've got all the incentive you need now to get up on the dance floor, Alex. Remember? The two Scotches and the—"

Alex shut him up with an I'm-going-to-kill-you look.

Jane paid no heed and hooked her arm through Alex's. "C'mon, Agent Dull. Let's kick up our heels."

The three of them danced to the Black Eyed Peas. Alex, despite her protestations, was an adept dancer, which seemed to surprise Jane, who was no slouch herself on the dance floor. Jane smiled and nodded encouragingly at Alex, moving rhythmically next to her. Jane's hips moved easily and fluidly, her long arms graceful in sync to the music. Her footwork was quick and flawless and perfectly timed. But it was her face that entranced Alex. Jane was radiant with an absolutely blissful, immovable smile. Alex had never seen her look so carefree, so self-permissive, so quick to slip the bonds of control and obligation. She stared in wonder at the transformation before her and thought how she had never seen Jane Kincaid—or any woman—look more beautiful.

They hardly noticed Carter meander away with a good-looking prospect, and when they did, Jane shrugged and laughed, hands upturned. "I think we've just been officially ditched."

Annie Lennox began singing a dance version of The Temptations' "I Can't Get Next To You," and the irony made Alex chuckle. She'd been next to this woman for two weeks and yet barely knew her. How was it possible to be so physically close to someone twelve hours a day—to the point where you knew what they took in their coffee and how many times in a day they yawned—and yet not really know them, Alex wondered for not the first time.

"What's so funny?"

In her alcoholic fog, Alex shook her head dismissively. Jane grabbed her hand and twirled beneath it. "You're a puzzle, Alex Warner."

"That's the pot calling the kettle," Alex boldly proclaimed, not quite sure if Jane had heard her.

Jane was a hundred miles away again in blissful oblivion, but when the song ended, she surprised Alex with an impulsive hug. Alex closed her eyes and breathed in the sweet, heady fusion of mild perfume, soap and clean sweat, and she squeezed Jane back, tighter than she ever would have in sobriety. It felt good to touch someone, even if it was just an innocent, friendly hug that she knew would never happen again in the light of day.

It was only seconds, but it felt like long, wonderful minutes before Jane pulled away, grinning. "Thank you for the dance, Alex. The Hawaiian shirt's a nice touch, by the way." Jane's hand loosely and innocently found Alex's, as though it were the most natural thing in the world, and she led her back to the table.

Alex felt herself blushing furiously, absurdly liking the tingly, electrifying feeling of Jane's touch. It was ridiculous, she knew. Jane was her protectee, her *job*, for God's sake, and yet, it was just so damned easy to like being with her this way.

"It's good to see you enjoying yourself, Alex."

Alex turned to her host, uncharacteristically not caring that her guard had been stripped away by the Scotch and the music and the heavenly hug and that wonderful, warm hand in hers. "I know I didn't want to come tonight, but I'm glad you talked me into it. I've missed . . ." Alex glanced around helplessly. What she really wanted to say was how much she missed being a normal person over the last two weeks—a person who needed comradeship and the occasional touch of a woman.

"I'm glad you came too, Alex." Jane's hand was still holding Alex's, squeezing tighter now. It felt soft, safe, encouraging, almost as though they were the only two people in the world . . . or at least in the club.

God, was Jane flirting with her? Alex blinked hard. She felt her thoughts muddying, wishing like hell Jane was. It would be so sweet, even just for a few minutes, to be the recipient of such a gorgeous and important woman's lascivious intentions. But Alex felt the dull ache of knowing reality was cruelly mingling with fantasy. *Jane can't possibly know what she's doing.*

"I know we haven't really had a chance to talk over the last two weeks, Alex. I don't even think I've officially welcomed you aboard, and for that, I'm sorry. I've been pretty preoccupied."

"Don't worry about it," Alex answered quickly. It had been foolish and selfish of her to want Jane's attention in this way, to have expected she somehow deserved to get to know Jane better. Jane had a job to do, and so did Alex. Sadly, Alex realized that after tonight, they would be strangers again. Jane would focus her attention and charm and boundless energy on everyone but the invisible Secret Service agents again.

"Alex? Tell me something."

Alex leaned closer, felt herself drunkenly sway toward Jane like a willow tree in a windstorm. With that hand in hers and those beseeching brown eyes intently searching hers, she would tell Jane anything. *Ask me, Jane. Ask me anything at all.*

"Yes?"

Jane was frowning now. "Am I just a job to you?"

Alex was stunned. Her mind tried to grasp the question, but failed to, like fingers trying to cup fine sand. "Pardon?"

The frown deepened. "When we're on the road, you're kind of distant with me. Like I'm just this object that has to be protected. Like a package of jewels, or money, or something like that." Jane looked mildly hurt—offended, almost. "I've been a bit intimidated by you. That's why I asked you here tonight. To see if . . . if you even really wanted to get to know me better."

Alex could barely breathe. *Intimidated? An object? Distant?* Could Jane be talking about *her*? *She* was not those things. It was Jane who had been that way with her . . . *Wasn't it?* Alex was confused. She longed for another Scotch to infuse some kind of synthetic clarity.

"I, I—," Alex stammered, her mind still slipping its gears. "No, it's not like that. It's not like that at all."

Jane's demeanor softened considerably. "I'm sorry, Alex. I've put you on the spot."

"No, it's . . . okay. I like you, Jane. Very much."

Jane's smile crested over Alex like sunshine ascending a horizon. "And I like you, Alex." She gave her a teasing wink. "And I definitely can't call you Agent Dull anymore."

Chapter 3

Jane had spent an emotionally grueling two days fighting with Steph and Jack about her latest pronouncement. Wait until after Pennsylvania, they'd insisted. Better yet, pick another cause, they'd pleaded. They did not want their candidate to become snared on a cause sure to alienate a good number of the electorate. She'd listened, she'd argued, but Jane would not budge. Finally, stubbornly, she hunkered down alone to write the speech that, whether it succeeded or failed, would be a watershed in presidential campaigning.

She flipped through the pages of her draft again, then threw them down impatiently. She cursed quietly and decided to ignore the faint tension headache. She was putting her ass on the proverbial line, and it was a lonely place to be. But with the Pennsylvania primary just a couple of days away, she was anxious to make good on what she'd recently pledged to herself and to the memory of her father—that she would speak to the issues that were important to her, that she would paint a picture of what she wanted *her* America to look like, and most important of all, that she would not be afraid to be herself. And if that failed to get her the Democratic nomination, then so be it. If nothing else, she would succeed in getting her agenda in the news and on people's minds, and maybe, just maybe, she could prick the national conscience along the way. Shifting the party a little more to the left couldn't hurt either.

She picked up the two-way radio on her desk and hit the call button. "Commander? Are you there?"

"Go ahead, Dr. Kincaid," Harry Johnson replied.

"Can you find Alex and send her to my suite?"

"Sure thing."

Jane absently picked up her reading glasses, then tossed them back onto the desk. She was nervous, unsettled about this whole thing, even though she had made up her mind and would not back down now. This would be big—the biggest proclamation she'd made, next to announcing her candidacy last summer. She stood then smoothed her slacks. Pacing, Jane undid the cuffs of her sleeves and rolled them up. It was good to be nervous, she reminded herself. Her speeches were always better when she was a little on edge, or even angry.

Following the quiet knock on the door, Jane ushered Alex in and motioned her toward a comfortable chair by the hotel room's large bay window. Alex's sport jacket bulged with her semi-automatic .357 as she sat down, and it struck Jane that the weapon must be as familiar as her right arm to someone as experienced in law enforcement as Alex was.

"Can I get you anything, Alex? Coffee? Juice?" Jane gestured toward the small kitchenette.

"I'm fine, thank you." Alex was aloof and polite, as usual.

"Oh hell, I could use something." Jane strode to the bar fridge and pulled out a carafe of orange juice. She poured it into a glass, then unceremoniously dumped a two-ounce bottle of vodka into it.

When she returned with the glass and sat down in the opposite chair, a quizzical frown greeted her.

"Is everything all right?" Alex asked warily. Even with her hackles up, she still looked calm and confident, her southern drawl smooth and gentle and a little enigmatic.

Jane tried to smile reassuringly and felt herself relaxing. "Yes, Alex. Everything is fine. But thank you for your concern."

Alex wasn't looking particularly convinced.

Jane took a long, steadying drink before setting the glass down on the table beside her. "Alex, as you know, I'm going to make a speech tonight at the Mellon Arena. And it's going to set off some shock waves. I just wanted you to know that the road is going to get a lot bumpier after tonight. It might make your job a little more challenging."

Jane knew she wasn't being completely truthful—that warning Alex wasn't the only reason she'd summoned her here.

Alex blinked but otherwise showed no expression. "Thank you for the warning, ma'am—Jane. How bumpy?" she asked mechanically.

Jane shrugged one shoulder. "There's no telling."

"I see." Alex's tone implied she didn't really see at all.

Drumming her fingers anxiously on the armrest, Jane said, "Alex, you may know that Pennsylvania is one of the few states in which a gay marriage bill is slowly making its way through the General Assembly. It's too early yet to say whether it will pass, but it's going to be a big issue here in the coming year. I'm going to jump into the fray tonight."

Alex looked entirely nonplussed, as though Jane had just said she planned on discussing the rising cost of lettuce. Jane took another drink, cradling the glass delicately, though she felt like squeezing it until it broke. She was disappointed she'd failed to get a reaction from Alex. "You don't think it's a good idea."

"No, I don't."

"Here in Pittsburgh, or in general?"

"I'm no expert on politics, Jane."

"I'm not asking you to be. I have plenty of people telling me I'm about to flush my political future down the toilet." Jane quietly despaired, feeling more alone than ever. If anyone would approve of her taking a stand on gay rights, she thought it would be Alex. Not only because Alex was gay, but because Alex had no personal stake in the success or failure of Jane's campaign. There would always be plenty of work for Alex, whether or not Jane's campaign continued.

Jane tried to rein in the self-doubt that was trying to gain a foothold and reminded herself that taking a stand on gay rights was the right thing to do, no matter what Alex or anyone else thought. She could not doubt her instincts now, and felt the passion for her conviction returning. She'd walked many political roads alone and she would do it again. "I'm not asking for your support or your permission, Alex," Jane blurted out, her voice rough as sandpaper.

She looked up and saw a flash of hurt sweep almost imperceptibly across Alex's face. *Shit.* This wasn't going well at all. She had not meant to be so snippy. It hadn't been fair to put Alex on the spot, to expect her to divulge her opinion on an issue that was obviously personal to her. She could see now that it had been a mistake, wanting Alex's opinion on the speech. Jane set her glass down and leaned closer to Alex, elbows resting on her thighs. "Alex, please tell me why you don't think this is a good idea tonight. I'd like to know."

Alex shrugged, looking indifferent, her Secret Service mask firmly in place again. Her voice was neutral, even if her words were not. "It's a hot-button issue. It's dangerous, Jane. There are so many nuts out there just waiting to pounce on something like this."

"But that's just it. If it's not this issue, it's something else they're ready to attack me on. The 'nuts,' as you say, already hate me anyway."

"Look. I'm no behavioral scientist, but this could push some fanatic over the edge."

Jane rubbed her hands together. "I can't play it safe, Alex. It's not who I am. I won't do it."

Alex stood to go. She nodded once. "I'm not leaving your side tonight, Jane."

Jane smiled as she escorted Alex to the door, and felt unexpected relief that tonight, while she made the most provocative political speech of her life, Alex would be only steps away, watching over her and out for her, every second. Jane might not have Alex's approval, but at least she had her attention, and it felt surprisingly comforting. "I feel better knowing that, Alex."

Alex turned to Jane at the door with a pained expression. "Can I ask you something?"

"Of course."

"Are you making this speech because you really believe it, or is it for the publicity?"

Jane gently touched Alex's arm and tried not to sound offended, even though her heart had sunk a little. "I know you don't know me very well, Alex. And I hope to change that. When you do know me better, you'll have your answer."

Alex smiled haltingly. "It's a heckuva thing you're doing. For your sake, I just wish you wouldn't."

The arena was jammed with seventeen thousand people, most of them members and supporters of Pennsylvania's AFL-CIO and the Steelworkers of America. It wasn't exactly a hostile audience for a left-leaning politician. Alex relaxed in her seat a little as first a State Assemblyman spoke, then the president of Pennsylvania's AFL-CIO. A Bruce Springsteen cover band had long ago warmed up the crowd, and now the pinnacle was Jane's speech.

Alex watched Jane stride confidently to the podium, acknowledging the applause with a grateful smile, then she graciously turned and nodded to the other speakers, who were sitting in chairs at the back of the stage. Alex was there too, but off to the side, near the edge of the stage. She had timed it precisely—she was two steps and a full-body leap from Jane, if need be. Other agents were placed at the exits and entrances, and a few had mixed in with the crowd.

"Wow. What a great city for a sports fan," Jane enthused, and the crowd roared in response. Then she made a point of scanning the rafters until she spotted the Stanley Cup banners hanging there. "It's wonderful to be in the house that Mario Lemieux built!" Again the crowd went wild. "And now I know how he must have felt when he hoisted the Stanley Cup here in front of wonderful fans like you!"

The audience collectively whistled and stamped their feet, and Jane half-heartedly tried to shush them with upraised palms. "I'm glad Mario's not running for the Democratic ticket, or I think I'd be in trouble!"

Jane laughed along with the crowd, all the while shuffling her speech notes into place behind the lectern. She would not use any electronic prompts or cue cards, Alex knew from experience. Jane always memorized her speeches and often spoke off the cuff, but seemed to like the security of having the papers close by.

Jane segued into a call for better health care coverage for the poor with anecdotal evidence of a professional hockey player being able to get an MRI exam within hours of an injury, while someone on Medicaid must wait many months.

Alex barely listened as she watched the faces of the crowd on the floor below. The audience was being kept back by flimsy barricades and Pittsburgh cops standing every twenty feet or so apart. She saw nothing but approval on the faces and in the gestures of the audience, but this was not unusual. Alex had seen little in the way of animosity directed toward Jane during her three weeks on the job so far. But Alex would not let that dull her senses. Crowds could be unpredictable. And individuals who looked the part of admirers could be terrorist plants or just plain lunatics waiting for their moment.

Alex and her colleagues used modern technology at every turn—sensitive metal detectors and personal searches at controlled entrances, bomb sniffing dogs inside and out, extensive background checks on suspicious people known to the authorities who might be in the area. Cops in and out of uniform as well as the Secret Service detail, were well positioned, all linked by small earpieces and microphones. There were cameras strategically placed too. But all of the measures, Alex knew, were very limited in their usefulness. Luck and circumstance played big roles, and their whim left Alex feeling helpless, no matter how choreographed the security for a simple speech before a friendly crowd.

Jane had launched into a call for increasing the minimum wage at the federal level. Many states had already gone far beyond the rate set by the federal government, she told them. "On this, ladies and gentlemen, the federal government should lead, not follow. I believe in leadership at the highest level. I believe in setting a good example. And most of all, I believe in simply doing what is right, and fair wages for a hard day's work is the right thing to do!"

The crowd cheered loudly. Alex noticed Jane's hands trembling beneath the lectern—probably from adrenaline rather than nervousness—yet she stood tall and erect and was the picture of poise and confidence.

Jane let the audience quiet down, until the arena became eerily silent with anticipation. "But ladies and gentlemen of Pittsburgh, there is something even more detestable than unfair wages, and that is the absence of basic human rights."

Alex felt her pulse automatically quicken. *Here it comes*, she thought with trepidation. She moved closer to the edge of her seat and felt her muscles twitch in readiness. She scanned the sea of faces again and looked for subtle movements in front of and along the sides of the stage. She knew the other agents would be doing the same.

"There is a segment of our society, right here in the United States of America, and even in a vibrant state like Pennsylvania, who are losing their jobs and their homes because of who they are. Every year, a good number of them kill themselves or are killed by others for who they are. Many of them are met, on a daily basis, with contempt and loathing or pity by people who don't even know them. And all just because they are different."

The crowd began a crescendo of anxious whispering. Jane had piqued their curiosity, and now, in an understated but rock-steady voice, she gave them what they were waiting for. "I'm talking, of course, about gays and lesbians."

There was a shocked, collective intake of breath. Even Alex, who'd known it was coming, felt her nerves prickle all over again. A mainstream presidential candidate talking about gay rights was pretty much uncharted waters, and the audience knew it. Tonight was history in the making.

The crowd quieted quickly, their attention riveted on Jane. They wanted her to continue, and she did not make them wait long. "Yes, gay people are different from most of us in one, and only one, unique way. But does that give us the legal and moral justification to deprive them of the same basic rights? To deprive them of holding joint property in some states? Of adopting children? Of getting married? Of bequeathing pensions? Of walking down the street with the expectation of being safe?"

Jane's right hand stabbed the air for emphasis. Her body was taut with emotion, her voice deep and rich and rising steadily. "When you teach people to hate and fear their fellow citizens, when you teach that those who differ from you threaten your freedom or your job or your family, then you also learn to confront others not as fellow human beings . . . but as enemies to be met not with cooperation but with conquest . . . to be subjugated and mastered. To be humiliated."

Jane paused in the dead quiet, looking earnestly at the faces in the first few rows, her body language visibly softening. "I'm asking you, brothers and sisters, to look into your own communities, and most of all, into your own hearts, and find love and understanding and justice there. And from those elements will come great leadership, from each of you, on one of the biggest moral issues of our generation. I talked about leadership earlier, and I said I believed in it. And I know you do, too."

Alex hadn't realized her own clammy fists were clenched tightly in her lap, until she felt them cramp. Jesus, Jane had really done it. Gone where no one else had before, and the audience seemed to sense it, too. They seemed shocked and awed by her ballsiness, but she kept at them, hammering her point, showing them she would not let them off the hook yet.

Jane was leaning over the lectern, hugging it. "Don't let differences divide your homes, your neighborhood, your city, your state—our country. We must celebrate our diversity, our individual strengths, and pull each other up from the mat when one of us stumbles." She looked intently at the faces in the crowd, then spoke slowly, enunciating each word. "And no matter what else, I want you to remember that your gay son or your lesbian neighbor or your bisexual coworker is simply sharing with you the same short movement of life, is seeking the same chance at happiness and purpose and fulfillment in this life as you."

Alex moved further to the edge of her seat, her breath lodged hard in her throat. She'd been watching the crowd for the most part, not Jane, but Jane's words had walloped her like a punch to the gut, and then they began to resonate in her mind. It was a stunning endorsement for gays and lesbians everywhere. For a presidential candidate to insist gay people not only be granted the same rights as everyone else, but to be accepted and loved and respected as well, was a bombshell that could have monumental and far-reaching effects. My God, Alex thought. This was huge. Jane's words, so thick with conviction, and yet so prosaic, made Alex feel incredibly proud and inspired. If she had not realized it before, she knew now that she could easily be a rabid supporter of Jane were she not on her security detail. And that was saying a lot, since Alex had rarely taken an interest in politics or politicians before now.

Jane was moving in for the kill, but her voice remained even, assuring, safe . . . like an evangelist who had given them a glimpse of the promised land and was now ready to take them there, if only they would give themselves up to her. "In giving, there is much to receive. When we give love, we receive it many times over. When we give understanding, we are met with cooperation. When we extend the same rights to all our fellow human beings . . . we all become just a little freer . . . and a heck of a lot richer in *here*." Jane clutched her fist to her chest.

The crowd jumped to its feet as one, cheering wildly in unison and chanting her name. "Jane! Jane! JANE!"

Alex noticed Jane look skyward for just an instant, then drop her shoulders in relief. She turned slightly to Alex, shot her a knowing wink and a smile as if to say 'what were you so worried about?', then opened her arms wide to the crowd below her to abstractly embrace them all.

"Thank you, Pittsburgh. I love you all!"

Alex made a beeline for Jane, grabbed her elbow as the crowd closed in like a knot around the stage, still chanting her name, reaching out their hands, wanting to touch her. Jane waved to them as Alex hustled her off the stage and through a steel door and into a labyrinth of hallways and more doors until they came to a back exit door, where Jane's limo squealed to a stop in front of them.

Steph and Carter were already inside. Jane scrambled in beside them, while Alex took a seat opposite.

Jane's two aides gave her a high five and Jane responded with a victory yelp.

"You did it, Jane, you really did it." Carter gave her a quick hug.

Steph couldn't stop grinning. "And they loved it, Jane. God! You had them eating out of your hand! I think you could have sold them a new Bill of Rights."

"Or at least a few used cars," Carter chimed in.

Jane smiled contentedly. "I guess that was pretty incredible, wasn't it?"

Carter smiled at Alex, reached over and tapped her knee. "What'd you think, sport?"

Alex was still stunned, her heart pounding wildly. She'd never been to a political rally or any sort of speech by a politician until she'd joined Jane's detail. She'd never met anyone so charismatic, so forceful with her words, so dynamic in personality, so able to stir a crowd with a look or a word or just by her mere presence. Jane could really move people, and Alex knew she was not an easy person to move. Could someone like Jane Kincaid really change the world? Alex had always thought such rhetoric nonsensical, but her feelings of political apathy and alienation had suddenly crumbled beneath the weight of Jane's speech.

There was a lump in Alex's throat she couldn't speak around.

"Oh, leave her alone, Carter," Jane urged, adrenaline still charging her voice. "She's probably worrying about how she's going to keep my butt safe tomorrow when the shit really hits the fan." She gave Alex a playful grin.

"Oh, Lord." Carter groaned, turning his attention back to Jane. "The media is going to go crazy tomorrow when we arrive in Philadelphia. Jack's already there, trying to smooth the way."

"An earthmover couldn't smooth the way after tonight," replied Steph, but she was laughing. "Still, we need to prepare ourselves for tomorrow's reception. It's going to be a zoo."

Alex turned her face toward the tinted window, lost in the

reflections. She felt oddly numbed. She knew she would never be the same person after tonight. Jane had reached in and touched something deep within her. It was more than just inspiring her and giving public credence to her sexual orientation. Alex had undeniably begun to care about Jane. And she cared about more than just keeping her safe. She wanted Jane to succeed, wanted her to have a chance to show the world what she could really do.

Oh, Jesus. Don't get so carried away, Warner, or you'll be wanting to campaign for her next.

Chapter 4

The campaign bus to Philadelphia left Pittsburgh before the sun had fully risen. It would be a grueling day for Jane. Upon arrival, there was to be a luncheon with city and school board officials, followed by a ribbon cutting, a rally at a park, a small dinner with a couple of dozen state party officials, and then an evening speech at Temple University. An itinerary from hell, Jane thought morosely. And it would be made worse because she knew she would be constantly plagued by aggressive reporters about last night's speech in Pittsburgh. She'd just unleashed a storm right before the primary vote, of that she was sure. But what was done was done, and she'd been right to do it, she reminded herself, no matter how much flak she was about to take. She'd handle the fallout, no matter how ugly it got. And ugly might just be an understatement.

Jane shoved the lunch speech printout into her briefcase and gazed at Alex, sitting alone four rows ahead and across the aisle. She was listening to an iPod, her eyes closed, her right foot tapping the floor. Alex was not a follower, Jane knew from her dossier. She was an Olympic athlete, a cop who'd been both lauded as a hero and yet rebuked for not doing things by the book. Jane liked that. Too often she was surrounded by eager followers, people without an original thought, or, if they did have one, they didn't have the gumption to express it. Alex Warner was an original, and it was damned refreshing. There was a quiet magnetic quality about the woman too, Jane thought appreciatively. Not the kind of showy, extroverted charisma, but a quiet, powerful confidence.

Jane slipped out of her seat and stood next to the empty one beside Alex. "May I?"

Alex tore the headphones from her ears and sat up straighter. "Of course. Please."

Jane sat down, stretching out her legs as much as the seat ahead would allow. "That bumpy road I was talking to you about yesterday? It definitely starts today."

Alex looked admiringly at Jane, yet the silent approval was too late, in Jane's mind. As much as Alex might approve today of what Jane had said last night, it still rankled her that Alex had been so opposed initially. "Yesterday, Alex, you cautioned me not to make that speech, because you said it would be dangerous." Jane studied Alex's face for any signs of regret, but saw none. "You've never for a moment shrunk from danger, have you?"

Alex shrugged casually, looking mildly surprised by Jane's question. "It's my job not to."

"Oh, no, you don't," Jane said curtly. "Don't give me that crap about just doing your job."

"Huh?" Alex looked like she'd just been slapped.

"When danger looks your way, Alex Warner, you stare right back at it. Just two nights ago, I watched the tape of you playing in the gold medal hockey game at the Nagano Olympics in ninety-eight." Jane couldn't help but smile. She'd been so impressed by Alex's athleticism and composure. "You were magnificent, scoring that winning goal all on your own, skating around three players to do it."

"It's easy to be brave when you're just playing a game."

"All right. What about when you were a state trooper, running into a burning house to save a trapped child. Was that just part of your job, too?"

Alex looked agitated, a little pissed off, but Jane didn't care. She would not be diverted from speaking her mind. Alex deserved to be put on the spot for being so opposed to the speech. "Alex, whether it's in sports, or in your job, or just you living your life, you're not afraid of danger. We both know that. And I admire that very much. But you know what? You're not the only one, okay?"

Alex gaped at Jane. Her jaw moved, but nothing came out.

"You need to accept that it's okay for others to do brave things, too. I'm not some shrinking violet, you know. And I'm not a cop and I'm not an athlete. But have you ever thought that my job also requires me to stand up and face danger sometimes?"

Jane let her words resonate. She was just beginning to think that perhaps she'd gone too far, when Alex suddenly began to laugh. It wasn't just a chuckle, either, but a full, chest-heaving laugh. *Well, I'm glad someone's enjoying this little chat*, Jane thought with a twinge of annoyance, but she was grateful the tension had evaporated.

"I think I just got taken out to the woodshed and spanked."

Jane laughed too and felt an unexpected flutter in her chest. *Alex Warner, you are damned charming when you look at me like that!* Jane wrinkled her nose playfully. "A spanking, no. A slap on the wrist, definitely!"

"Darn it all," Alex replied in her southern drawl, teasing. "Spankings are much more fun."

Jane's voice dropped an octave. "Ooh, I'll remember that,

Agent Warner."

Alex immediately looked sheepish and slightly mortified. Having had her fun, Jane decided to take pity on Alex's embarrassment by changing the subject.

"So how did a southern girl like you come to settle in my home state of Michigan?"

"So you *did* read the dossier on me."

"Of course. You're surprised that I'm thorough?"

"Not anymore."

"Well?" Jane was serious. She'd been meaning to get to know Alex better.

Alex shifted uncomfortably under Jane's scrutiny. She stalled and fidgeted with the headphones of her iPod. "Not a very exciting story, I'm afraid. After college, my girlfriend took a job with the Michigan State Police. So I followed her out there and joined the force as well."

Jane felt it before she thought it. She sensed with unexplained certainty that Alex had been hurt. Badly. It explained Alex's well-practiced ability to retreat within herself, to hold back her emotions, to remain aloof. "She hurt you, didn't she?" Jane said softly, matter-of-factly. *I'll bet you didn't even see it coming.*

By the way she looked, Alex might have just been hit between the eyes by a two-by-four, and Jane was immediately sorry she'd evoked such raw pain. She knew this vulnerable display in front of her must be killing Alex, and it pulled at Jane's heartstrings.

With visible effort, Alex gathered herself and forced a wisp of a smile. "That was almost five years ago. The funny thing is, she's the reason I became a cop, and now she's not even a cop anymore."

"Oh?"

"I heard she quit and moved to Florida. Met somebody on the Internet and decided to change her whole life, I guess." Alex's voice was thick with disbelief and hurt.

"I'm sorry, Alex. Were you together long?"

"Eight years."

Jane was moved by the depth of hurt in Alex's face, the almost imperceptible tremor in her voice. After all these years, she was still reeling from it. "That's why you quit the state police and joined the Secret Service four years ago, isn't it?"

Alex flashed a look of mild disbelief. "When you said you were thorough, you weren't kidding."

"Nah, that stuff wasn't in your dossier."

Alex looked perplexed. "You specialized in psychiatry, is that it?"

Jane replied softly, "No, Alex. I just know what it's like to be hurt and to want to run away from it." Jane felt her voice grow distant. "To know it's the only way to cope with loss."

She looked past Alex and stared, almost unseeing, at the blurred countryside whizzing past. *God.* She'd missed Dan so much after his death. Had the life sucked right out of her. She'd stumbled through her medical practice for a few more months until she knew she had to make wholesale changes to her life if she were to survive. She joined Doctors Without Borders and served in North Africa for a year. And after that, well, there was no way she could go back to private practice in Chicago. Life had become starkly different in so many ways. Maybe it was her father's death shortly after her return stateside, and the political legacy he'd left her—not to mention the starving, sick bodies and hopeless faces she'd seen in Africa. In any case, Jane knew she had to help people on a grander scale. So she'd formed DOORS—Doctors For a Responsible Society—and spent a couple of years lobbying multinationals, Congress, the Senate, state assemblies, the American Medical Association, pharmaceutical companies. She had even been the subject of a short, award-winning documentary. But when she'd begun to hit brick wall after brick wall, she decided the best way to make changes was from within the system. So she ran for the Senate and won, thanks to her growing public profile and her father's reputation.

And now, at the age of forty-three, she was running for the top job in the country. It still floored her sometimes, this life she'd carved out since Dan's death, and her father's.

"Are you still running away?"

Alex's question ripped Jane from her reverie. She swallowed hard. Her thoughts tumbled. *Is that what this is all about? Dear God, could Alex be right?* Panic knotted in her like a fist. Was she still running from grief? Was running for the Democratic nomination just another distraction, another form of anesthetizing herself? Another way to keep herself so busy that she didn't have time to think? She hadn't wanted to consider it before, this idea that she might be overachieving to suppress her grief, her pain.

Jane felt unexpected tears welling. She couldn't afford doubts like this creeping into her psyche, her campaign. It would be disastrous. *Damn you, Alex Warner.*

She rose abruptly and irritably. "Excuse me, Alex. I need to get back to my work. We'll be arriving soon."

Alex had a sinking feeling as the bus pulled into the hotel parking lot. It was teeming with throngs of people, all looking antsy for probably different reasons. There were hundreds of people. Many were clearly reporters and photographers, but others were holding up signs, both of support and protest. A couple of rainbow flags waved distantly in the chilly February air.

Sweet Jesus. How were they ever going to get Jane through this and into the hotel, where she was already due for her lunch meeting? Alex shot an exasperated look at Commander Harry Johnson across the bus aisle. He shrugged, looking ornery.

The bus door hissed opened and Alex peeked out. *Yep, a zoo.* The dozen or so police officers on hand looked overwhelmed and cranky, as though the spontaneous gathering were a total imposition. She waved a sergeant over and asked if they could send more backup. The sergeant replied with the barest civility that they were doing the best they could, and Alex reminded her that with the mayor inside and a presidential candidate on hand, it wouldn't look good for things to go badly.

Jane was impatient to get off the bus and made it known she would not wait for further negotiations. Harry hastily led the way outside, breaking a path, followed by Steph and Carter, another agent, then Jane. Alex fell in half a step behind Jane, who looked remarkably unrumpled for such a long bus ride. She was the picture of energy and poise, and walked with casual confidence and purpose, as though the boisterous greeting was both expected and welcome.

"Good morning, good to see you," Jane repeated countless times to the anonymous people she passed, even though many were shouting and chanting, calling out things like "Remember What the Bible Says" and "Homosexuality is a Sin!" Reporters scurried alongside, thrusting microphones and tape recorders into Jane's face. They pelted her with questions like hail in a thunderstorm.

Alex was getting poked in the ribs and elbowed in the gut as she swatted away cameras, arms, microphones and even picket signs. She could feel scratches and bruises swelling on her arms already.

Jane halted just outside the Marriott's huge glass doors and turned to the crowd. Reporters jammed themselves around her in an unruly semi-circle while the police tried desperately to keep the others back. Alex urged Jane to just go inside, as did the rest of her entourage, but Jane would not hear of it. She had that look that Alex had become so familiar with, the one that said she had made up her mind. Alex tucked herself in just behind Jane and braced herself for whatever came next. She always had to be ready for the unscripted, and with Jane, there were plenty of those moments.

"I'll take a couple of questions," Jane yelled over the din to the journalists, "but since I hadn't planned on a scrum, I'm afraid it will have to be brief."

Questions were lobbed at her simultaneously, but one stood out. "Is your campaign being financed by the gay rights movement?"

Jane visibly flinched. "My campaign receives donations from many organizations and individuals, but it is certainly not financed by any particular movement, as you put it."

"Is your speech last night going to hurt your campaign?"

"I have no idea," Jane answered tersely. There was no sign of her usual characteristic humor when she sparred with journalists.

"Why have you taken up the gay cause?"

"I have taken up many causes in this campaign. There are many wrongs I want to see righted. Gay rights is just one of those."

"Are you a lesbian, Dr. Kincaid?"

Silence fell like a guillotine.

Jane glared at the male questioner. Alex automatically tensed. "I fail to see any connection between a person's sexual orientation and their support for gay rights. Do you have to be impoverished yourself to be in favor of food stamps? Are only women in favor of women's rights? I don't think so."

"You didn't answer the question," someone else shouted.

Jane's staff exchanged nervous glances. Jane was striking out like a snake that had just been stepped on, and it was putting them all on edge.

"That's right," Jane replied testily. "I didn't. And I won't."

Alex heard Jack and Steph quietly mumble as Jane abruptly ended the press conference and made for the hotel door. Relieved the moment was over, Alex allowed herself to feel secretly pleased that Jane hadn't fallen into the trap of declaring that she was straight, or acting as though it would be the worst insult in the world to be mistaken for gay. More proof, as if Alex needed any, that this woman had guts.

Alex took a seat next to Carter at the luncheon, close enough to keep an eye on Jane at the head table with the mayor and other local officials. Other agents were interspersed throughout the room, while uniformed cops manned the exits.

"Jesus, she's like a bear with a sore ass today," Carter whispered to Alex. "I don't think I've ever seen her this grouchy. She seemed so happy after her speech last night. I hope she's not regretting it."

"I don't think that's it," Alex replied coyly.

"What makes you say that?"

Alex shifted in her seat. "I think I'm the one who put her in a bad mood."

"What?" Carter narrowed his eyes at Alex. "What'd you do to her, stud, make a pass at her?"

Alex whacked him lightly on the arm. "Be serious, Carter. Jesus. I opened up my big yap and said something I shouldn't have." She briefly recounted their conversation on the bus. "And then I asked her if she was still running away . . . you know . . . from her past."

"You did *what*!" Carter exclaimed a little too loudly. A few heads turned in their direction.

"Well, she started it all," Alex protested.

Carter nervously chewed his bottom lip. He was clearly not pleased. "If she doesn't get in a better mood, and quickly, she's going to come across looking too defensive, too touchy over that speech last night. And that's very bad, Alex."

"It is?"

"The press will think there's a hell of a lot more behind this whole gay rights thing if she starts putting up walls. Whatever else, Jane can never look like she flip flops on issues, especially as big an issue as this."

The day's newspapers had produced a mixed reaction to Jane's Pittsburgh speech, but they'd all agreed it was monumental. A media furor was quickly building throughout the day. "She's got to continue to be cool and confident about this or she'll kill any good to come from that speech," he added needlessly.

Alex stared into her soup, feeling horrible. Who knew that a single, little innocent question from her, an inconsequential Secret Service agent, could throw a presidential campaign into a tailspin? She'd have to get Jane alone and tell her she was sorry, that she'd acted unprofessionally . . . that she hadn't meant to pry, let alone imply a judgment.

The day passed in a typical chaotic blur of speeches, shunting around and handshaking. It wasn't until early in the evening, when it was time to fetch Jane in her hotel room for the short drive to Temple University, that Alex saw her first opportunity to get her alone.

Alex shouldn't have been surprised by the sight of Jane, not after all this time, but she was. Jane was breathtakingly gorgeous and looked far too rested and radiant than she had a right to. A tight-fitting, forest green thigh-length dress clung to her long, slim body. A bare shoulder glowed tantalizingly where the dress dropped off on a slant, a string of pearls glimmering around her smooth neck. Alex found herself wishing the dress were shorter, more mid-thigh than just above the knee. She was being juvenile, Alex knew. It was wrong and forbidden. But Jane was a very attractive woman, and Alex *was* human. She could pretend all she wanted that she hadn't noticed how Jane looked, but it would be a sham. Oblivious to Alex's appreciative appraisal, Jane slipped into a stark, white blazer, covering that luscious shoulder. Her usual lightning-quick smile was still absent and Alex felt a fresh wave of concern. For the hundredth time, she berated herself for having offended Jane.

"Jane, before we go down, can I have a minute?"

Dark eyebrows rose. "Of course," Jane answered flatly. "What's on your mind, Alex?"

They stood several feet apart, Alex feeling awkward. For a moment, she considered high-tailing it out of there and forgetting the whole thing. But she'd come to make amends, and that's what she would do, whatever the cost. "I owe you an apology."

"For what?"

Alex blinked her surprise. "For what I said on the bus."

Jane looked at Alex as if she were speaking another language.

"I—I asked you if you were still running away. From what happened to you. I'm sorry. I know I upset you. It wasn't my place. It won't happen again." The words fell out all at once.

"Oh, Alex." Jane winced. "I'm not upset with you."

"You're not?"

"No, of course not. I was the one asking you all kinds of personal questions, remember?"

Alex nodded and suddenly felt utterly ridiculous. "I'm sorry. I misjudged."

Jane leaned back against a low mahogany table, crossing her arms in front of her, looking miserable again. "No, you didn't entirely misjudge. I have been upset today."

"Then it is my fault."

Jane smiled reassuringly, graciously, and Alex's worries began to lift, like a balloon.

"Alex, you didn't do anything wrong. It's just that, what you said—it did make me examine some things, ask myself some hard questions." Jane turned her back to Alex, her hands spread across the table, her shoulders slumped. "It got me questioning if that's what this campaign is about, in part. Me running away from my loneliness, my pain. Overreaching. Trying to prove to myself and to everyone else that I've got my shit together enough to run this country, when in reality, I am no more together than anyone else."

Alex stepped closer and gently touched Jane's shoulder, which was stiff with tension. Jane slowly turned around and Alex saw that she was on the verge of tears. A surge of panic welled up. *Sweet Jesus, I did this to her! If she quits this race, it's all my fault. I've got to make this right.*

Alex mustered her courage. She wasn't so good with words.

She preferred brute force to this nurturing business. Please let me say the right thing, she prayed. Her hand was still resting lightly on Jane's shoulder. Holding Jane's watery gaze, she took her time, mentally rehearsing her words. *The very future of this country might depend on what I say next.* She swallowed before she spoke, and hoped Jane didn't notice how nervous she was.

"Jane, you are not running away from anything. You have been running *to* something, to serving this country in the highest form possible. And you were right this morning when you said I wasn't the only one who faced up to danger. You're not afraid of anything either. Don't you see that what you're doing is the most courageous, responsible, admirable thing you could possibly do with your life?"

Jane flinched but she said nothing.

"Jesus!" Alex exclaimed, her own emotions surfacing. "I would run naked into ten burning buildings before I'd do what you're doing."

Jane's lips curled into a slow, knowing smirk, much to Alex's relief. "Okay, now you're giving me a mental image."

Alex laughed. "Sorry."

Jane was looking devastated again, her face contorted in a private pain that was beyond Alex's comprehension. Alex quickly closed the few inches between them and, without hesitation, wrapped her arms tightly around Jane's shoulders and pulled her into a hug.

Jane began to clutch back so tightly, it almost hurt. She buried her face in Alex's shoulder, and Alex smiled at the faint, sweet and now-familiar fragrance. Alex breathed in, trying to capture the unique scent, wanting to store it in her memory. Having Jane so intimately in her arms didn't feel nearly as strange as it should have. On the contrary, it felt incredibly easy. And nice. Alex felt a comfortable warmth settling softly in her belly, like the little snowflakes in a glass bubble ornament. *Oh, I could get used to this!*

"Oh, Alex," Jane murmured into Alex's expensive suit, obviously unaware of the pleasurable sensations she'd aroused. "Those people who look up to me . . . Sometimes I think—I *know*—I don't deserve their admiration."

"Now that's where you're wrong." Alex pulled back just enough to look into Jane's flushed face. "I see how you affect people, how you give them hope and inspiration. Do you think that comes along every day?"

Jane shrugged defiantly.

"Trust me," Alex said quietly, wanting to say so much more. "When you walk into a room, it's like a comet zooming through the atmosphere."

Jane smiled, still tightly ensconced in Alex's arms. "You don't have to do this, Alex," Jane said, but her tone and her body language told Alex she wasn't through needing comfort and assurance. Jane needed whatever strength Alex could give her at this moment.

"It's your calling, Jane, your duty. It would be running away if you *didn't* do this. I truly believe that."

This consoling thing wasn't so bad after all, Alex thought with bemusement. *Who knew?* She fought the urge to tenderly stroke Jane's hair, to protectively run her hands down her back, to gently wipe the wetness from her cheeks. She could easily imagine the smoothness of Jane's skin beneath her fingertips. *God!* What she wouldn't give to be able to touch her that way. Alex's heart pounded wildly. It felt wonderful having another woman in her arms—and not just any woman, but this woman! This beautiful, dynamic, charismatic, intelligent, desirable woman.

Jesus, Alex, get a grip! What was she thinking? This was a presidential candidate—a candidate she was supposed to be protecting. And the fact that she smelled so good and looked so good and was so soft and vulnerable right now . . . *Oh, Alex, this is going to get you into big trouble if you don't stop this.*

Alex drew away self-consciously, admonishing herself, but Jane was too busy straightening up and dabbing at her cheeks to notice the mortification Alex was sure must be all over her face.

"I'm sorry I had this little meltdown, Alex," Jane said calmly. "I think maybe it's been building for awhile." She smiled a little bashfully. "It wasn't very 'presidential' of me, was it?"

Alex commanded herself to relax and forced what she hoped was a reassuring smile. She'd play it cool and try to lighten the moment for Jane's sake. "Hey, I have broad shoulders."

Jane gave her a bold once-over that caused Alex to blush to the bottom of her polished shoes. "I know." For a moment she looked like she might say something more, but she just smiled benignly. "It was very kind of you. Thank you for being there for me. I feel so much better, Alex."

"Good. Do I get a raise? That oath to secrecy's got to be worth a lot right about now."

"Don't push your luck, Agent Warner." Jane was still chuckling as they gathered themselves and strode to the bank of elevators. All evidence of her tears had quickly vanished. She looked stunning again and thoroughly composed.

"You know something, Jane?" Alex said in the empty elevator, feeling brave again. "I think you're very brave. And as for having all your shit together, as you put it, I'm afraid no one's a pro at that. Not you and certainly not me."

The doors clamped shut and Jane shot Alex a grateful look.

"Promise me you'll remind me of that every now and again."

"Sure. I'm awfully good at reminding people that I'm not perfect."

"Alex, you're a clown. And to think, when I first met you, I was afraid you had no sense of humor."

"I'm glad I proved you wrong."

The elevator opened onto the lobby, where a frantic Steph and Carter were motioning at them. Jane rebelliously hit the button to freeze the doors for a moment.

"Alex, the Secret Service is still looking for a code name for me. I think I like your suggestion."

"Huh? What suggestion?"

Jane's familiar, mischievous smile spread delightfully across her face. "Comet!"

Alex laughed. "Okay, Comet, you got it."

The beckoning from afar grew more frantic and a brief look of regret flashed across Jane's face. "Duty calls."

The four of them climbed into the limousine. Alex grinned across the seat at Jane. "Did you actually go out and find a tape of my gold medal hockey game from the ninety-eight Olympics?" She was secretly tickled at the idea, though a little bewildered.

"Well," Jane hedged. "*I* didn't actually go out and hunt it down. That's what I have loyal staff for." She winked at Steph.

Jane's speech lasted nearly an hour. With just the right blend of idealism and detail, she unveiled her "Blueprint for America" to the receptive audience of mostly students, who cheered each point she ticked off. As the speech wound down, Jane suddenly left the lectern and her notes, pulled the cordless mic from its stand and carried it to the edge of the stage, where she plopped down and dangled her long legs over the edge.

Alex was in an agonizing state of near convulsions at the sight of Jane's precarious perch.

"Last night, in Pittsburgh—" Jane was cut off by sporadic cheers from somewhere in the back of the auditorium. She smiled and shielded her eyes from the blinding stage lights. "I'm glad to know there are at least three people in the audience who didn't mind that speech!"

The crowd laughed as one, Jane joining in. She let the jocularity die down naturally. "When I spoke about gay rights last night, it appears I made some people uncomfortable." Jane's tone was one of mock surprise, and the crowd twittered. Her smile slowly faded. "Seriously, folks. I'm sorry if what I said upset some people, but I think those things needed to be said. Actually . . ." Jane paused, a clenched fist in her lap. "You know what? I take that back. I'm not sorry at all." She leaned toward the crowd and made eye contact with as many people as she could. "I think a little discomfort *should* precede changes that make our society better." Her voice was stentorian. "It is not easy to unlock the chains of bondage, to unhitch the yoke of subjugation, to—" She wiggled for emphasis. "To make room for a new order, to slough off our comfortable skin in our ivory towers."

Damn, she's good, Alex marveled. *And the audience knows it, too.*

"Change is never easy. Self-examination is never painless."

Alex knew that last bit was a reference to their private moment together earlier, and she moved to the edge of her seat as Jane paused.

Brimming with emotion, Jane said, "But we are all just human. None of us is perfect." She smiled sheepishly at the crowd. She could do that so effortlessly—look bold and serious one moment, shy and humble the next. "Believe me, I know. In fact, a friend just reminded me of that earlier tonight."

Alex nearly fell off her chair. She felt her face warming.

"As human beings, with all our imperfections, we are constantly called to change. And yes, we fight it and protest it and think the world is going to end. But you know what? Change *comes*, ladies and gentlemen. Whether we like it or not. Whether we embrace it or not. And I'll tell you one thing, I'm still learning myself." She lowered her voice to a near-whisper. "It's a helluva lot easier to embrace change than to fight it."

The crowd roared and surged. Hands reached up and pulled Jane down.

Alex leapt up and looked down. *Jesus Christ!* Jane was gone! She'd disappeared into the jaws of that live, writhing, unpredictable beast known as a mob. Alex dove in after her, yelling uselessly, pushing and pulling bodies away. And there was Jane, on her ass on the floor, where anonymous arms were in the midst of pulling her up. She was beaming like a kid.

"Hey, sailor," Jane shouted at Alex, still grinning. "Going my way? I could use a lift outta here."

Alex wasn't the least bit amused. Roughly, she hauled Jane up, batted a couple of bodies out of the way and signaled for backup.

"You guys didn't need to be so rough with those kids," Jane admonished later in the back seat of the leased Chevy Tahoe. She was looking uncharacteristically rumpled from all the jostling and more than a little displeased.

"I'm sorry, but I don't agree. I know those kids meant well, but you could still get hurt."

The tension in her body, the clenched expression told Alex that Jane was still seething. Her words only punctuated it. "If I was concerned, I would have yelled for you. Did I look concerned?"

"No, but I can't wait for you to decide if you're in trouble or not. It's my job to anticipate trouble before it happens." Alex refused to feed Jane's anger by getting angry herself. She spoke reasonably, because she knew she was right. Looking at everyone as a potential threat to Jane was an unpleasant but necessary part of her job.

"Well, you can't run over people just because you think I might get hurt, Alex. I won't have it. I won't have a goon squad around me."

Alex would have laughed were Jane not so angry. She'd never thought of herself as belonging to a goon squad. It just wasn't true, but it was best to let Jane blow off a little steam rather than keep arguing with her.

"I'll keep that in mind, Jane. I certainly don't want my tactics causing you any embarrassment or discomfort."

Alex watched Jane's anger slowly deflate. Contriteness did it every time.

The celebration party went on for hours the next night in the hotel ballroom, a prolonged and raucous affair with Jane spending an interminable amount of time personally thanking each of the hundreds of supporters there.

The day's Pennsylvania primary win was huge for Jane, and Alex was pleased for her. The aides had been nervous wrecks hours earlier as they waited for results. They still looked bedraggled, as though they'd run a marathon, but they were a hell of a lot happier. It was like a tremendous weight had been lifted from the campaign.

"How're you feeling?" Alex asked Carter, her attention never leaving Jane in the crowd.

"Never mind me. Isn't it great? Life hasn't been this good since New Hampshire."

Jane had finished a close second to Dennis Collins in most of the primaries, but all-out wins like this one were rare—too rare.

"So you think she's really got something going now?" Alex asked, hoping it was true. Maybe she would soon be able to topple Collins from his lead.

Carter looked a little skeptical in spite of his enthusiasm. "These primaries she's won are pretty small potatoes in terms of the delegates."

"Huh? You lost me there, Carter." Alex figured a win was a win, no matter which primary it was.

"See, each primary is worth so many delegates at the national convention. So each vote she's picking up in the primaries now means those delegates will be voting for her in July. The problem is, Collins has more delegates right now. He's been winning the bigger primaries, like Florida, which is worth over a hundred delegates. Pennsylvania's worth a good couple of dozen less. It's all about the numbers, baby."

"Jeez. I didn't know you had to be a math whiz to figure all this out."

Carter was watching Jane too as she moved through the crowd. "The numbers game can wait. What's important right now is that Jane knows she can win primaries. Especially with those Super Tuesdays coming up."

Alex inwardly groaned. She knew a Super Tuesday was when a whole pile of states held their primaries at once, and there would be two of them in the upcoming weeks. On those days, it wasn't uncommon for candidates to cram in as many campaign appearances as they could, even if it meant visiting three or four states in a day.

But if Jane was up to the demand, so was she. Alex was continually amazed by Jane's stamina. Even now, as she worked the room after such a long day, she chatted with each person, asked their name, asked them something about themselves. There were special words and hugs or handshakes for each. Jane's hands would be scratched and swollen because everyone, it seemed, wanted to touch her. Her smile rarely wavered and somehow, miraculously, she still managed to look fresh and interested.

Finally, Jane signaled that she was going upstairs to the suite of rooms her team had rented for the more private celebration. Alex hoped it wouldn't go on all night.

She and Carter shared a look of helpless exhaustion, but quickly fell into place behind Jane.

Upstairs in the large suite, champagne was flowing, music was playing, and Jane had begun disappearing into a bedroom in turn with each of her closest staffers for a few minutes at a time. Alex dutifully stood around, making small talk, wondering what Jane wanted her for. She was growing more bored by the minute, and yet she was curious. The next time Jane emerged, she crooked her finger at Alex and motioned her in.

Alex felt like a kid being called before the teacher. Was Jane still pissed at her over last night's scene at the university? Her imagination began to run wild with the possibilities. Was Jane going to have her removed from her security detail? Could she even do that? Alex didn't think so, but still . . .

Jane closed the door and told Alex to take a seat on the bed. Unsmiling, Jane sat down opposite Alex on the facing bed, her impassive expression giving no hint of what lay ahead. Now Alex was really worried.

"Alex, tonight is one of my biggest primary wins. It was crucial at this point in my campaign and I wanted to do something a little special."

Whew, so she wasn't in trouble. Alex relaxed her shoulders and felt her exhaustion ebb. "Congratulations, Jane. You deserved it." Alex knew Jane had heard those words a million times tonight, but she could think of nothing more original to say. She just hoped it didn't sound trite coming from her. She meant it far more than she was able to express. She knew Jane had no idea just how much she had affected her these last few weeks . . . how much she had inspired and infused her with her enthusiasm, her energy, her compassion, her beliefs. She'd almost blurted out how much Jane was beginning to matter to her, and yet thankfully she hadn't. It would be inappropriate, unprofessional. Jane needed a bodyguard, not another fan.

Jane was grinning like it was Christmas morning.

"Alex, you might just be my good luck charm."

"What?" Okay, that wasn't what she'd expected.

"Well, here you are on my detail, and suddenly things are looking up."

Alex laughed in relief. "I surely do wish I had such magical powers, but I'm just an average North Carolinian and an ex-cop who never paid any attention to politics until now."

"Well then, Agent Warner, I'm glad to be your first political tutor."

"Well, my mama always said, if you're going to learn something, learn from the best."

Jane smiled modestly. "Well, let's not get too carried away.

I'm afraid your lessons don't come with a guarantee for success."

Alex felt smug and shot a wink at Jane. "Don't worry, I'm not exactly in the business of guarantees, either."

"Ah, good point, Alex."

Alex resisted looking at her watch. She'd already been in here with Jane for as long or longer than Jane had spent with anyone else, yet she hadn't come to the point yet, Alex knew. She tapped her foot nervously.

As if reading her mind, Jane said, "Alex, I've been giving everyone close to me a small token of my appreciation for how hard they've been working. And I have something special for you."

Alex hid her surprise as Jane reached into her jacket pocket and pulled out a small stone, flat and round and black. She pressed it into Alex's hand and squeezed gently.

"What is it?" Alex asked, still a little breathless from the anticipation.

"It's from the Pacific Ocean. Take a look at it. I picked it up when we were campaigning in Oregon a couple of months ago. I'd taken an early morning walk on the beach and found it."

Alex held the stone up to examine it. It was smooth as glass and had a double ring that went all the way around it, one red, the other orange. It was beautiful, and felt instantly warm and sure and so smooth in her hand. "It's awesome," she said.

Jane was digging into her pocket again for a second stone, this one amber with two black, perfect rings around it.

"This one's from the Atlantic Ocean. I picked it up in Maine."

Alex touched it, and it was equally as worn as the other. "It's beautiful, Jane. They both are."

Jane looked at Alex in that skilled way she had that made Alex feel like she was the only thought on Jane's mind, the only person who mattered at that moment. "I've carried these two stones with me every day since I found them, to remind me how beautiful and big this country of ours is, and how far I've traveled across it."

"But, that means they're a set. I can't take this," Alex said.

Jane put the second stone back in her pocket and reached for Alex's hand. "I want you to keep this one, Alex, because last night was probably the lowest moment I've had in this campaign, and our talk helped me find my place again. I'm not sure that tonight would have been possible without you, Alex."

Alex could not find her breath. She desperately wanted to say something. She yearned to tell Jane how touched she was by this symbolic gesture, how thoughtful it was. But she just looked at Jane, dumbfounded and stoic.

"Just promise me you'll take good care of it. It's lucky, you know. The rings around these stones mean luck. Did you know that, Alex?"

Alex shook her head dumbly.

"Keep it in your pocket, and if you're feeling a little stressed, it's comforting just to rub it with your fingers and use it to ground yourself." Jane's smile curled into a frown. "I bet you didn't know I don't like flying."

Alex wouldn't have guessed. Jane rarely showed any sort of fear.

"I feel much better having a little bit of planet earth in my pocket when I fly."

"I—I don't what to say," Alex sputtered. "It's—are you sure? There must be someone more deserving of this."

Jane stood up and gave Alex a lengthy hug that made her weak in the knees. Alex marveled at how their bodies seemed to fit so perfectly, how Jane slid so easily into her arms and how she felt so soft and yet so firm, like she belonged there.

At the door, Jane turned to Alex. "Alex, you keep me both lucky and safe. That makes you the most deserving person I know."

Chapter 5

Alex reclined on the couch at the home of her friends, Kim and Linny. It was cold and gray outside—typical for February in Detroit. It wasn't at all enticing to be out in it, and besides, her body needed the rest, even if it was only for a couple of days. Alex had requested and been granted the brief respite while Jane's campaign stopped in Michigan. And now she was trying hard to be a good guest, but it was a strain when she was so dog-tired. She really just wanted to cocoon herself from the world, but she'd promised her friends a visit.

Kim set another cold beer down on the table beside Alex, and the couple pulled chairs up close, unaware of Alex's exhaustion. They were bubbling over with eagerness and curiosity about Alex's first month on the campaign. Linny, a high school English teacher with a secret desire to be a novelist, was being particularly annoying, pumping Alex for every detail—especially any lurid ones.

They'd shown Alex their collection of the latest magazine covers featuring Jane Kincaid—everything from *The Advocate* to *Vanity Fair* to *Time*. They'd gotten particularly animated about the *People* magazine piece called, appropriately, "This Jane is Anything But Plain."

Kim took a hurried pull on her beer bottle and indicated the stack of magazines in the corner. "I tell you, Al, she's doing way better than anyone thought she would. I mean, that win in Pennsylvania last week was huge. They're saying now she might actually go all the way."

"Yeah," Linny gushed. "And the way she's come out for gay rights. Man, what a gamble! She's got balls, I'll say that."

Alex shrugged noncommittally. Speculating about Jane's fortunes almost seemed a betrayal, or maybe just bad luck. You didn't talk about a teammate to someone who wasn't on the team. You didn't talk about winning until the game was over.

Kim, usually the more cynical of any of them, was clearly impressed. "I gotta give her credit. She really knows how to inspire people, how to make them believe in her. Even the media are tripping over themselves lately to give her good press."

"She certainly gives them something to write about," Alex said cryptically. The journalists were like sadistic roller-coaster operators—they'd send you up and then let the bottom drop out when you least expected it. Alex gave little credence to what the media thought of Jane at any given moment, but Jane and her staff couldn't afford to be so cavalier. The news stories were a weathervane, and at the same time, they shaped public opinion. Politicians lived and died by it, Alex knew, but the necessity of it didn't make it any more palatable to her.

"I think she's marvelous," said Linny, holding up a particularly flattering magazine photo of Jane in faded jeans, cowboy boots and a loose denim shirt unbuttoned just enough to reveal a hint of tantalizing cleavage. "She's smart and she's brassy. And she's sooo hot! My *God*, Alex. I want your job just so I can stare at her all day."

Alex was growing crankier by the minute. She didn't want to talk about Jane that way, nor did she want to share her with her friends. Everyone wanted a piece of Jane, it seemed. It was like she was some remarkable, rare ornament to look at, to covet, to talk about, and not the real person she was. It wasn't right.

Irritated, Alex abruptly rose and made an excuse about needing a nap.

Kim flicked on the television. The Detroit Red Wings were about to play the Boston Bruins. "Hey, Al, Jane Kincaid's about to drop the ceremonial puck at Joe Louis Arena."

Alex slung the tea towel, still wet from the supper dishes, over her shoulder. Sure enough, there was Jane at center ice, looking fresh and relaxed in form-fitting jeans and a Red Wings jersey. Her hair was pulled back in a ponytail, giving her a youthful, athletic look. Alex marveled at how incredibly stunning Jane looked, even when she wasn't trying to.

And then it hit her like a sucker punch, that unmistakable pull of wishing she were there. With *her*. At Jane's side, holding her elbow so she didn't slip on the ice, close enough to smell Jane's sweet-scented shampoo and lilac soap. A flutter awoke in her chest. She could call a cab and be at the arena in twenty minutes. *And tell Jane what, that you were just in the neighborhood and wanted to say hi?*

Alex immediately felt silly and childish and pissed at herself for churning inside like some heartsick kid instead of the professional she was. Hell, Jane wouldn't even be noticing her absence right now. She had plenty of other agents at her side, and protection was protection. What difference would it make to Jane who was standing next to her?

All three women's attention was riveted on the television set as Jane steadied herself, the two hockey players in the ready stance before her. A closeup showed the concentration etched on her face. *She's worried right now. She doesn't want to slip up.* Alex felt the anticipation and stepped closer to the screen. Jane had jokingly disclosed to Alex her fear of falling or fumbling the puck. She'd tried to make light of it, but Alex knew the nervousness was genuine. She'd tried her best to reassure Jane and even promised she would not watch it on television, which, of course, she'd had every intention of doing.

Jane seamlessly dropped the puck, shook each player's hand and even joked with the referee, making a pretend grab for his whistle. The crowd roared its approval and Jane's smile was full of pride and relief.

You did it, darlin'! Alex felt ridiculously pleased. She realized she was grinning like some kind of lunatic.

"You okay, Alex?" Kim asked.

"Sure. Fine. Why?"

Kim and Linny exchanged a look, and Alex knew they were up to something.

"I've got an idea," Linny said cheerily, as if the idea had just occurred to her. "How about the three of us go out to our old haunt?"

"Huh?" Alex replied, distracted. She had no idea what they were talking about and didn't much care.

"You know. The dyke bar on Crescent Avenue."

Alex groaned. "Why don't we just stay in and watch some really bad movie or something?"

"Oh, no," Kim said. "You can watch a movie any old time."

"Actually, I can't," Alex grumbled, but her friends weren't listening. They were already pulling coats off the rack.

"Indulge us, my friend." Kim's suggestion was more like an order, and Alex decided not to fight it.

৵৵

The years hadn't left much of a mark on the place, other than a slightly more worn sheen. Colored spotlights splashed across the dance floor, where bodies writhed to the latest dance tracks pounding from oversized speakers. A pool table in the corner was occupied by three butches in denim and a cute little femme in a black leather mini.

The three friends had no sooner bought drinks and claimed a table before Linny was off socializing, undoubtedly getting her gossip fix. They wouldn't see her much the rest of the evening, Alex knew from experience.

"So," Kim directed at Alex after a long silence. "What's wrong, kid?"

"Huh?" Alex could play dumb all night if she had to.

"Don't try to deny it, either."

"Deny what?"

Kim rolled her eyes. "There you go again, impenetrable as steel."

"I don't have the slightest idea what you're talkin' 'bout," Alex drawled. Her accent was always thicker when she chilled with friends or had a few drinks, and especially when she was tired, like tonight.

"We've been friends now for, what, ten or eleven years? And patrol partners for five of those. I can tell your little moods better than anyone else."

"Hmmm, and just what little mood am I supposedly in, since y'all seem to have the answers," Alex replied innocently, conveniently ignoring the anxious knot in her stomach. She knew Kim was tenacious as hell and would mercilessly keep at her if she had it in her mind to.

"I'm serious, Alex. You've barely strung together a sentence since you've been visiting us, and you're wound up tighter than my granny's old clock. You're not yourself and you know it. You look completely preoccupied."

Alex stared at her drink. "Aww, Kimmy, just leave it be.

Nothin's goin' on." She reached into her pocket and fingered the stone Jane had given her.

"Bullshit we're leaving it be. Whatever it is, I can tell you haven't talked to anybody about it. So talk to me."

Alex sighed loudly. "You sure you weren't my older sister in a past life?"

"No, I was your frigging mother. C'mon, talk to mama. And quit hiding behind humor."

Alex watched couples pair up to dance to Elton John's "Tiny Dancer," and she felt a longing ache lodge in her throat. She pictured Jane magically appearing, walking wordlessly up to her, extending her hand, leading her out to the dance floor . . .

Alex sipped her drink, jolted back to the very demanding presence of her friend. Kim was right. She hadn't been herself lately. Sometimes her concentration would slip for no apparent reason. Emotions unexpectedly welled. The problem was, she just didn't quite know how to articulate what she was feeling. She hadn't felt this out-of-sorts since her breakup with Julia, but at least then she'd known the cause. How could she tell Kim what she was feeling when she wasn't even quite sure herself?

"Well, I'm waaaaiting."

"I don't have anything to say. Honest." Alex wanted Kim to take the hint and drop it.

"Then I guess I'll have to play a guessing game. And I'm going to start with the name Jane Kincaid."

"What?"

Kim quietly drank, letting Alex stew for a few minutes. "Are you falling for our lovely senator, Alex?"

Alex nearly choked on her beer. "No!" she quickly protested.

"Be honest. Tell me how you feel about her." Kim's voice had softened considerably. *Maybe the interrogation's just about over.*

"Oh, Lord, Kim. Can't you leave it be?"

"Just play along with me, Al. Please?"

Alex took a deep breath and held it for a long time. *I am not falling for Jane Kincaid. That's ridiculous! I'm her bodyguard . . . a paid member of the United States government.*

"Don't think, Al, just tell me what comes to mind when I say her name."

"Oh, hell, Kimmy. That psychology degree of yours is nothing but a pain in the ass. Maybe you could get your own TV show if you ever stop being a cop. You can be the next Dr. Phil!"

"Aleeex."

Alex took a huge gulp before staring unwaveringly back at Kim. "She's the most fascinating, exciting, interesting person I've ever fucking met, okay? She's—she's just like nobody else. Period. As in, that's all there is to it. Satisfied?"

"No. Tell me more."

Alex's voice grew strained. "Ah, Kimmy. What can I tell you? It's like when you're in a dark room and you're blindly feeling around because you can't see a goddamned thing. And then all of a sudden a bright light is switched on and the whole world is suddenly right there before you. That's what she's like."

Kim whistled, a look of wonder on her face. "Huh. She's that good?"

"No. She's that special."

Kim looked sternly at Alex. "She's also straight, Alex."

"She was married once, if that's what you mean."

"Oh, no, you don't. Don't go there, Alex. I hear what you're *not* saying, loud and clear."

"What in blazes are you talking 'bout?"

Kim frowned. "That maybe she's not straight. That having been married to a man doesn't necessarily mean anything."

"You're putting words in my mouth."

"Whatever. Just don't fall for a straight woman, Alex. We've all been through that shit before, and it's not worth it. No matter how fascinating or gorgeous or wonderful or talented!"

But Alex wasn't listening anymore. Her gaze was following a tall, gorgeous brunette at the bar who bore more than a passing resemblance to Jane Kincaid.

"Forget it, Alex."

"What?" she asked innocently, still tracking the woman.

"She looks like a Republican to me," Kim spat.

"Well, she looks like lunch to me." Alex couldn't deny the sudden arousal rocketing through her body. It'd been a long time—too long. And Kim was right. She *was* wound up too tight lately.

"Don't do it, girl. She looks too much like our candidate. You're asking for trouble."

But Alex was already off her chair, striding quickly to the bar. It didn't take her more than a few seconds to garner the long-haired beauty's attention.

Alex nuzzled into the woman, planting delicate kisses on her long, smooth neck, eager for a second round.

"My, my, Alex," the woman growled. "You are a persistent one, aren't you?"

Alex's kisses grew more demanding, trailing down the woman's collarbone, then down to an erect, sumptuous nipple, which Alex sucked ravenously. It wasn't long before her mouth busily traveled south again, eliciting sharp moans with each nip and sure stroke. The naked body beneath hers predictably squirmed with delight.

But emotionally, Alex was making love to the woman by rote. Her mind had long ago drifted away—to Jane, to the campaign, to work. She'd hoped a roll in the sack would put her right again, suck away some of that loneliness, fill some of that emptiness she felt more often than not these days. But it wasn't working. She just wanted to get on with it and go.

Kim warned you this would be trouble, you moron.

❧

Kim waggled her eyebrows teasingly. "Must have been some night, Stud. Strolling in here at the bright hour of . . ." She made a big show of looking at her watch. "Ten a.m."

Alex grimaced and glanced around. "Where's Linny?"

"My dear Caroline has gone out grocery shopping. I bribed her, of course. Want some breakfast?"

Alex wasn't hungry. Her funk had only grown, despite the distractions of her wonderful friends and the lovely piece of ass known as Gillian.

Kim stood before her, hands on her hips, worry etched onto her face. "Want to talk?"

Alex considered for long moment. "Walk with me?"

They picked their way silently through a neighboring graveyard, Alex stopping briefly at random headstones, reading the names and dates to herself and wondering absently about the life stories behind those names. When she was a kid, she would entertain herself by spending hours walking through centuries-old gravesites, her imagination easily making up faces and elaborate histories. North Carolina was fertile ground for a kid with an interest in history and an elaborate imagination.

Alex finally let out an exaggerated sigh, signaling that she was ready to talk. "I think I should ask to be reassigned."

Kim's jaw dropped. "Why?"

Alex hedged. "It's just . . . I dunno."

"What? I thought it was pretty obvious you liked working with Jane."

"That's just it, Kim." Alex wished that for once she didn't have to explain it all. She hated spilling her guts like this about something so personal, but she needed a friend's advice right now. And Kim would understand—she always did.

Kim reached over and clutched her arm as they walked. "I see," she said in quiet acknowledgement. "You think you can't be a good agent unless you maintain detachment from your subject."

Alex winced. "Something like that."

"You know, it's probably not that uncommon for Secret Service agents to like their subjects. Think how horrible it'd be if you hated her. It'd be even harder to do your job, don't you think?"

"I just . . . I just wasn't figuring on this."

Kim chuckled. "Yeah, well, life's full of stuff we didn't figure on, sister."

Alex's mood was as dark as their surroundings. "I get the feeling you think I'm making a huge deal out of this."

"Something like that." Kim slowed them to a stop. "Look, Al. So you like the candidate. A lot. And why not? Sounds like she's pretty incredible, which means another fifty million people probably feel exactly as you do." Kim couldn't truly understand the depth of Alex's growing feelings for Jane. Even Alex didn't, but at least Kim was trying. "I know I gave you a hard time last night . . . and I'm not saying you shouldn't be careful. But I think you've got yourself too worked up about all this."

Alex nodded tightly. It was true. Sometimes she felt like a coiled spring that might snap.

"If you truly think your feelings are getting in the way of doing your job, you'll know when to ask for a transfer. You won't even have to question it like you're doing now. You're too good a cop not to know if that happens."

"You sound pretty darned sure of me." *I just hope you're right.*

"Alex, you know what I think is really going on here?"

Alex wavered between wanting and not wanting to hear what Kim had to say next. She acquiesced with her silence.

"It's your first big protection detail. They've made you the number one of someone who's incredibly dynamic, charming, smart and gorgeous to boot. Throw in the glitter and grind of a presidential campaign, and it's no wonder you're feeling out of your league. You gotta give it some time to get used to it all, girl." A wide grin broke out on Kim's face. "Hey. Remember your first fuck?"

Alex jerked in surprise. *How could anyone forget that?*

"It's, like, the biggest thing that's ever happened in your life up to that point, right? Of course it's overwhelming at first. And you even mistake it for love. And then after awhile, you see it for what it really is—just a moment in your life. And this moment you're having over Jane will pass, too. Pretty soon, you'll see all her warts and you'll deny you were ever smitten with her."

Alex smiled and let her shoulders relax. With luck, the rest of her would relax, too. Maybe Kim was right. Any day now she probably *would* get sick to death of Jane and her campaign. "Kim, what would I do without you and Linny?"

"That, my dear, you'll hopefully never have to find out." They resumed walking, arm in arm, Kim tugging Alex a bit. "Speaking of . . . ah-hem . . . the dirty deed, how was the Republican last night?"

Alex laughed and punched Kim lightly in the arm. "You never told me how you guessed she was a Republican."

Kim smirked. "She looked like the type who thinks her own shit doesn't stink."

Alex laughed again, feeling a lightness she hadn't felt in weeks. "Sometimes, those ones are the best—" Her chirping cell phone interrupted.

"Warner here."

Alex listened intently to Commander Harry Johnson on the other end, her body tensing with every word. It was only seeing her distress mirrored in Kim's anxious face that forced her to calm down.

"I'll meet you at the airport in an hour," she said evenly into the phone, then clicked it shut.

"Anything wrong?" Kim asked.

"Maybe."

Chapter 6

Jane's spontaneous embrace, though abrupt, was spirited, and it made the clearly surprised Alex jump like a nervous cat. Jane secretly enjoyed seeing her put off her feet like that, and made a mental note that if boredom ever struck, she just might try something like that again.

Jane had missed Alex these last couple of days, and it only just occurred to her, like the sudden flash of remembering a dream from the night before. Now she turned her razor sharp mind to Alex, who still baffled her, in spite of their growing closeness. Alex could be so funny and warm and open one minute, then stiff and aloof the next. It was puzzling, and the only puzzles Jane liked were the ones she could solve. This one she wanted to solve. Perhaps a little emotional nudge now and again, like a hug, might go a long way in making Alex trust her enough to be more at ease.

"It's good to see you, Agent Warner."

"Thank you, ma'am." A polite smile. "It's good to see you, too."

Jane frowned a little. She couldn't seem to entirely break Alex of that "ma'am" thing and the syrupy, southern way it came out. Jane found it surprisingly sweet, charming even. That polite reticence was a fascinating contradiction to the tough cop persona that Alex usually wore like a uniform. But it was also one of the many little walls Alex habitually put up between them.

"Did you have fun visiting your friends, Alex?"

Alex's face had begun turning an interesting shade of red.

"Okay, don't answer that." Jane laughed to hide her curiosity. "Listen, I'm sorry to have to pull you away. Apparently my mother has had a little accident and wants to see me at the family home up north." She held up a forestalling hand. "Nothing serious. But my very bossy staff members are insisting that I go check on her, spend a couple of days with her. Okay by you?"

"My pleasure," Alex answered automatically. "Will this be a little vacation for you as well?"

Jane grimaced. "Not if I can help it. With our first Super Tuesday next week, I've got a million things to do. And then some, but who's counting?"

The two women climbed into the small commuter jet where they were met by two other agents. They were a small group because Jane's staff was on their way back to Washington to firm up plans for the coming days. It would just be Jane, the three agents and her mother on the island, and even that was three people too many. Well, two anyway, Jane thought, stealing a glance at Alex.

"Maybe a little vacation would be a good idea, then," Alex suggested.

"Funny, that's exactly what my staff said, too." Jane fastened her lap belt and looked skeptically at Alex. "Did they tell you to say that?"

"Of course not," Alex answered quickly. "I just thought, you know, with things getting even busier—"

Jane waved her agreement. "I could use a little time to recharge my batteries." She said it more to herself than to Alex. It felt like such a foreign idea.

The plane darted into the sky, heading north by way of the Lake Huron shoreline. The lake below, with its snow-covered icy crust, looked like a white desert.

"You didn't happen to see my big moment at Joe Louis Arena, did you?" Jane glanced a little sheepishly at Alex.

Alex bit back a smile. "Um, well . . . Do you really want me to answer that?"

They were sitting side-by-side for the forty-minute flight to Mackinac Island, with the other agents at the back of the plane. Jane didn't know them as well as she knew Alex and didn't feel like inviting them to sit closer. She was rather looking forward to having Alex to herself for a little while. Their banter came much easier these days, and it pleased Jane. She let out a deep sigh for effect and summoned her most scolding tone. "You promised you wouldn't watch, Agent Warner!"

Alex looked remorseful for all of about two seconds. "Sorry. My friends made me. But you did great. You looked like a real pro!"

Jane giggled, pleased. "Well, let's not get too carried away, Alex." She'd been afraid of making a fool of herself, and yet it had gone much better than she'd expected. "It was a blast, actually."

"Hey, maybe refereeing could be, you know, your . . ."

"Fall-back job if I don't win the nomination?"

Alex's smile was a little doubtful, as if she weren't quite sure she should be teasing Jane this way. *Oh, Alex, you're so damn cute sometimes.*

Jane patted Alex's knee reassuringly. "Good idea, Alex. With your connections in the hockey world, maybe you could get me some work."

"Actually, my rec league is always looking for a good ref."

Jane laughed, feeling unusually relaxed. Maybe she really was on her way to solving Alex. "So," she began lightly. "Anything exciting happen on your days off?" She almost chuckled out loud at the slow, adorable blush working its way up Alex's neck. *Oh, yes, I've got you now, Alex!*

"Nah. Nothing much." A tiny shrug, but Alex couldn't seem to look at Jane.

Jane was smug. *So, Alex is hiding something.* "You don't kiss and tell, is that it?"

Alex let out a small gasp and did turn to Jane this time, her eyes wide with surprise.

Jane chuckled, enjoying herself. "Discretion is always a good quality, Alex. I admire that."

In fact, in the month or more since Alex had joined her security detail, Jane hadn't heard a single word from anyone about any exploits on the agent's part. She was charming, handsome, bright, athletic . . . she couldn't possibly have any trouble in the girlfriend department, and yet there had not been a peep of gossip about her. Alex had been all business on the campaign trail as far as Jane could see . . . until now, it seemed.

"At least someone's having some fun, I hope," Jane quipped, refusing to consider how long it had been since she'd even been on a date herself, let alone something more. Her personal life, as usual, would just have to wait.

Jane's thoughts began to drift to work, as they always did eventually. She didn't like taking time out of her campaign, even if it was to spend a couple of days with her mother, whom she'd seen so little of the last few months. She couldn't help but feel there was some good-natured conspiracy afoot to force her to take a timeout from her hectic schedule. She just wished they'd all been honest about it so she could at least act like she was doing all of *them* a favor by taking a break.

Jane turned to Alex, determined to call the bluff, if there was one. "Alex, I really think my mother is using an injury ruse to get me to visit. And yes, a little vacation is probably a good idea, but I'm not sure that I can afford one right now." Time off was just another sacrifice Jane was used to making without a second thought.

Alex sighed quietly but said nothing.

"I might just stay a few hours. I want you guys ready to roll on short notice."

Alex remained silent, but her jaw had visibly tightened.

Jane leaned closer, her Spidey sense tingling. She sniffed the air like a bloodhound on the trail of a scent. "Alex, by chance is there something you are neglecting to tell me?"

Alex was the picture of wide-eyed innocence. The act was a little too good, in Jane's opinion.

Oh, yeah, something's definitely up. "Let me guess. My rivals have planned some big television debate and didn't want to invite me."

Alex chuckled. "Damn. I knew you'd figure it out. I understand they were afraid they were no match for you in front of the cameras."

"Hah. I hope they realize they're no match for me, period. Cameras or no cameras!"

"Good point," Alex replied. "But I'll bet the cameras *love* you."

"Hmmm, you're not trying to distract me by paying me compliments, are you, Agent Warner?"

"Distract you from what?" Alex asked, playing dumb, but her tone was mischievous.

"Oh, never mind." Jane sighed. Tempted as she was to get to the bottom of things, she considered the precarious and frustrating position of being ten thousand feet off the ground in this cigar tube they called an airplane—not to mention that no one was giving her a straight answer anyway. She would let it go, let them all have their fun. For the moment.

The amount of snow on the ground surprised Jane a little. She hadn't seen the island in winter for a few years, because usually her mother wintered on the mainland. This year, because of the campaign and all its publicity, her mother had chosen to stay at the quiet retreat.

Jane had always loved Mackinac Island. When she was a kid and her father was governor of Michigan, the family spent summers at the governor's mansion on the island that separated the northern and southern parts of the state, where Lakes Huron and Michigan converged. Twelve years after they first started coming to Mackinac, when Joe Kincaid retired from politics, the family purchased a 140-year-old, sixteen-room Victorian mansion so that they could keep returning to their beloved island. Jane's time there now was so infrequent—sometimes a couple of years passed before she visited—that she couldn't help now but yield to a sense of yearning and nostalgia. It was a beautiful place, with beautiful family memories. And it was always wonderful to return, no matter what the reason. She just wished the timing were a little better.

To Jane's surprise, Commander Harry Johnson was waiting inside a horse-driven carriage at the airport's small parking area.

"Hello, Harry. I didn't expect to find you here." Jane's voice was even, masking her growing suspicion. She watched Alex and the two other agents quickly pile luggage into a second carriage.

Harry's smile was innocuous, his overcoat bulging where his pistol was holstered. *God.* She hated those damned things. She didn't know how Alex could stand having one sticking in her side all the time.

"When they said I had the chance to come spend some time here . . ." He gestured broadly, a grin plastered on his hang-dog face. " . . . I couldn't pass it up. Hell, why should Alex get all the plum jobs?"

Jane smiled more hospitably than she felt. So much for a quiet getaway. And not only that, but she'd been mislead about the number of agents who would be accompanying her, for some inexplicable reason. Harry's presence meant he'd probably been supervising an advance team.

As she, Alex and Harry climbed into the enclosed buggy, Jane realized with a pang of nostalgia how much she'd missed the sharp smell of horses. There were advantages to not having any motorized vehicles on the island, and the big beautiful beasts clomping down the streets always filled her with a sense of wonder and comfort. *Though a warm car would be nice right about now, too.*

The buggy threaded its way down narrow, winding streets, past the majestic Grand Hotel. The sight of the huge, ostentatious white building, its long, covered porch that, in summer, was decorated with large American flags, always awed Jane. It was only a short hop from there, on an escarpment that dropped starkly off into the straits, that the buggy came to a halt in front of the Kincaid mansion. It was one of several old Victorian homes from the nineteenth century, all of which the locals referred to as the "cottages" of the wealthy.

Few people lived on the island during winter, and it was almost ghostly in its serenity. Even the Kincaid home looked somehow lonely and sad.

Jane jumped down from the buggy and ran to her mother, who stood patiently waiting on the steps. Maria Kincaid was an elegant woman, tall and slender and beautiful, as always.

"Hi, Mom." Jane hugged her mother tightly. E-mails and phone calls were no replacement for this, Jane realized with a twinge of regret. *God. How long had it been?* Jane did the mental math and realized they hadn't seen each other in almost six months. "It's so good to see you, Mom."

"It's good to see you, Janey. Let me look at you." She pulled back and studied Jane with a careful eye. "You need to eat. Have you been eating properly?"

Jane didn't know how her mother could possibly tell anything about her weight through her heavy overcoat. It was that Italian heritage of her mother that placed so much emphasis on food. "Yes, I've been eating. But you—" Jane noticed for the first time the bandaged wrist peeking out of her mother's sleeve. "So you really did hurt yourself. Or is this just for show?"

"Your mother would never lie about such a thing, dear."

"Is it sprained or broken?" Jane asked, instantly in doctor mode.

"Just sprained, dear. I'll be good as new in a few weeks, the doctor tells me."

Jane was instantly relieved. "Mom, I don't like you spending the winter here. It's dangerous, all this ice and snow."

"Oh, shush, dear. What's a little ice and snow? Anyone could take a tumble down these steps, even you. Now," Maria Kincaid turned to Alex, and raised a finely shaped silver eyebrow. "Who is this good-looking young woman you've brought? I've already met Harry. And yes, Harry, you're good-looking, too." She winked at the commander in jest, before casting curious dark eyes back to Alex.

Jane did the introductions, explaining that Alex would be staying in the house with them. She assumed Harry and the other two agents, who'd already taken the other carriage to the back of the house, would set up shop nearby.

"Yes, I already figured that," her mother replied hastily, still checking Alex out with a thoroughness that was almost embarrassing. "All the other agents are staying in the guest house over the stable. It'll be just us girls in the big house."

"*All* the other agents? I thought this was going to be a low-key thing?" She glared at Harry and Alex, not as surprised as she sounded. "There's more I don't know about?"

"We threw in a couple more for the hell of it. I needed the extra help just to handle all your luggage," Harry joked.

Hands on her hips, Jane's indulgence had run out. The gloves were off. "Okay. I want some answers, because something is going on. Mom." She stared sternly at her mother, then softened just a touch. "I know a sprained wrist isn't exactly a family emergency that requires my presence. Though it is nice to be here," she added grudgingly before turning her sights on Alex and Harry. "You two have managed to spirit me away up here with a truckload of agents, apparently, while my staff have all conveniently stayed in Washington. I'm getting the distinct feeling this isn't a little vacation after all." Jane crossed her arms over her chest for effect. "Now, is someone going to tell me what's going on, or am I going to have to make some phone calls? Or I could just beat it out of the two of you."

The two agents exchanged wary glances before Jane's mother intervened. "How about the four of us go inside and chat over some hot chocolate, shall we?"

Maria Kincaid was already heading for the door, the three of them having no choice but to follow.

"Well?" Jane impatiently prompted over the hot mugs.

Harry loosened his tie, then clasped his hands in front of him on the kitchen table. "There's been a threat against you, Jane."

Jane waved a dismissive hand. "Is that all? I'm sure there are threats against me every day. What's the big deal about this one?"

"A thirty-year-old man from Alabama just escaped from jail," Harry said. "He phoned your campaign office twice in the past week from prison and said he would kill you before you ever got to be president. There was other stuff too, of course. More detailed stuff. But suffice it to say that we had reasonable grounds to believe your life was in danger."

"What was he in jail for?"

Alex answered this time, her tone official. "For bombing an abortion clinic. He also has a long criminal record for assaulting women."

"Anybody killed in the bombing?"

"Fortunately, no. But a clinic worker lost a leg."

"And so you think squirreling me away up here is a good idea?"

"We have reason to believe the perp is in Washington right now, which is why you're not," Harry interjected. "And we can't assume he's working alone, either. Your staff is back in Washington as part of a decoy plan. They're making it look like business as usual."

Jane thought it sounded like something out of a bad movie. "This is all sounding rather complicated and cryptic. He's supposed to think I'm there when I'm actually here? Will it even work?"

Alex looked a lot more calm than Jane felt. "The media will be told that you're suffering from the flu and are holed up in your Georgetown residence. We're hoping it will help flush this guy out. Police, the FBI and the Secret Service are combing the city for him as we speak."

Jane looked pointedly at both agents. "Tell me something. Are you truly worried or are you just following protocol?" Jane needed the truth, because if she were going to stay here under guard, the threat had to be credible in her mind, too. More than credible. She'd need to be downright scared.

Alex and Harry shared an indecipherable look.

"Yes," the commander answered after a moment. "We feel it is a serious threat, Dr. Kincaid."

Jane felt a mild headache coming on as anger began a slow and steady burn. *Great. Just great. I'm stuck here at the whim of some asshole while the race for the nomination goes on without me! And I'm going to look like a wimp who's run away.*

She slumped back in her chair, needing to settle her voice and her emotions. She summoned what shred of patience she still had. "So why bring me here and bring my mother into this? I mean, isn't her safety in jeopardy now?"

"No," Alex said evenly. "Your mother is actually safer here with a half dozen Secret Service agents around her. And you're safer out of Washington. As you know, in winter the airport is the only way to get to the island. And the population is so sparse, we'll know exactly who's coming and going."

"What if the press finds out I'm here instead of Washington?"

"We hope that doesn't happen," Harry answered. "But if it does, your staff will tell them that a family emergency required your sudden presence here. And that you wanted it to be private."

"Jesus Christ," Jane said quietly, still trying to grasp what was happening to her. It was such a helpless feeling. This lunatic was already victimizing her, even if he never came near her. "Just how long, exactly, am I supposed to be here?"

Harry looked almost as miserable as Jane felt. "Until this guy is caught."

Jane held up a palm, though she felt like smashing something. "Goddammit, no! I will *not* be held hostage here indefinitely. No way! We've got to have a better plan than that."

"Jane," Maria Kincaid lightly scolded. "This is *not* a prison! For God's sake, it's your home. Our home."

Jane rubbed her aching forehead. *Shit*. "I'm sorry, Mother. I didn't mean it like that. It's just that, I can't hide here like some kind of . . . of hunted prey or something while everyone else goes on campaigning." She stood up, signaling that the discussion was over. She'd made up her mind. "All right. I will give the authorities twenty-four hours to find this nut. Either way, I'm heading back to Washington tomorrow afternoon, even if I have to take an air taxi. I will not stop this campaign any longer than that."

Alex was blown away by the charm and character of the Kincaid "cottage." Gleaming oak hardwood floors throughout

84

were covered with intermittent, colorful area rugs that Alex figured were worth a small fortune. Elegant light fixtures hung from the vaulted ceilings, and stained glass wall sconces cast ambient light along every hallway. Elaborate wood-burning fireplaces graced the dining room, living room, the library and at least two of the upstairs bedrooms. The main staircase curved through the center of the house, its balustrade made of black walnut and hand-carved in ornate detail—like something straight out of *Gone With The Wind*. The furniture was all antique, much of it made from black walnut or oak and polished to within an inch of its life.

It was poles apart from the pre-fab, post-war bungalow in North Carolina she grew up in. In full admiration, Alex caressed the smooth wood of the stairway's banister, a vague yearning in her deepest recesses. The place was warm and homey in a way Alex had little experience with. She had no close family to speak of anymore, and her own Washington townhouse was functional and tidy and *nice*. But *home* was mostly an abstract idea for her.

Maria Kincaid called Alex's name from somewhere distant, pulling her reluctantly from her thoughts, and beckoned her to join mother and daughter in the library for an after-dinner drink.

Each woman was quietly sipping a glass of brandy, seated in high, blood-red, leather wingback chairs flanking a roaring fire. Maria gestured to a matching loveseat across from them and offered Alex a drink, which she politely refused.

"We're discussing Janey's campaign, and I'd really like your opinion, Alex."

Oh, boy. She'd been warned by other agents never to engage in political talk with or about candidates. And here she was, put on the spot by a lovely woman who had just fed her the best roast beef she'd ever tasted.

Alex cast a covert glance at Jane and felt a distinct frostiness. *Great. She's still pissed off at me over deceiving her with this whole mess.* The decision to trick Jane into coming to the island was none of Alex's doing, yet she'd gone along with it because she was confident it was the right thing to do. Jane's safety had to trump everything else. Getting her out of Washington *was* the prudent thing to do.

"I'm sorry, ma'am, but it's really not my place to offer opinions about your daughter's or anyone else's campaign." Alex quietly held her breath, knowing and hating how mechanical her words sounded. She felt sweat beading on the back of her neck.

"But you're in the perfect position to offer an opinion," Maria pressed, her smile pinning Alex. "You've heard every speech over the last month; you've seen Jane with the crowds." She nodded proudly at Jane, who sat stone-faced, silently sipping her brandy as the flames threw dancing orange light across her face. She looked ridiculously beautiful in spite of her unhappiness, Alex thought with a mild start.

"She has a wonderful, special rapport with people, don't you think?" Maria was leaning forward in earnestness.

Alex tried not to grin like a fool as she thought of Jane's magnetic pull on crowds, how she could mesmerize them with a few poignant words, or with her voice, her gestures, her smile, or even just a playful twinkle in her eye. Alex had followed Jane in a rope line just last week in Cleveland, and they had come across a family whose younger child was a paraplegic. Jane had spoken to them all, touched them all with a pat or a warm handshake, but it was her words to the older, healthy child that had nearly choked Alex up. Jane told him never to forget that his parents loved him equally too. That sometimes it seemed parents played favorites, but that in their hearts, it wasn't true.

"Yes," Alex finally answered in a voice thick with the emotion of the memory. She did not—could not—look at Jane right now for fear of becoming a blubbering idiot. "She has a wonderful relationship with the crowds."

"Ah-ha!" Maria exclaimed triumphantly, turning to Jane. "You see, dear, you're a natural at that, and I'm not just saying it because you're my daughter." Maria shot a wink at Alex. "I've been around a politician or two in my life."

"Mother, please—"

"Listen, dear, because I'm going to tell you this anyway."

From her periphery, Alex could see Jane clench her jaw in reluctant resignation.

"What you're *not* a natural at is working with television," Jane's mother continued. "You need to embrace more opportunities, do some live interviews, like *Larry King Live*, or *Oprah*. You come through so well on television."

"Mom—"

"I know, dear, you don't like being a media slut."

Alex stifled a laugh and risked a quick glance at Jane, whose face had softened into a suppressed chortle.

"The people who get the chance to see you and hear you in person already love you. It's everyone else that needs to fall in love with you, too. And to reach them, you've got to go through the mass media. Mass media equal mass audiences." Maria looked directly at Alex. "Alex, don't you agree that Jane is easy to fall in love with once you know her?"

Alex thought the ground had just literally shifted under her. *Goddamn, I could use that drink right now.* She was at a loss as to how she was supposed to answer a question like that. What was she supposed to do, say no and risk having to come up with some elaborate explanation? Or worse yet, say yes and watch them laugh at her as she got all hot and flustered and embarrassed? But Maria was still looking at her, waiting. "I, ah, ah, y-yes, of course she is, ma'am," Alex stammered. She felt their curious stares and prayed for the floor to somehow open up and swallow her.

"You see, Jane? That's exactly what I'm talking about. It's time to think nationally, instead of one or two states at a time, or a few thousand people at a time. You need to think of yourself as running for the presidency now, not just for the Democratic nomination."

But Jane was clearly preoccupied, staring sightlessly into her empty snifter. "Christ, I wish they'd hurry up and find that nutcase so I can get back to work. I hate this." She looked up at Alex, impatience creasing her forehead.

Maria stood awkwardly. "They're doing all they can, dear. Right, Alex?"

"Yes, ma'am, they are."

"Now, if you two will excuse me, brandy and pain pills really don't mix very well. Alex, dear, will you help me navigate the stairs to my room?"

Maria leaned on Alex as they slowly climbed the stairs. "My daughter speaks very highly of you, you know."

Alex was shocked. "She does?"

"She says you're a very good agent. She trusts you."

Alex smiled. "I'm glad she thinks so."

"She says she can talk to you. That you listen."

They stopped outside Maria Kincaid's bedroom door.

"I don't think she has too much to say to me right now, not after today." Alex hoped she didn't sound as dreadful about it as she felt.

Maria snickered. "She'll get over it. She's just frustrated. But listen." She squeezed Alex's arm with her good hand. "I don't mind telling you that she does need someone she can talk to every now and then . . . someone whose fortunes are not so tied to the success of her campaign. Do you know what I mean?"

"I think so, ma'am."

Maria rolled her eyes. "Oh, Alex. Always the polite but evasive southerner."

"Pardon?"

"Never mind. What I'm trying to say, Alex, is this. Be there for my daughter if she needs to talk. Just listen, offer your best advice, or even just your shoulder. I know it's not part of your duties, but will you do this for me?"

"I—I'm not sure what to say, Mrs. Kincaid. I would surely

like to say yes, but I reckon I may not be the best one to—"

"Oh, please, Alex." Maria's jaw was set uncompromisingly— the same look Alex had seen so many times on Jane when she'd set her mind to something. "Jane says you're a very bright woman. You're grounded and unflappable, and I think she relies on you. Maybe more than you think." She shrugged. "Maybe more than *she* thinks."

"Your daughter seems to have quite a lot to say about me. More than she's ever told me." She felt an odd sense of relief. Perhaps the intimate talk they'd had in Philadelphia hadn't been just a fluke. She hoped it wasn't. She hoped Jane really did think of her as more than just a bodyguard.

"Alex, there's chemistry between the two of you. When you walked into the room earlier, I felt a change in my daughter. A kind of calmness, but electricity, too." She looked a little per- plexed. "Anyway, that's why I've asked you to look out for her. I want you to be her friend."

"I'll do my best, ma'am. And, for the record, I think your daughter . . ." *is the most incredible, wonderful woman I've ever met!* " . . . is a tremendous person."

"Well, you're right about that. She just needs to be reminded now and again." Maria's hand rested on the doorknob. "There is one more thing. You will keep my daughter safe, won't you, Alex?"

Alex had no trouble with *that* question. "If it's the last thing I do, ma'am."

Alex jogged down the stairs, planning on a quick goodnight, since Jane wasn't really talking to her anyway. But when she got to the library, Jane was pouring brandy into two snifters. Her look was both appraising and summoning, a slight smile pulling at the corners of her mouth. She silently walked over to Alex and held out a glass, as if it were a routine they'd done many times. "I know you're on duty, but one drink won't kill you . . . I mean *us*." She laughed hollowly at her own joke, and Alex guessed Jane was a little drunk.

"You're not angry with me?" Alex ventured before hesitantly accepting the glass. A few sips couldn't hurt.

"Yes, I am," Jane said matter-of-factly from behind the rim of her glass. "Pissed as hell at you and Harry for manipulating me *and* bringing my mother into this."

"But we feel we didn't have any other—"

Jane held up a hand. "Relax. I know you're just doing your job and following orders. It's not your fault. So have a drink with me and consider yourself absolved."

Alex raised her glass in mock salute and took a quick sip. "You Catholic women always know just the thing to say to a girl."

Jane laughed so hard, Alex had to reach over and steady her.

"Alex." Jane's eyes glistened with tears of laughter. "I don't think I could ever truly stay angry at you."

"Can I have that notarized for future reference?"

Jane scolded Alex with her eyes, but she didn't mean it. "Do you see a judge around here?"

Alex took another sip, the warm burning sensation giving her instant courage. "No, but doesn't the next President of the United States have that power?"

Alex watched Jane silently move to a wall of framed photos. She paused pensively in front of a picture of President Kennedy and a youthful looking man Alex knew from old news articles was Jane's father, the former governor. On the wall beside it was another photo of Joe Kincaid, this time with Bobby Kennedy. He was more aged in the picture with Jimmy Carter.

A grandfather clock chimed nine times, breaking the silence.

"My mother's right, of course." Jane sighed, running a finger tenderly around a wood picture frame.

"Right about what?" Alex swallowed nervously. *There's chemistry between the two of you . . . Electricity.* Maria Kincaid's words repeated in her mind. *Was it true?*

Jane still had her back to Alex, was still staring at the old photos that she surely must have studied hundreds of times before. "About playing to a more national audience. She's very astute about those things. I guess I'm more like my father. I relate better to people one-on-one or in small groups. Not millions at a time."

Alex took a step closer to Jane and tried to ignore the very powerful desire to reach out and touch her. She felt her chest constrict painfully. "Did your father ever want to run for president?"

"Yes. Several times. He never did, though. He thought he had a good chance of being Bobby Kennedy's running mate, but of course . . ." Jane's voice trailed off.

Yes. Bobby Kennedy. He was the reason Alex was even here. Until his assassination, candidates didn't come under Secret Service protection before the party nomination was complete. Now, almost all declared candidates got protection.

"He loved being governor of Michigan, and once his third term was over, he knew that his brand of politics had become antiquated. So he threw his energies into mentoring others and being a power broker behind the scenes."

Jane turned around, languidly leaned against a bookshelf, and sipped her drink with deliberation. She looked far more intense than an after-dinner drink called for. Perhaps she was considering her father's legacy and all its dauntless burdens and gifts.

Alex was struck by the power in Jane's stillness, and she felt the startling realization that it was as if destiny were at work. It felt like some sort of brush with greatness or royalty, being in Jane's presence. Alex had seen it, felt it many times before with Jane. A word, a look, a touch, was often magical. She spoke from the heart. Always. And she was attentive, thoughtful. She made people feel as if they were the most important person in the world in that single moment. It was truly a natural-born gift.

Yet part of Jane's power was also in what she held back. Alex had seen Jane readily reveal a feeling or a thought or an experience that was meaningful to her in a substantial way, even to strangers. But there was always the sense that it was really only a fraction of what Jane wasn't revealing, and might never reveal to anyone. There always seemed to be so much more there, so many more layers. It was damn alluring.

Jesus, Kim. You're wrong. The way this woman affects me . . . I'm not starstruck because I'm new to the job or new to a presidential campaign. She's really got to me because she's so incredibly special.

Mute panic seized Alex like a fist, and her heart thudded in her ears. She felt helpless in the face of her own feelings. They frightened the hell out of her. She ached for Jane to tell her things—things she didn't tell anyone else. She wanted to be scooped up and carried off into Jane's intimate and heady journey toward destiny, to greatness. To be there, by her side. To matter to Jane, as Jane mattered to her.

Alex felt nauseous. Sweat was beading thickly on her forehead. This couldn't be happening. In her job, she was supposed to be immune to such things, to such people, to such feelings. It just wasn't acceptable. Professional detachment was expected. It was vital. And in spite of what she'd just promised to Jane's mother, she had to get a grip and remember why she was here.

"Alex, you've gone all pale on me," Jane said worriedly. "You okay? You look like you're about to have an anxiety attack."

Yes, I am, and I need you to take me in your arms and tell me that I'm not losing my sanity, that everything is okay. Alex blinked harshly to clear her mind, but the effort was futile. She took a drink of the warm, bronze liquid and tried to sound casual. "I'm fine. Sorry. We were talking about your father." Alex desperately needed the conversation to be so *not* about her right now. "Did he want you to go into politics?"

Jane's eyes widened almost imperceptibly. She finished off the rest of her drink and went for a refill. "More?" she asked without turning around.

"No, thank you." It was a lie, she did want more of the calming elixir, but she needed to keep her wits about her.

Jane took a drink from her refilled glass, held it for a long, savoring moment before swallowing. She reclaimed her wingback chair by the fire, and Alex followed her cue, still feeling slightly dazed, and sat in the matching chair.

Jane slowly brushed her hair from her shoulder, as if she were in no hurry to answer Alex's question. She studied the contents of her glass in the flickering firelight. "My father . . . He always had grand designs for at least one of us to follow him into politics. I absolutely loathed the idea in the early part of my life."

Alex felt disbelief. "You did? But . . ." Jane was so damn good at politics. A natural, as if she'd been born to do it.

Jane laughed. "I know what you're thinking. Why would I fight something I seem so suited to?"

"Exactly."

"My brother . . . he was two years older than me." Jane took another long sip and stared into the fading fire, cloaked in her own private memories. "He was the anointed one," she said, barely loud enough for Alex to hear. "But he died of leukemia when he was twenty-three."

"I'm sorry." Alex could hear the unmistakable grief in Jane's voice, even after so many years.

"And my little sister was seven years younger than me . . . she was just a kid. So I became my father's obsession."

A long, uncomfortable silence ensued, leaving Alex to wonder if she should end the conversation, say goodnight. But then Jane suddenly laughed dolefully, her voice low.

"My lazy, aimless days ended in a hurry, that's for sure. You see, the year before my brother died, I'd dropped out of college to travel around Europe. I was just basically a lazy, rich kid, going where I wanted, doing whatever pleased me, having affairs, drinking too much, smoking dope, hanging out with other aimless rich kids." She took another drink, then looked up at Alex with an expression that was hard to read. "My brother was the rising star in the family . . . he was in law school before he died. He was playing the role of prodigy . . . the smart, ambitious kid who never disappointed. While he was getting all that attention, I could just kind of melt into the background. Do my own thing." Jane took a deep breath. "Then, once he was gone . . . I couldn't very well sit on my ass anymore and hide. There was suddenly this huge vacuum in the family, this role to fulfill. There was an unspoken, but very clear pressure, to take on that responsibility."

Jane quieted again, studying the diminishing contents in her glass. Alex leaned closer.

"In the back of my mind, I had always wanted to be a doctor . . . *some day*. Like, way down the road, once I had my fun and grew up. After my brother died, I figured it was a way for me to make my parents proud without trying to emulate him. So I got on my horse and that's what I did."

"And your father was okay with your choice?"

"Yeah, he was okay with it, as long as I promised to consider politics eventually. But man, I resisted. Big time. No way was I going into politics. We argued and fought over it for years. I mean, I had my calling, you know?"

Alex drained her glass. "So, what made you finally do it?"

Jane's faint smile turned bitter. She stared at the glowing embers. "Circumstances in my life changed. My husband died. I got disenchanted with my profession. Then my father died. All those awful things in quick succession. Suddenly, I had no harness on me. Nobody with any expectations of me. I could do whatever I wanted. I was totally free for the first time since just before my brother died." She looked at Alex again, this time with resolve. Her right hand curled into a fist. "And that's when I wanted it. Like I'd never wanted anything before. If I was going to make a difference in the world, I knew it had to be in the political arena."

Alex stared, transfixed, delighted to see the familiar spark and fierceness in Jane. She felt awed and honored that Jane had just shared something so special with her. Was she becoming a friend, someone Jane could talk to, like Maria said? *Oh, Lord. This is all so wrong, but I can't seem to stop it. And I don't want to stop it!*

Jane stood up somewhat awkwardly. She smiled tiredly. "Alex, I'm sorry to have talked your ear off."

Alex stood, too. She smiled, reached out and squeezed Jane's arm affectionately, answering the urge to touch Jane in some silent seal of acknowledgement of what Jane had just shared with her. "I'm glad you did."

Jane smiled again. "I'm glad, too. Alex?"

"Yes?"

"For some time now, I've felt I really do have a special talent for politics, a sort of gift with people. I know that sounds totally immodest of me, but I'm being truthful."

"I know."

"Alex, I really *was* born to do this. I'm doing what I was meant to do, even though I fought it for so long. I hope I convey that to people. That they don't look at me as a phony, an opportunist. Someone just riding on daddy's coattails." She looked unsurely at Alex.

Alex swallowed around the lump in her throat, reminded of their moment in Philadelphia, when Jane had tearfully confided in her that she didn't always feel worthy of her ambitions. Alex inherently felt such moments of human misgivings were very rare for Jane, and rarer yet for her to express them.

"Jane, you are not a phony. And you don't ever come across that way. Just keep being yourself."

Jane winked at Alex. "Whether I can do that on TV is the big question, isn't it?"

Alex laughed. "Hey, with your looks and . . ." She felt herself blushing, and then her words got caught up in her throat. "Ah, I just mean . . ."

Jane laughed. "Oh, Alex. You don't have to *mean* anything. I won't take offense. You're far too polite, you know." She set her empty glass down on the nearby table. "Now, I do believe I'm well on my way to getting drunk. Will you help me up to my bedroom, or do you only reserve such special treatment for my mother?"

Alex dutifully began guiding Jane out of the room, smirking at the hint of jealousy in her voice. "Just show me the way, ma'am."

Jane chuckled, shooting a wickedly flirtatious grin at Alex. "I didn't know it would be so easy to get you to my boudoir."

Alex gasped. "Did you just—"

Jane laughed, louder this time. "Yes, Alex, I just made an inappropriate joke. You're not going to sue me for sexual harassment, are you? I dare say that would put an end to my campaign in one hell of a hurry."

"What, and put myself out of a job? No way!"

Alex was still pleasantly buzzing from their joking when Jane beckoned her into her spacious bedroom. She closed the door behind them and leaned against it, her humor clearly gone. Alex felt nervous in the glare of Jane's suddenly acute appraisal.

"Alex, I get a funny feeling at times that I make you uncomfortable. Do I?"

Alex reeled in surprise. "I'm not sure what you mean."

"I think you do." Jane moved to the four-poster bed and sat down on its edge. "I think I make you nervous for some reason."

"You think so?" Oh, God, Alex thought, trying to buy time. *Am I being that obvious?* It felt like déjà vu all over again with her friend Kim's pointed questions.

Jane sighed impatiently. "Okay. You drift off, Alex. You go to another place. You get all quiet and nervous on me. Just in these little flashes, and then you're fine again. Have there been other threats against me? Is that it?"

"No," Alex said quickly, surprised by Jane's astuteness. "We've told you everything."

Jane patted the bed beside her until Alex obediently sat down. "C'mon, Alex. I want to help make this better."

Alex felt her body sag in defeat. She propped her elbows on her knees. *You can't help, Jane, not when you're the cause of it!*

An arm snaked around Alex's shoulders and the warmth and intimacy of the one-armed embrace immediately weakened Alex's resistance. It reminded her of the close contact they'd had in Philadelphia, when Alex had consoled Jane. Now it was the other way around.

"It's me, isn't it?"

"Yes," she blurted out, unable to stop herself.

"Dammit," Jane snapped. "I knew it."

Alex jumped up, suddenly needing to put distance between them. "I mean, no, that's not what I meant." She needed to set things straight—somehow.

"Alex, what have I done that's upset you so?" Jane's voice had turned soothing, like warm liquid. "Please. I want to know."

"It's me, not you." Alex knew she wasn't doing a good job of hiding the anguish she felt. "I don't feel I can protect you properly. That I can do a good job anymore."

"What are you talking about, Alex?"

Alex leaned against a low, thick windowsill. Her heart was pounding like a freight train. Foot chases and armed takedowns had never been this hard, but it was too late now. Jane needed an honest explanation. "I'm not sure I can do this anymore. I'm going to ask for a transfer when we get back to Washington."

"What?" Jane jumped to her feet, hands on her hips. Bewilderment was quickly morphing into anger. "What the hell is going on, Alex? Jesus Christ! Tell me this is a bad joke."

Alex jammed jittery hands into her pockets. Now she'd done it. Gone and pissed Jane off, and in such a personal way. *That's twice in one day, Alex.* "Jane, I . . ."

Jane stepped closer, her arms crossed over her chest. "This is not the confident, super-human Alex Warner I've come to know and rely on. Why are you wanting off my detail?"

Alex spoke haltingly. "I . . . I feel like I'm in way over my head, Jane."

Jane's expression softened. She dropped her arms. "Oh, honey." It was spoken so naturally that Alex almost thought she hadn't heard it. *Honey?* Alex soared at the endearing term. "Some days I feel like I'm in so deep, I can't even see the sky anymore," Jane said. "It's normal in this business. You just have to trust that you're doing what you were meant to do. Didn't you tell me words to that effect in Philadelphia? And didn't we just discuss that a few minutes ago downstairs? You're good at what you do, Alex. Very good."

"I can't do this anymore, Jane. I have no choice."

Jane tenderly touched Alex's arm. "Honey, you've got to tell me what's wrong. I can help you."

"No, Jane. You can't." *And if you keep calling me honey, I'm going to melt into a little puddle on the floor.*

"Alex, I can fix anything."

Alex was adamant. "Dammit, Jane. You can't fix this. Don't you know what I'm trying to tell you?"

Her feelings were bubbling so close to the surface now. Tears threatened and she shoved them down with sheer determination. *Goddammit, I will not cry!*

Jane cocked her head but said nothing.

"Jane, I'm too close."

"To what?"

"To you. I care about you, more than I should. I care whether you're doing well in the campaign. I care if you're unhappy, or upset. I care what you think. What you feel. It's affecting the way I do my job, it's . . . I don't know what's happening to me anymore. I can't think clearly." An unwelcome tear slid down Alex's cheek, and she angrily brushed it away. She hadn't felt this out of control, this exposed, since Julia had left her more than four years ago.

Jane stepped closer until she was just inches from Alex. "Oh, Alex. I care for you, too. You've been there when I needed you. You're always there, Alex. A rock. *My* rock."

Jane reached up and unabashedly touched Alex's cheek, brushing the wetness still there. Her caress was soft, tender, affectionate—everything Alex knew it would be, and she melted into Jane's palm, nuzzling it, embracing the warm sensation coursing through her. She'd stopped breathing. Everything had stopped. All that mattered was the soft, warm fingers gently stroking her face, sending tiny jolts of electricity through her. *My God, Jane.*

And then Jane's arms tightly threaded around her, and she clutched Alex tightly. "It's okay to care, Alex," she whispered into Alex's neck. "I want you to care for me. If I thought you didn't, I'd never feel safe with you. I'd never trust you. Don't you see?"

Alex was silently choking back more tears, feeling numb in Jane's arms. She was afraid to return the hug, afraid of needing it so badly. "No. You don't understand. It makes me weak," she rasped. "It could get us hurt. Killed."

Jane pulled away abruptly, her face reddening with each pulse. "This is all my fault, Alex."

Alex stood stunned as Jane rushed to an empty suitcase and began haphazardly throwing clothes into it.

"What are you doing?" Alex was quickly regaining her composure. This was not going well. Not going well at all!

"This wouldn't be happening if we weren't stuck here like hostages. I'm leaving, Alex. I'm going back to Washington, where we can forget all of this ever happened."

"No, Jane. You can't. I'm sorry, but you can't go anywhere."

Jane had that immovable look about her and Alex knew it was going to be a fight. "Yes, I can," Jane ground out through clenched teeth. "I'm getting the fuck out of here, now, Alex. And you can't stop me."

She threw the half-filled suitcase to the floor and made a dash for the door, but Alex deftly jumped in front of her and barred the way.

"Get out of my way, Alex."

"No."

Jane tried to push past her, but she was no match for Alex, who probably had a good thirty pounds on her. They struggled, Jane pushing and pulling to try to free herself. Finally, Alex wrapped her in a bear hug, and still Jane squirmed and fought like a desperate animal caught in a trap. They were both breathing hard, both straining with all their strength, but Alex was winning an inch at a time, pulling them both away from the door. Momentum finally landed them on the bed. They were still locked together, Jane on top. Alex expertly rolled them over so that she was on top, and pinned the bucking woman beneath her.

"Goddammit, Jane." She was forced to pin Jane's arms at the wrists and use her superior weight and strength to keep Jane beneath her. "Stop it. Stop fighting me."

Jane suddenly went still, except for her rapidly rising and falling chest. Her face was beet red and still full of anger. She stared, unblinking, at Alex, still hell-bent.

"Jane, listen to me. I am not letting you up until you calm down and realize that you are not going anywhere tonight."

Jane said nothing, but she was clearly seething. Alex would simply wait her out. It was several tense moments before she felt Jane's breathing grow shallower and her muscles begin to relax. Resisting was exhausting business.

"You can't leave me, Alex," Jane finally said softly, her voice trembling, her face collapsing in anguish. "You're the only agent I've ever let get this close to me. The only one I ever will. I'll be in more danger if you don't stay."

"No, Jane. Don't do that to me."

"No, Alex. Don't *you* do this to *me*, damn you." Anger reared up again.

Alex pressed her body more firmly into Jane's. She stared hard into Jane's eyes, which were growing more watery by the second. It was the first time she'd ever seen such fear there, and it startled her. No, she could not leave this woman. She would not.

Jane's body finally went limp beneath her, the fight mercifully extinguished. Alex loosened her grip from Jane's wrists, but still pressed down with her body. "Jane, darlin'," she said. "I won't leave you."

Jane threw her arms around Alex's neck, burying her face in her shoulder, and Alex felt Jane's body softly trembling beneath her. She held Jane patiently, gently. She inhaled the sweet perfume of Jane's hair, her skin, the faint smell of brandy, and tried hard to forget they were lying on a bed, until a jolt of fire pierced her. Jane was arching into her, breasts and pelvis pressing lightly but surely against her. Alex knew the signal well. Her hands twitched at the thought of sliding them down to Jane's ass and pulling her even more tightly to her, until their bodies melded and moved together in frantic, sweet harmony. *God!* How she wanted to. Is that what Jane wanted, too? Or was she not even aware of what she was doing, of what her body was saying to Alex?

Alex knew she had to put an end to this while she still could. She began to protest when Jane suddenly pressed a finger to her lips.

"Shh. Don't say anything, Alex."

Only that one finger separated their mouths. Alex searched for a sign of reluctance or hesitation in Jane. Anything to stop what was happening, because her own body had begun responding. But she saw only capitulation and desire in Jane, and it both scared and thrilled her.

Alex began helplessly moving in sync with Jane's body—slowly, sweetly pressing her pulsing, engorged crotch into Jane's.

Denim roughly caressed denim. *Oh, God, Jane. I could take you right now. Loosen those buttons and press my mouth to your warm breasts, part your legs with my hand, and . . .*

She pressed her mouth harder against Jane's finger. It was almost like kissing her, and she began imagining how it would really feel. They were both breathing hard again, as if the wrestling match had reignited. *A little harder and I'll come right here in my jeans,* Alex thought as she continued to respond to the body answering hers. She stifled a moan and considered the very real possibility of a furtive orgasm.

The cell phone clipped to her belt suddenly chirped to life. It took at least three rings for them both to recognize and respond to the intrusion. Alex forcefully pulled herself away from the clenching of their bodies and sat up. *Fuck!* Jane was hastily sitting up too.

More slowly than it should have, duty reasserted itself and Alex answered her phone.

She looked at Jane a moment later, disappointment and relief fighting an internal battle. "They caught the guy in Washington. He's back in custody."

Chapter 7

Jane closed her laptop computer and looked at Steph and Carter, the three of them jammed into the small office at the back of her campaign bus. Jane had spontaneously decided to have the bus and her staff meet her in Detroit before heading straight to Indianapolis. They had lost a day, maybe two, and Jane intended to make it up.

Her staff had her back on course with a town hall-style meeting that was just hours away. The three had gone over the issues Jane would address, both aides throwing questions at her that might be expected from the audience, then critiquing her responses. She'd thrown herself into the exercise with a sense of relief and satisfaction at having something tangible to occupy her mind with.

Leaning back in her seat, Jane clasped her hands behind her head. "Damn, it's good to be back on the trail." She liked being busy, loved the frenetic challenges of the campaign. And today, she needed it more than ever—needed to feel the normalcy of the fevered pace she'd become accustomed to. Mackinac Island had been . . . *crazy. But this* . . . Jane glanced happily out the diesel-blackened window at the blurring countryside. *This I can handle. This is what it's all about.*

"I'm glad they caught that nutcase so soon, Jane, but I still wish you could have had more time on the island," Steph said.

Jane shrugged and massaged her temples, where a brandy-induced headache faintly persisted. Unwelcome thoughts of the island again pulled at her, viscous and cloying, like molasses. She didn't want to deal with the confusion and shock of what had happened there with Alex, not to mention the surreal brush—even if it was at a distance—with someone who wanted to assassinate her.

For almost twenty-four hours, Jane's world had been knocked off its axis. What had once felt solid and sure, she now struggled to gain a foothold on. It was as though the ground were no longer there, and she didn't like the unfamiliar territory—this feeling of slipping, of losing control of her feelings. That was why it was so important to throw herself headlong into the campaign again . . . back into what was comfortable.

"Jane?" Steph was looking intently at her. "Are you okay?"

Jane barely managed a nod. She stared back out the window and forced herself for the hundredth time to try to make sense out of the senseless. She hadn't expected to feel such a wellspring of emotion when Alex had announced that she wanted a transfer. She'd felt surprisingly frightened and lost by the prospect of losing her. It had been a horrible time for Alex to spring it on her. She'd been so vulnerable, in her family home, talking about her family to Alex, about her feelings and fears. *Damn it. She makes me want to tell her things.* Everything about Alex, from her strong arms to her patient eyes, made Jane feel safe and trusting.

The bus hit a bump and the jolt momentarily dislodged the

fog from Jane's mind.

"Steph, really. I'm fine."

The aide frowned and hesitated. "Did something happen . . . something to frighten you? I mean, besides the obvious."

Oh, God, Alex. Jesus. Jane's pulse quickened. She couldn't help but remember the warmth and electricity of Alex's body when they'd hugged, and then the taut muscles and the strength of her body as she'd held Jane down on the bed. Their heated physical exchange had somehow but very surely shifted and transformed into desire that was so pure and acute. It had nearly answered the throbbing hunger that had welled in Jane so unexpectedly.

Jane felt her stomach do a slow, painfully sweet roll. Recalling her arousal sparked tiny shock waves, even now. She had nearly come, right there against Alex. That had never happened before with another woman, or even with a man. It had been years since she had been that turned on. Jane had thought that part of her was dormant, like a field left fallow that would need careful turning and seeding before it would bear fruit again. But Alex's rock-hard body, moving perfectly in time against hers, had quickly proved that theory wrong.

Jesus, Alex. What have you done to me?

Jane looked up, determined not to let any of her feelings or confusion show. "Nothing happened there, Steph. Everything's fine."

It wasn't fine, not really. But she would make it fine. *It will be fine.* Jane's chest felt heavy, as though she were sucking air through a straw. With sheer stubbornness and will, she calmed herself.

"I'm sorry, Steph. I'm just a little distracted about tonight." She smiled. "Well, that and a little hangover."

Steph grinned. "Good. It sounds like you did relax after all."

"Yeah. A little." *If you call getting half-drunk and nearly sleeping with my bodyguard relaxing.*

Jane knew she needed to get ahold of herself. Now. *A little scare from some nutcase and some alcohol-infused alone time with Alex, and look what happens.*

If only it were so easy to chalk it up to alcohol and fear. Jane was realistic enough to know she couldn't blame it on anyone but herself. Sure, Alex was good looking and nice and charming and . . . *so strong and yet so vulnerable. God, and those sweet green eyes that could melt a glacier!* No. It wasn't Alex's fault. It was Jane who had been needy and weak. It had to stop, those raw emotions Alex seemed to tweak. She needed to get back to the grueling campaign work and focus. *And to stop feeling so pathetically lonely.*

"Jane?" It was Carter.

"Hmm?"

"How do you want to play the assassination attempt? It'll be all the media will want to talk about today . . . and tomorrow and the next day."

The question was enough to shake Jane from her introspection. "First of all, it wasn't an assassination attempt. I was supposedly the intended target of an unstable person who got nowhere near me and who is now in police custody. That's how we'll play it, because that's the way it is. It was nothing."

"You know," Steph suggested cautiously, "these kinds of things can really play on people's sympa—"

"No!" Jane snapped. "I will not use this as political currency. And neither will any of you." She pinned her aides with a piercing glare. "We are moving on from this right now."

Jane relaxed back in her seat again. The words "moving on" reverberated in her mind, and they felt reassuring. Right. *Yes, it's time to move on.*

"So, what's on tomorrow's agenda?" Jane asked nonchalantly.

"We have an anti-poverty breakfast in Gary, and then we're flying to New York," Steph answered. "You've got *Larry King* there in a little more than forty-eight hours."

"You got me on Larry?" Jane asked, astonished. *Shit. Mother must have given Steph that idea!*

Steph grinned. "You're also going to read to a first grade class in Harlem tomorrow."

Jane drummed her fingers nervously on her desk. "You're sure about this?"

"The school?" Steph asked innocently.

Jane threw a pen at her aide in jest.

Carter and Steph stood to leave. "You'll be great, Jane." Carter grinned reassuringly at her. "You'll charm the pants off Larry. Anything else, boss?"

"I still want to go over next week's Super Tuesday itinerary with you. After lunch?"

"Right, boss." Carter cheerfully saluted and left.

"Steph? Can you stay behind for a second?"

Stephanie Cameron reclaimed her seat.

"Remember Keith Henderson?"

The aide smiled enthusiastically. "That tall, blond, good-looking juvenile court judge in New York? How could I forget? I'd thought maybe you and he might get something going a while back."

"Yeah, well, there just wasn't time," Jane said benignly, not nearly as excited about the prospect as Steph, but he did seem like a decent guy. She was being pathetic and she knew it. Lonely and turned on and grasping at the first man she could think of for some sort of quick sexual fix. Still, she had to do something to get last night out of her system, to show herself and Alex that their brief moment had been a mistake, an aberration. "I wonder if he's still single?" She tried to sound casual about it.

Steph shrugged, smiled and took the bait. "I'm sure I can make some discreet inquiries."

Alex waited anxiously first for Carter, then Steph, to leave Jane's office. She squared her shoulders stalked down the aisle of the swaying bus, not at all sure of what she was going to say to

Jane, but they had to talk about what had happened between them. Alex needed to know where things stood, even if she did dread what lay ahead.

She hesitated, then rapped firmly on the door.

"Come in."

Alex opened the door and stepped in, shutting it quickly behind her. When Jane looked up from her computer, a frown instantaneously streaked across her forehead, a faint look of chagrin darkening her eyes.

Oh, boy.

"Alex," Jane said, a slight question in her tone.

Alex stood rooted in place. Her legs felt so heavy, she didn't think she could move if she wanted to. *Oh, Christ, what am I going to say?*

"Would you like to sit down?" The question was more out of obligation than welcome, Alex could tell. Jane seemed peeved, as though Alex's presence were an imposition.

With effort, Alex commanded her legs to move to the bolted down seat facing Jane. She would much rather have remained standing. "Jane, I . . ." Alex stalled, clasping her hands tightly together, trying to formulate her words, corral her thoughts. She hated feeling so awkward with Jane. Just last night, things had been so hot between them. Alex had been seconds away from ripping Jane's clothes off and having her way with her . . . and she knew Jane wouldn't have stopped her. They had wanted each other; their bodies had certainly made *that* clear. But now . . . Now things were so frosty between them.

"What's on your mind, Alex?"

Besides how much you turn me on? And how much I hate how different things are between us now? Alex mentally shook herself. Clearly Jane wasn't going to initiate the discussion. It would be up to Alex to put things right, to make sense of things for them both. There was only one thing to do. "If you want me to leave your detail, I will." Thankfully, there was no trace in her voice of the emotions

108

that could easily overwhelm her if she were not careful.

Jane silently contemplated Alex, her fingers steepled on the desktop, her eyes unreadable. She looked about as indifferent as a CEO who had just been handed her eighteenth business proposal of the day.

Please don't say yes, Jane. I need to be near you. I need to be around your energy, your warmth, your beauty, your tireless ambition, your intelligence, your humor, your altruism. I need your friendship, your voice, your touch. Alex had never felt such a powerful attraction to anyone before, had never felt so *affected* by anyone. She hadn't completely confessed to Jane last night just how much she meant to her, but she would now, if that's what it took. *I'll tell her I think I'm falling in love with her . . .*

"No, Alex." Jane was looking less composed. A vague sort of sadness seemed to have quietly descended on her. "I want you to stay."

Alex didn't realize she'd been holding her breath. She'd been squeezing her hands so tightly, they were cramping. "Are you sure?"

"Yes, I'm sure." Jane's gaze slid from Alex. There was a slight tremor in her hands, and she must have noticed it at the same time as Alex. She quickly stuffed her hands beneath her desk.

Alex swallowed nervously. "I think maybe there're some things we should—"

"No, Alex." Jane shot her a withering look, her voice low and absolute. "I don't want to talk about last night. Ever. I don't know what exactly happened or why, but I do know it will *never* happen again."

The sting of Jane's words were like a slap that left Alex instantly reeling.

The anti-poverty breakfast was going even better than last night's town hall meeting, and that was pretty damned good.

Jane had found receptive, rapt audiences at each. She'd laid out more of her "Blueprint For America"—as she and now the press had dubbed it—and the crowds had eagerly approved. She talked candidly about devoting more of the federal budget to schools and food programs, health clinics for the poor, and creating jobs.

"Action in adequate measures can wait no longer," she passionately told the morning's audience of about five hundred people. "There are children suffering in this country, who go to school with empty stomachs and deflated spirits. It is a form of abuse, caused by institutional indifference and inaction. With resolve and action, we can change this now. We must change this now."

Before the last of the applause had died down, Jane's aides and a gaggle of Secret Service agents quickly descended on her and ushered her away.

"My, aren't we in a hurry," Jane grumbled.

"We have that plane to catch for New York," Steph replied coolly. "And a crisis is brewing."

Steph, Carter, Jane and her chief of staff, Jack Wilson, tucked themselves into a corner of the plane, where the aides told Jane that a couple of Web sites and blogs had popped up a few hours ago, claiming that Jane was a closet lesbian.

"Oh, hell, that's not a crisis," Jane said crustily, her political skin firmly intact. "That's just entertainment."

"I'm afraid not," Jack said sternly. "After your stance on gay rights last week in Pennsylvania, some people will buy this crap, unfortunately."

Jane cursed a blue streak, but only in her head. Five more minutes alone with Alex the other night, and the rumors might have been true. What had she been thinking? Had she really been willing to throw her future away over a sudden impulse?

"It's just the conservative Right trying to distract us and the voters," Jane said, frustrated. "And the timing's rather suspicious, with our first Super Tuesday just a few days away."

"Yes, it is," Jack said. "Which gives it all the more reason to take it seriously."

"It's just bullshit, and we all know it."

"Right again," Jack said. "Now our job is to make sure everyone else knows it, too."

Jane looked at the three of them. "So what are you suggesting? And for God's sake, don't tell me some quick march to the altar."

Carter laughed hollowly. "Look, Jane. There'll likely be the usual scrum of reporters when we arrive shortly at JFK. If they don't bring it up, neither do we. But late this afternoon—after the school reading—you have an editorial board meeting with *The Times*. I think you should bring it up with them. Say that there're these rumors going around and that it's bullshit. That you've got nothing against being gay, but that you just don't happen to *be* gay."

The others voiced their agreement, and Jane could think of no other suggestions. "Okay, sounds like a plan. And for the record . . ." Jane could no longer stem the anger slowly rising within. "It pisses me off that they make it sound like such a dirty accusation," she said quietly, looking away. Sadness tugged at her heartstrings as she thought of Alex, who didn't have the luxury of denying that she was gay. How often had she had to put up with this sort of crap, Jane wondered. For Jane, the accusation was a mere distraction, an irritant, an untruth. For Alex, it was her life, and there were people out there who would think less of her because of it. It wasn't fair.

"Jane." Carter smiled and reached for her hand. "You don't have to defend yourself to us. But let's not forget the business we're in, okay?"

She nodded and squared her shoulders. It was moments like these that she wondered what she was doing in this snake pit called politics. Sometimes, like now, it was only the fact that the end sometimes justified the means that kept her going.

Only one reporter among the two dozen or so at the airport brought up the question of "vague rumors" about Jane's personal life. She dismissed the question with a warning that the right wing elements in the country would say or do anything to distract her from her agenda, to send her "Blueprint For America" to the back pages.

"Isn't any publicity good publicity?" a reporter she knew well asked jokingly.

Jane chuckled harshly. "Oh, I think history over the years has proven that theory wrong, my friend. And if you don't believe me, ask the high-profile Republicans who have had to resign over the last couple of years because of unwanted publicity."

Later, with *The New York Times*, Jane brought up the rumors more specifically. She dared her anonymous detractors to show their faces and provide evidence. Ultimately, she blamed it on people who were afraid that she was on the right track with her support for gay rights. They felt threatened, and rightly so.

By nightfall, Jane was emotionally exhausted. She was ready to climb into bed when the doorbell in her hotel suite rang. Steph called out, asking to come in for a minute.

"What's up?" Jane asked as she let her in. "And please don't tell me some other crisis has come up. There's nothing left on the crisis quotient meter tonight."

Steph beamed. "No. This time I have good news."

"Well, I could certainly use some. C'mon, spill it, woman."

"Remember that good-looking judge we were talking about? Keith Henderson?"

Jane nodded.

"Well, you're taking him out for dinner tomorrow night."

"What? Steph! I didn't mean for you to actually—"

"Oh, come on, Jane. I can read between the lines."

Her signals had been pretty clear, even if she did feel a little mixed about them herself. "But I thought I had *Larry King* tomorrow night?"

"You do, but you'll be done in plenty of time, don't worry." Steph was looking far too happy about it all. "Since tomorrow's Saturday, you and Larry have the studio to yourselves. The show won't air until Monday night. You're with Larry from six til seven, and then you're on a date." She waggled her eyebrows for effect.

"Steph, you're impossible."

"I know. You can thank me after your date with Prince Charming."

Jane closed the door after Steph and leaned heavily against it. She didn't know whether to be pissed off or relieved to have a bona fide date with a man. And then she thought of Alex again, for about the thirtieth time today, and could not dislodge the disconcerting feeling that she was somehow betraying her. She'd been cruel to Alex with her aloofness and her little speech about nothing ever happening between them again. Truthfully, she'd wanted nothing more than to take Alex's hand during their discussion in the bus, caress her fingers over the roughened palm, tell Alex that she cared about her too. Maybe even concede that she was attracted to her. But it was just fantasy and it was time to stop this silliness.

I'm sorry, Alex, but I have to move on.

Jane awoke the next morning to a full-blown campaign crisis. Over breakfast in her room, her staff broke the news to her, replete with a stack of newspapers. The front pages were covered with bold headlines claiming that not only was Jane a closet lesbian, but that she was having an affair with her very out personal bodyguard, Secret Service Agent Alex Warner.

"Fuck!" Jane was incensed that Alex was being swept into this mess. Her temples throbbed as anger bubbled hot through her veins. She threw the nearest newspaper across the room and watched it flutter to the floor. "How could this have happened?"

Her aides were just as stunned and outraged. They had no answers.

"These are legitimate newspapers, not gossip rags. What the hell's going on? I want answers, goddammit."

Carter looked uncharacteristically helpless. "They're saying the proof is that the two of you snuck off to Mackinac Island for a tryst."

"Yeah, with my mother and a whole host of other agents," Jane muttered. "How did they even find out I was there?"

"Who knows?" Steph supplied. "Could have been an airport worker, one of the islanders. Does it really matter?"

Carter tossed the *Detroit Free Press* on top of the pile. Staring out at Jane was a closeup photo of Alex, along with a very candid story about her. Jane picked it up.

"My God," Jane gasped in fresh outrage as she read. The article recounted Alex's Olympic hockey playing days when she was in her early twenties, her heroics with the Michigan State Police, her lengthy live-in relationship with a fellow cop named Julia that ended a few years ago. The article went on to say that just days before sneaking off to the "Mackinac love nest" with Jane, Alex had had a one-night stand in Detroit with a Republican senator's very beautiful and very talkative assistant. It quoted her, and Jane was happy to read it out in her most vitriolic tone. "I would never have gone to bed with her if I'd known she worked so closely with Senator Kincaid."

Jane threw the paper to the floor. "Those bastards! I'm going to sue their asses."

"No, you're not," Jack said. "We all need to calm down here."

"Does Alex know about any of this yet?"

Carter shook his head.

Jane pushed her cold eggs away, feeling her stomach rebel. "I'll talk to her."

"Meantime," Jack offered, "the best thing we can do is respond calmly and intelligently to this."

Steph nodded. "We'll answer every question truthfully and factually. Without emotion."

"Don't expect me to act like this shit is just part of the game. That it's okay, because it's not," Jane huffed. "People get hurt by this crap."

"I know, Jane," Carter said softly. "It's fucking low. But Steph is right. If we stoop to their level or act like we're trying to put up a smokescreen, we'll be in trouble. It's best to just carry on and let it pass. Give it the factual attention it deserves and nothing more."

"We'll stick to the schedule," Steph added. "You'll do *Larry King* tonight." She lowered her voice " . . . and the other thing."

Steph and Jack rose to leave, but Carter didn't move.

"What?" Jane looked pointedly at Carter.

He waited for the others to leave and fidgeted in his chair.

"Well?" Jane prodded impatiently. The team was close. They were like siblings, and she knew he wouldn't be offended by her grumpiness. "Are you going to spit it out or do I have to beat it out of you?"

He sighed loudly, stalling for time. "Jane, I need to ask you something personal." He leaned forward in his chair. "Has anything happened between you and Alex?"

"What are you talking about, Carter?"

"Like, girlfriend, have you slept with her?"

"Jesus, Carter, no!" But almost immediately, Jane felt the shock of his question begin to flatten out, blur around the edges, lose its impact. She had almost slept with Alex, she reminded herself. If that cell phone hadn't gone off, they might have made love, and there would have been no taking it back. No denying these vicious rumors. She felt the chill again of having almost done irreversible damage to her campaign.

"Are you attracted to her?" he persisted.

"Carter, what the hell does this line of questioning have to do with anything?" *Goddammit, I will not answer that!*

"She *is* a very attractive woman, Jane. There's a real, you know, sexual power about her. And she can be very sweet and charming. Even *I* can see that!"

Jane's hands were on her hips. She stared down at Carter like she were a strict schoolteacher and he a kid she was about to order into detention.

"What?" He shrugged innocently.

"Are you switching teams for Alex, Carter?" Jane feigned seriousness.

Carter's reaction didn't disappoint. His eyes nearly popped out of his head and he began to sputter comically. "Wh-what? Me? Switch teams? Are you kidding? Jesus, Jane. Alex is very nice. And good looking. But I am not turning straight!"

Jane laughed. "All right, all right. So, Alex is sweet and good looking." *Yes, there's no denying that.* "So what's your point?"

Carter sighed with a flourish. "I'm just saying, she might be hard to resist."

If only he knew how close to the truth he really was. But he didn't, and Jane wasn't about to enlighten him. "That sexual power of hers must be pretty damned potent, Carter, if you think I'm powerless to resist." *Except I almost wasn't!*

"Look, Jane. I'm not trying to give you a hard time," he said gently. "My point is, you know what this could mean to your campaign, to your career, if there's any merit to this stuff."

Jane felt her face reddening. She was scared of the truth. Scared that, indeed, she might not be able to resist Alex if there was a next time. But she certainly didn't need a lecture about how a serious attraction to Alex would be the death of her campaign. "Carter, how many ways do I have to spell it out to you? I am not having an affair with Alex, okay?"

"No, it's not okay," he said quietly. "Because I think Alex might be in love with you."

Jane reeled mentally. *In love with me? No. No.* Alex had said she cared for Jane, but *love?* That was one hell of a leap. Sure, there was something special between them, something unique, but . . . *love?* "Has . . . has she told you this?" *Please don't let it be so.*

"No."

Jane collapsed back in her chair, relieved, and tried to ignore the thin shadow of disappointment. "See? Nothing to worry about, Carter."

"Jane. This is dangerous." There was a hint of desperation in his voice. "I'm sensing something, and I don't know if it's coming from you, or her, or from both of you. But you've got to be careful."

Jane stood up. "Carter, don't be such a worrywart. Everything's under control." And if it wasn't, she would make damn sure she put it that way.

He raised a skeptical eyebrow.

"Look, I'm even going on a date with someone tonight. And Alex is busy having her own flings, remember?" She couldn't keep the iciness out of her voice. "Now send Lover Girl in here, would you? I'd better tell her what's going on before she sees the papers."

Jane, still in silk pajamas and a terry cloth bathrobe, paced until Alex appeared.

"Looks like a tornado's hit in here." Alex pointed to the newspapers scattered like leaves on the floor. She grinned at Jane, looking more like her old self. "It's a good thing your campaign isn't as disorganized as this room."

But Jane was already thinking about how she was going to break the news to Alex, and how that silly grin was about to come to an abrupt end. She didn't want to have to do this, but it needed to come from her. "Sit down, Alex. Something's happened."

A look of alarm raced across Alex's face. Obediently, she sat on the couch, adjusting her gun in that habitual way she had. Jane sat down beside her, clutching a couple of newspapers to her chest.

"I'm afraid the papers have gotten a little nasty with us, Alex." She looked at Alex and was disheartened to see that she had a look of sullen expectation about her, as if she had come to expect disappointment from Jane lately.

Jane winced. "Alex, I'm sure you heard about the rumors yesterday—the ones about me being a closet lesbian."

Jane could see Alex mentally shift her gears, even force a smile. "Well, we're always looking for new recruits, you know."

Jane didn't laugh at the joke. "It's worse today. They're saying I'm having an affair . . . with you."

"What?" The color swiftly drained from Alex's face.

Jane tossed the newspapers to the floor with a thud. She scrubbed her cheeks and tried not to think about wanting to take Alex's hand in hers and caress it soothingly. She wished so much that she could take the last few days back, start over with Alex. Things had been so messed up between them lately. They might never be right again.

"I'm sorry, Alex. It's absolutely dreadful, and I never meant for you to get hurt. I just hope you're out with your family, because if you weren't, you are now."

"I . . ." Alex looked numb. "There's just my brother and we're not exactly on speaking terms," she answered quietly. "How did this . . . ?"

Jane reached for the Detroit paper and felt new bitterness toward the nameless woman Alex had supposedly taken to bed. "Looks like your bedmate from last week in Detroit got talkative."

Alex's face was turning from white to red. She looked devastated in a way Jane had never seen before. "Sweet Jesus. I had no idea she'd . . . God!"

"It's true, then. That you slept with her," Jane said tersely, knowing she sounded accusatory, but she couldn't help herself. What she really wanted to do was berate Alex for having been so careless, so indiscreet. It was practically begging for this sort of shit to happen. *And if she's supposed to be pining for me, as Carter thinks, then why is she fucking someone else!*

Alex was shaking her head slowly from side to side, staring, transfixed, at the floor. "It was a mistake," she answered quietly.

"Obviously." Jane felt more hurt than she knew she had a right to. "Alex," she said and waited until their eyes met. "The best thing you can do is just carry on as though nothing's happened. We're sticking to the same schedule. We're not going to blow this out of proportion. And if anyone asks you questions, defer them to me or my staff, okay?"

Alex nodded absently, still lost in her thoughts.

"There's one more thing. Steph will give you the details, but I have a special dinner engagement tonight. And I need you guys to hang back on this one as much as possible."

Alex looked questioningly at her, but Jane jumped up and began cleaning up the papers. She could not bring herself to explain.

Alex tapped her foot impatiently and tried not to stare at Jane and her date across the room. They were dining on shrimp and drinking Cristal, smiling and laughing at quiet jokes, and it was burning Alex up. She and Commander Harry Johnson ate their dinner, trying their best not to look like Secret Service agents. What Alex really wanted to do was march over there and dump her Perrier all over poster boy's head. He looked far too contented, like he'd just won the lottery or something. *The bastard!*

"Alex, I wish you'd get out of this mood," Harry said over his heaping plate of steak and mushrooms. "I know it's been a hell of a day, but—"

"You have no idea," Alex ground out. She looked across the

room again. *Christ! Was that form-fitting black, come-fuck-me cocktail dress really necessary?*

"Boy, Jane really handled that Larry King interview well, didn't she?" Harry said appreciatively.

Alex stared at her untouched plate. Indeed, Jane had handled herself exceptionally well. She'd responded calmly and cleverly to the gay controversy, looking very presidential with just the right mix of indignation, analytical detachment and even humor. The only hint of anger she'd shown was when she told King how unfair it was that an innocent person was harmed in all of this . . . how she herself was fair game, and maybe even her hired staff. But Alex, as a member of the Secret Service, was not. She'd even made the crack that she figured the only way her sex life would ever make the news was if celibacy suddenly became trendy.

Alex had to hand it to her. Jane was spectacular under fire. But why did she feel compelled to go on a date with this guy? Especially after doing such a good job of deflecting the controversy. Now it was going to look like she was trying to prove something. Alex glared at them again. *That smug bastard's trying to get her drunk so he can get into her pants, I know it. And then he'll probably sell the story. Wouldn't put it past the creep.*

Harry's chuckling finally got Alex's attention.

"What's so funny?"

"Nothing. I'm just astonished, that's all. Jane's staff says this is the first date Jane's been on in, like, years. Can you believe that?"

Alex silently fumed. *And it's all my fault!* "I don't find that particularly amusing or astonishing, Harry." She sipped her Perrier in a full-blown sulk.

"Sorry, but I beg to differ. A woman as good looking and smart and funny and successful as her . . ." He took another savoring bite. "What the hell is wrong with the men of America? *People* magazine even voted her the country's most eligible woman last year." He nodded in the direction of Keith Henderson. "At least that guy's got the brains to go after her."

Alex shoved her food around her plate, not the least bit interested in it. *The brains? What's so damned brainy about a man wanting to stick his dick up some gorgeous woman? He doesn't even know her for God's sake.* "He's an asshole." Alex bristled.

Harry polished off the last of his food and even looked like he might lick the plate. "What'd he ever do to you, slugger?"

"Just look at him, Harry. He's a wolf. And he's been gloating and smirking all night."

Harry pointed his finger at Alex. "You go acting all jealous, and it's gonna look like there's something to those stories in the papers today."

Alex threw down her napkin. "Fuck those stories."

"Look, kid, I know it's been—"

"I don't want to talk it about it, Harry," Alex snapped, louder than she intended.

Harry pushed his chair back and spoke into the tiny microphone in his sleeve to alert the other agents. "Looks like Comet's on the move."

Paparazzi waited outside the restaurant for the couple and furiously snapped pictures as they emerged. Somebody must have tipped them off . . . probably Jane's staff, Alex thought with bitter cynicism. Sure couldn't hurt the campaign for Jane to be seen on a date with some good-looking dude.

"Fuck this politics bullshit," Alex grumbled to no one. She was not cut out for this, and the sooner this fucking campaign was over, the better!

Jane slipped out of her heels and went to pour them both a brandy. She was not entirely sure bringing her date back to her room was a good idea. Keith Henderson had already served at least one purpose, and that was testing Alex. She had glared at them throughout dinner, full of pent-up resentment and tension. *So, Alex is jealous.* The thought fluttered in the pit of Jane's stomach, sending a small, undeniable shiver through her. Alex's jealousy should have felt disconcerting, but it didn't. Somehow, it almost seemed as though Jane had been expecting this. *Carter's right. She does have a thing for me*. She hadn't been sure until now. She'd done a pretty good job of talking herself into believing their heated wrestling match on Mackinac was nothing more than mild attraction that had simply gotten out of hand. Now Jane had at least a shred of evidence that to Alex, it was much more than that.

My God, she wants me. She drew in a deep breath, felt the powerful surge of heat gather between her legs. Her pulse had begun to race . . . she could almost feel Alex beside her, taking her hand . . .

Jane returned to the couch with the two brandy snifters.

"Jane." Keith was looking at her like she was dessert. He moved his hand to her thigh.

Alex paced her end of the hallway, unlike her counterpart at the opposite end, who stood stock-still. He might even be asleep standing up, except for the tiny movement of his eyes every now and again.

Alex could not force the images from her mind of what Jane and her date might be doing in that room just steps away. She couldn't stop remembering that it was she and Jane just a few nights ago, in each other's arms. And it hurt that now it was *him* and not *her* in there with Jane—touching her in secret, warm places, feeling the excitement in her body as it responded.

Alex wanted to scream with every cell in her body. She knew as surely as she breathed that she wanted Jane again. Wanted all of her. And if there *was* a next time for them, there would be no stopping. And no excuses afterward, no regrets. No taking it back.

I shouldn't have let her off the hook with that little speech she made in the bus, Alex rebuked herself. *I should have made her own up to what happened, to what she felt, to what we both felt, to what she wanted to happen, however much the truth might make her uncomfortable. Jane can't just dismiss it the way she did. She can't!*

But then . . . Alex sighed in frustration. She knew she hadn't been entirely truthful, either. Sure, she'd told Jane she cared for her, but that was like saying she sort of liked hot fudge sundaes. She had not put it all out there, had not admitted that she was crazy about her. How she wanted to be near Jane, wanted to be the object of her attention, her touch, her smile, wanted to share her thoughts, wanted to touch that incredible body in a way that only she surely knew how. Wanted Jane to look at her in that special way, like they were the only two people in the world. She wanted a future with Jane. It was incredibly simple and yet it was the most complex, unattainable thing she'd ever desired.

She felt in her pants pocket for the stone Jane had given her and rubbed its smooth surface. It was supposed to make you feel better, Jane had told her. *Well, it's not working, Jane.*

Much as she wanted to believe differently, Alex knew there was no use in pining for Jane, in building up some fantasy world in her mind. It was ridiculous, in fact. *She'd never risk everything for you, Alex. She wouldn't risk a single damned thing for you. You might as well have a crush on the Woman on the Moon.*

With a feeling of profound hopelessness, Alex leaned against the wall and wished for her shift to end.

Jane's date was playfully grinding against her as he lay on top of her. They'd moved to her bedroom, both stripped to their underwear. His kisses were rough, his cheeks like sandpaper. A film of sweat covered his body, and his hardness poked at Jane, demanding removal of her cotton panties. He already had a condom on, Jane confirmed as she reached down to grab hold of him. *When had he put that on?* She squeezed him lightly and tried to convince herself that she was ready. She pushed her underwear aside and mechanically guided his cock slowly into her. He let out a groan as he entered and it wasn't long before he was moving inside her.

Shit, Jane thought. She wasn't ready. It hurt. *Dammit*! She cast about in her mind for sexy thoughts, to will the wetness she had so thoroughly felt the other night. *With Alex. Jesus!* She'd been so wet. So full of wanting. *Oh, Alex.* The handsome face—those eyes like tropical pools—ascended in Jane's mind like a heavenly but grainy vision, as though she were under water. *Sweet, sweet Alex.* A small shiver ran through Jane and she felt her thoughts begin to crystallize.

Keith was grunting and sweating and pumping for all he was worth, but it was no use. It was all wrong. She did not want this. Did not want him. *This is not what I want!*

"Keith, stop, please."

He continued, oblivious.

"Keith! Stop it!" She tried to pull away, her body stiff with revulsion, which only made the pain worse. "Keith, get off me!"

He looked at her, stunned, as her words registered. "What the hell?"

"Get off me! You're hurting me. I can't do this."

He pulled out of her. "Jesus, Jane. What's the fucking problem?"

"I just can't, Keith."

"Christ! What's wrong with you?" He leapt up from the bed and reached for his clothes. "I thought you wanted this?"

Jane sat up. She wouldn't apologize or explain. "Please, go."

"Goddamn right, I'll go." He was pulling his clothes on quickly. His confusion was clearly turning to anger. "I'll tell your girlfriend on the way out to come and finish the job."

He was halfway out the bedroom door when Jane reached for the glass vase on her nightstand and threw it. It missed him, but shattered loudly as it hit the door frame. He slammed the door hard on his way out.

"Bastard!" Jane yelled, feeling as empty as the echo in the room.

Seconds later, Jane's bedroom door flew open. It was Alex, breathless and wild-eyed, one hand resting on the butt of her holstered pistol. "Jane! Are you okay?"

A yelp of surprise died in Jane's throat as she awkwardly tugged the sheet up around her bare breasts, knowing she hadn't quite covered herself in time. She'd seen Alex's eyes quickly rake over her.

"Did he hurt you, Jane?" Her voice was choked, on the edge of rage.

Jane shook her head lamely. She felt ashamed, embarrassed. *She must think I'm a slut.* Jane felt her cheeks burning, less with embarrassment now and more with irrational petulance. *It's because of you that this happened, Alex . . . because I can't quite get what happened between us out of my fucking mind!*

Alex was still breathing hard from the adrenaline and the sprint to Jane's room. She was still looking skeptically at Jane, as though she didn't quite believe she was okay. Her thorough scrutiny of her was not entirely clinical, Jane knew. She felt gratitude—vindication even—for the brief flicker of appreciation she'd seen in Alex's eyes as they'd swept over her naked chest.

"It's okay, Alex. I'm fine."

"If he did anything to you, I'll kill the son-of-a-bitch."

"Alex, no!" Jane shot up from the bed, holding the sheet loosely around her, and remembered at the last second to leap over the broken glass. She caught up to Alex in the living room and grabbed her arm. "Stop, please."

Alex threw her hands up in exasperation. "Dammit, Jane. When I heard the crashing, I thought . . . I thought he was hurting you. What the hell happened?" Her words came out like automatic gunfire.

Jane moved to the couch and sat down, carefully tucking the sheet in around her. "Alex, I'm sorry. I can't explain right now."

"Yes, you can," Alex replied, her voice tight, like a kite string. Jane had never seen her so furious. "What the *fuck* were you doing with that guy?"

Jane inwardly recoiled from the sting of Alex's tone. What business was it of hers, anyway? What right did she have to question Jane's judgment, her actions? *How dare she be so imperious!* "The same thing you were doing with that Republican in Detroit last week," Jane ground out through clenched teeth. *She would not take the entire blame for this.*

Alex stood perfectly still, looking numbly at Jane for the longest time, her face a blank. "I told you that was a mistake," she finally answered. "Was this a mistake for you tonight? With *him*?"

"Alex, what makes you think I need to answer that?" Jane asked with indignation.

Alex sat down next to Jane and spoke in soft tones. "You need to answer it, Jane. Because I'm being completely honest with you."

Jane laughed without mirth. "I see. Okay, Alex, since you're being *completely* honest, tell me why you're acting so jealous tonight? And why it matters to you who I sleep with?"

"Why do you think?" Alex rasped.

Jane shrugged uncooperatively. She was in no mood for a lengthy verbal jousting. "I have no idea. You tell me what this is all about."

Alex's face was clenched in misery. "The other night. On the island." She dropped her eyes momentarily. "Something happened between us, Jane. Or at least, for me, it did. And now you go and end up in bed with . . . *him*!" Alex didn't even try to hide the hurt she was feeling. "I don't understand."

Jane felt herself yielding to Alex's vulnerability. She was being honest, which, for the moment, was more than Jane was being.

"Alex." Jane tried to corral her thoughts, which had scattered like confetti. "I don't know why I turned to him. I thought . . . I thought that's what I needed."

Alex squeezed her eyes shut as though she were imagining something painful. "Tell me what you do need, Jane."

Jane reached for Alex's hand, which felt cold and stiff. "Alex, I just . . . I can't answer that." *Oh, God. How can I tell you when I don't even know myself?* "My life is very complicated right now. We're into the heaviest part of the primaries." Jane grew more impassioned. "There's so much to do over the next few weeks, and I'm so close, Alex. I really feel I have a good chance of getting past Collins. It has to be my priority, don't you see?"

Alex slipped her hand free. She reached for Jane's face and tenderly cupped her chin. Her touch was gentle, but firm, like her voice. "Jane, stop. Just tell me what's going on in your heart. I need to know. I'm not asking for anything else."

Jane's eyelids slid shut. She could not look at Alex. Another second, and she would absolutely melt into that raw vulnerability of Alex's. Her defenses were nearly shattered. She would not do that, she told herself. There was not another soul on this earth with whom she shared absolutely every facet of her life, her thoughts, her feelings. And she was not about to completely open herself up now. Especially not in the middle of a campaign. She had to stay strong, focused. "No," she said.

"I can't do this alone, Jane."

"Do what, Alex?"

"This."

Jane suddenly felt soft lips pressing lightly against hers. She flinched in surprise. Her eyes flew open. *My God, she's kissing me!* Indisputably, irrevocably, Alex was slowly but soundly kissing her into heavenly oblivion. Jane's eyelids fluttered closed again. She hardly knew if she was even breathing anymore. Alex's lips were so soft, so agonizingly tender against her own, that Jane felt herself gasp in surprise and delight. It felt so damned good, so perfect. The kiss persisted and deepened in sweet exploration. It was like nothing she'd ever experienced before, and Jane found herself happily surrendering to it. Fire swept through her veins, the warmth lodging deep in her belly as Alex's tongue parted her lips. *My God, Alex, I am physically powerless against you.*

Jane heard herself moaning softly as Alex's tongue playfully engaged hers, and hands at her waist pulled her closer. She lost all track of time and space, her mind completely forfeiting any attempts to form a single thought. But her sense of feel had certainly not abandoned her. The sensual mouth on hers, the eager tongue sent sweet tremors up and down her spine. When she felt Alex faintly pull back, Jane pushed her mouth harder into Alex's, beckoning it back. She wanted the kiss to continue and it did . . . nothing else mattered for the moment. *Nothing.*

"Jane," Alex finally murmured, slightly out of breath. She disengaged reluctantly and stood up, a slow smile of self-satisfaction on her lips. "I'll see you in the morning," she said lightly before turning on her heel.

Jane leaned back on the couch, feeling like she'd just been flattened by a Mack truck. She was still breathing heavily, still trembling with pleasure and unfulfilled longing. What just happened, she wondered in astonishment, not sure she really wanted to know.

Hours later, Alex was still buzzing with the effects of the mind-blowing kiss when she sat down at the hotel's nearly empty restaurant and ordered a coffee. She really didn't need the caffeine fix because she was nowhere near ready for sleep, even though she was off duty now. But since she wasn't going to be able to sleep, coffee wouldn't hurt.

She still wasn't sure what had come over her, to kiss Jane senseless like that. She had never been that reckless with a straight woman before. But Jane had looked so cute sitting there, all hot and stubborn and indignant and half naked. That thin cotton sheet had been so sexy on her, clinging to every curve, only lightly concealing incredibly erect nipples. Admittedly, Alex had lost her head, but it had felt like a victory, especially because Jane had fully reciprocated.

Alex held onto the cup placed in front of her as if it were some sort of crystal ball. *If only Jane would tell me what she feels, goddammit!* She had told Alex in Mackinac that she cared for her, too. But it went deeper than that. Much deeper. Jane desired Alex as much as Alex desired her, and Jane's reaction to the kiss only proved that. The signals were all there, just not the words Alex needed to hear.

"Hey, you. This seat taken?" It was Carter, grinning coyly as though he had some private knowledge of what had just happened upstairs in Jane's room.

Alex smiled belatedly. "What are you doing up so early?"

Carter sat down on the bar stool next to Alex and ordered a coffee and full breakfast. "Are you kidding? I won't be getting any sleep for the next seventy-two hours. Super Tuesday's going to be a killer."

Alex wasn't ready to dismiss the thrilling memory of the kiss. She knew she was grinning like a fool.

"Whatever you were doing, I hope there were no reporters sneaking around," Carter joked.

Alex's grin curled into a scowl. "I am *so* not used to this fish bowl crap."

Carter winced. "Sorry. That was a really shitty thing that happened to you in the papers. I know Jane feels horrible about it. We all do. I know it wasn't what you expected—or deserved."

Alex's thoughts wandered, recalling the annoyance, anger even, in Jane's voice, as though Alex had brought the publicity on herself because of her indiscretion with the Republican. Maybe Jane just couldn't stand the idea of Alex in bed with anyone. Well, I know how that feels, Alex thought sullenly. She'd wanted to kill that Keith guy . . . tear the bastard's head off, and then when she'd drunk Cristal from the asshole's skull, she'd carry

Jane off and make mad, passionate love to her. Alex smiled. She'd been so tempted to pull that sheet down, to kiss that luscious neck. And those perky, round breasts—

"Something else bothering you, Alex?" Carter interrupted.

She didn't feel like lying. Didn't feel like telling the truth, either. She was so damned confused. Jane seemed at once to both want her and reject her and she had no idea what to do about it.

"Look, Alex. I have to be honest with you, okay?"

With effort, Alex shifted her attention back to Carter with a profound sense of foreboding. Whatever he was about to say, it wasn't going to be good.

Carter took a sip of his coffee and started out haltingly. "I know . . . I know this is none of my business. But I consider you my friend. And I'm Jane's friend, too, of course."

He shifted in his seat, looking as though a catastrophe might strike at any moment. And it just might. But Alex felt strangely calm. "It's okay, Carter, go on."

"Alex, I think you're falling in love with Jane." He paused, as if expecting a denial, but Alex couldn't give him one. "It's not like I blame you."

"Carter, I don't want to talk about this right now." Alex wished she had a little bottle of Bailey's or Irish whiskey for her coffee. She needed something a lot stronger than caffeine about now.

"I know you don't, hon, but you have to. See, it's about more than just you falling for Jane."

"Huh?"

Carter looked as bleak as his creamless coffee. "See, I think Jane might be falling for you too, even if she doesn't know it yet."

Alex had to remind herself to breathe. Oh, God, she wished it were so. But by the look on Carter's face, his vote was definitely against it. "So you think this would be a horrible thing for Jane?"

"Right now, yes."

Alex felt her temper rising. "I never expected homophobia from you, Carter."

"Alex, my friend, I'm not being homophobic. I'm being honest. And I'm in your corner, as well as Jane's. I think it would be wonderful if the two of you got together. Some day. I really do. But not now." He sipped his coffee again. "Christ, Alex, this is the most important time in Jane's life. She's worked very hard for this."

"And I could ruin it for her, is that it?"

"In a word, yes."

They looked at each for a long time, Alex feeling like she'd just had the stuffing knocked out of her. There was no denying Jane had absolutely everything to lose. Alex knew she was being selfish, wanting to love Jane and wanting Jane to love her back. But it would all be on Jane, not her.

"Alex," Carter said, "if you care for her, and I know you do, then you'll let her go. For now, at least. Until we see where this campaign leads."

"And if it leads all the way to the White House?"

He shook his head helplessly.

Alex recognized the futility of her position. *Great.* If she wanted any chance with Jane, she would have to hope the woman failed. It felt like some sort of punishment, coming this close to happiness, then having it snatched away. It wasn't fair. But she knew Carter was right.

"Do you have an empty envelope, Carter?"

"No, but I can get one." He asked the waiter for one and handed it to Alex, along with a pen.

Alex reached into her pocket and pinched the smooth stone between her fingers. She withdrew it, stuffed it into the envelope and sealed it. On the front, she wrote Jane's name. On the back she scrawled: "I'm sorry for everything, A.W."

"Carter, will you give this to Jane later?"

He looked at her curiously, but took the envelope. "What

should I tell her?"

Alex felt close to tears and knew she would end up crying if she stayed any longer, and she would not do that. At least not in public.

She stood up on suddenly wobbly legs. "See you around sometime, Carter."

Chapter 8

Jane and her staff made it through their first Super Tuesday and its hellish demands . . . though for much of it they were like automatons, rushing to appearances, churning out speeches, trying to be seen by as many people as possible. Jane didn't think she'd ever drunk so much coffee. Or smiled so much. She could hardly remember eating and she knew she'd barely slept. But it had been worth it, and she'd do it all again in two weeks for the second and final big block of primaries.

Jane was in the home stretch of the campaign. In a few weeks, she'd know whether she had enough delegates to make her the party's nomination for president. Right now, she was still running a close second to Dennis Collins. Out of hundreds of delegates' votes so far, only a few dozen separated them. Predictably, Collins was getting the nod from the southern states and the conservative midwestern and western states like Nebraska, Iowa and Oregon. Jane had won Michigan, Ohio, New York and some of the smaller, more liberal states.

The upcoming California primary would be the biggest prize yet. Jane would need an outright landslide there to send her over the top, and while she wasn't hopeful of that, she was counting on a solid win to launch a domino effect into the remaining primaries.

Jane's staff were faithfully taking her cue and working every bit as hard as her. Bleary-eyed with exhaustion, her voice scratched raw, Jane was putting in sixteen-hour days, always cramming in one last speech or one last meeting, another handshake, another interview. Her staff buoyed her, gave her the energy and affirmation she needed because they believed in the whole package that was Jane Kincaid—the platform, the purpose, the person. She knew she couldn't have kept on without them.

In a hotel room in Los Angeles, like battle strategists, they were plotting a speech Jane would give the next day to the city's Muslim community that was expected to be covered widely by the media. It was a delicate discussion, especially now that Jane was insisting on discarding her original topic, immigration policy, and substituting it with a speech on terrorism.

A suicide bus bombing in Paris had killed six people just days ago, and there would be no better time to address Islamic terrorism to Islamic Americans, Jane argued. She knew they were hurting, too.

Jack Wilson, her chief of staff, privately agreed with Jane but he wasn't keen on the speech. It was just too thorny an issue, he argued. "Our opponents will castigate us for trading tragedy for political opportunity, and the Muslim community will say we're outsiders who should mind our own business. It's a no-win situation."

Jane silently mulled over his argument, chewing on a pencil. "It is a gamble, of course. But maybe, just maybe, the Muslim community *wants* to talk about it. Maybe they're tired of being ignored, pigeonholed. Maybe they're tired of people like us assuming what they want and don't want."

Steph and Carter jumped into the fray, each taking opposing positions. Attentively, Jane listened to the three of them in full debate mode, each of them throwing out arguments like darts—some hitting the mark, some not. Jane's mind was nimble enough that, simultaneously, she could extract the relevant points from each argument and build them into the foundation of her own decision. She could drift in and out of a discussion, verbally or mentally, and still keep pace. She was like a runner who could veer off course and then veer back in, never losing step.

It was in those moments of drifting off that she would think of Alex, and it felt like falling off a cliff. She had been shocked and deeply hurt when Alex had abruptly left her campaign seven days ago—right after that unexpected, mind-blowing kiss. No note, no phone call, no e-mail, no explanation. No good-bye. Just the returned stone in an envelope with a vague apology scrawled on it.

What was that supposed to mean anyway, Jane wondered pointlessly and bitterly for about the four-hundredth time. Was Alex sorry they had kissed? Was she sorry she'd come upon that stupid scene with Keith Henderson? Was she sorry she'd ever met Jane? Or had she been apologizing in advance for defecting to Collins's team? The curt declaration hurt. Badly. It felt like complete rejection. Betrayal, even.

"There's no time for a poll," Jane interjected, gravitating seamlessly back to the discussion. "And besides, I won't have polls dictating my decisions." Her mood was still black with thoughts of Alex's departure. "I swear Dennis Collins runs his campaign on nothing but polls."

And now Alex is on his detail. Jane mentally chafed at the idea that Alex had chosen to join her opponent's security detail. Not only did the defection feel like a slap in the face, it cast the contest in a whole new personal light, as far as Jane was concerned. It gave her even more reason to want to win this fight. It bothered her whenever she saw newspaper photos or television footage of Alex standing dutifully behind Collins. She was both angered by and yet helplessly drawn to the images—Alex in her ubiquitous dark glasses, perfectly tailored suit, her short hair slightly windblown. She always looked composed and calm and in a perpetual state of alert readiness. She looked good, as always, but surely she couldn't be happy working with *him*, Jane thought bitterly. *Why did you do it, Alex? What went so wrong? You said you cared for me. Was it a lie?*

Jane weaved back into the debate. "Look, we're going to do this. Let's get to it and write that speech, shall we?"

Jane's staff unquestioningly rallied behind her decision. She expected and got nothing less than total loyalty once her mind was made up. Her team was a family and they would do their utmost to defend her decisions and make them a success. They trusted her fully and she, in turn, trusted them.

Jane opened her notebook and picked up the gnawed pencil. "Okay. I want to stress that we all belong to the human family, and that this shared humanity unites us and transcends divisions." She looked around the room, waiting for a response.

"Yes, that's good," Steph said with feeling. "And how about this . . . that suicide bombings and the killing of innocent people alienates an individual both from God and their human family."

Jane felt energized by the whirlpool of ideas. "Carter, I need some background on Islamic religion," she said. "I don't know a lot about it, but I'm sure Islam no more condones murder than Christianity."

Carter smiled confidently. "I happen to know a very handy verse from the Koran. It says, 'Whoever kills a person has killed the whole of humanity'."

"Excellent!" Jane exclaimed, scribbling furiously. "I'll use that. But I'm not going to get too mired in religion. I want to stress that we all need to differentiate and not generalize the minority from the majority, that we not brand a whole group of people as killers or haters of Christians. We all want the same things in life—basic freedom—and that's going to be my theme."

Jack stood up. "How about we all break for an hour and see what each of us comes up with?" He made a show of balling up Jane's now-discarded speech on immigration. A slow smile spread across his craggy face. "Jane, this will either be a brilliant move or a flop. But either way, you'll show you've got a lot more balls than Collins. Or the president, for that matter. Neither of them has ever stepped a toe into the Muslim community, let alone addressed terrorism with them."

Jane nodded absently and resumed chewing on her pencil. "Steph, when are we back in Washington?"

"Day after tomorrow, we go home for a couple of days."

"And what's Collins's itinerary this week?"

Steph quickly checked her handheld computer. "He's in Seattle today, Denver tomorrow, then it looks like he's back in Washington, too, for a few days."

Jane relaxed back in her seat, immersed in new thoughts.

Alex idly watched the passing ocean through the window as the limousine zipped along the freeway toward Seattle, where Dennis Collins was to visit a hospital before being feted at a dinner. She swung her gaze to the Democratic frontrunner, in whispered conversation with an aide, and wondered, without emotion, if she were looking at the next President of the United States. The incumbent president was beatable, and the nation seemed to be in the mood for change. Alex had heard enough talk and read enough newspapers to know that President Charles Howard had few loyal supporters anymore—that those groups and individuals he could typically count on as a Republican and a sitting president had begun casting about for someone else to get behind. For various reasons, America had become disillusioned with its one-term president, and the media had already begun labeling him a loser. What's more, President Howard had started looking the part of a hunted animal, which left the door wide open for Dennis Collins. Or Jane Kincaid.

Jane. Just thinking about her evoked a strange blend of longing and nostalgia. And pain. What had transpired between them was so personal and so deep, that Alex found it hard to objectively analyze Jane's prospects. She did know without a doubt that Jane was likeable. She had the air of a winner when she walked into a room or parted a crowd. She was smart, funny, honest, compassionate, tough when she needed to be, genuinely warm and patient when it mattered. Stunningly gorgeous. Men wanted to bed her. Women wanted to be her. Could she be any more perfect for the part? *Could she be any more perfect?*

And then there was Collins. He looked like a winner too, with his tanned, masculine good looks and fatherly gray hair. He was the ultimate professional politician—a senator for more than twelve years, a Congressman before that. He was slick, polished, never muffed a line, never got into hot water, said all the right things in perfect pitch. He came across as even-tempered, patient but decisive. Yet in almost a week of following him around on his protection detail, Alex never once saw him say or do anything spontaneous. He was scripted up the yin yang, and Alex saw no evidence that he was as brilliant and dynamic as Jane. He was cool, lusterless, formulaic. Not a man to really love or hate. *But the son-of-a-bitch will probably win, because he's a male and he's a transparent package and he hasn't really made an enemy of anyone.* There were no surprises with Collins, no risks, no excitement. What you saw was what you got—a manufactured winner with little substance, as far as Alex was concerned.

It was a tragedy that the best person for the job might not win, and though Alex was supposed to be impartial, she knew that was a load of crap. Especially in her case. Tears coalesced just below the surface and Alex slipped her dark glasses on. She would love Jane, always. She knew that, felt it with all her being. Jane had settled softly but surely into her heart, like silt floating to the bottom of a riverbed. Her feelings for Jane would always be there, just below the surface of her life. And that's where they would have to remain. She could never again show Jane that she cared for her, could never put Jane at risk of falling in love with her.

Yet she missed Jane. Terribly. It was made worse by the fact that she didn't even know when she might see her next. The two candidates were rarely in the same city at the same time, and never at the same event, and Alex felt reasonably sure that it would be weeks, maybe even months before she'd get a glimpse of Jane.

Maybe it's just as well, Alex thought despondently. She had no idea whether Jane would even want to talk to her again, after leaving the way she did. *I never even said good-bye. Oh, Jane, I couldn't have, don't you see? I wouldn't have been strong enough.*

Alex stared out the window again, watching the scenery slide past and losing a bit of herself with each mile that was farther from Jane. She was not the same person, the same agent she was a week ago, because the part of her that cared was gone. She hoped Jane still cared passionately about what *she* was doing, that she was still focused. The sacrifice of their permanent separation would all be worth it if somehow Jane could earn the nomination. She most certainly would have been a lock to lose had Alex stayed on her detail. The temptation of more of those searing kisses was too strong, and the lure of what Alex felt certain was mutual sexual attraction was just too great. Silly rumors had been one thing, but a full-blown love affair would be fatal to the campaign. And Alex would not be responsible for that. She would stay the course no matter how much it hurt. It was her—and Jane's—only option.

Jane straightened her ponytail, then nervously pressed her palms down the pleats of her khaki Capri pants. Her canary yellow cashmere top was already sticking to her and she wished she'd picked something lighter. March in Washington was unusually warm this year, and the cherry blossoms were full out, making the trees look like giant white, sweet-scented flowers in bloom.

She stood on the small stoop of Alex's brick, two-story, Georgian-style rowhouse and admired the heavy door, which glowed blood red in the setting sun. *Nice touch, Alex.* She smiled at Alex's adventurous choice of color, enjoying the momentary mental detour from the apprehension she felt. Jane took a deep breath against the flood of anger, hurt and anticipation, then rapped firmly on the door.

It seemed like an eternity before it was pulled open, and Alex was suddenly and breathtakingly there in wide-eyed surprise. A fist dove for sanctuary in the front pocket of her baggy, Adidas shorts, her other hand firmly holding the door. Her face was unreadable but for her shock at seeing Jane. God, it was good to see her again.

Any thoughts of being angry at Alex had vanished at the sight of her. Jane smiled weakly and lowered her voice to a teasing octave. "Would you believe me if I told you I was in the neighborhood?"

Alex looked at her disbelievingly, then sharply scanned the street behind her. Only Jane's black, Audi S4 was in sight. "Where are your bodyguards?"

Jane shrugged. "I actually convinced them to wait at the end of the block."

Alex's eyebrows jumped. "How did you manage that?"

Jane laughed and took a step closer, somehow successfully vanquishing her desire to reach out and stroke Alex's tanned cheek. "I had to promise that from now on, I would be so cooperative that I would actually start following *them* around."

Alex finally smiled, and Jane felt absurdly happy. "I see. I just may have to remember that little deal in the future."

Jane felt like doing cartwheels right there on the tiny front yard. *Did she say future? Is she coming back?*

Jane grinned and lightly shook her finger at Alex. "Believe it or not, I do know how to cooperate with the Secret Service."

Alex tossed her a knowing grin that hinted at the intimacy they'd shared. She was all butch sex appeal as she leaned casually against the door frame. "Well, personally I'd like to think that the level of cooperation depends on the agent."

Oh, God, she's flirting with me. Jane felt a rush of heat deep in her center. She could not resist admiring Alex's muscular, tanned arms, and her thick shoulders beneath the tight black T-shirt. The quadriceps of her legs bulged. It was enough to spark the same pleasurable ache she'd felt the night Alex kissed her so soundly.

Jane knew they were in dangerous territory here, looking at each other like that, both signaling that they were very much aware of their mutual attraction. She had to keep things moving along, show that she was in control, show Alex that she hadn't forgiven her for walking out of her life like she were simply trading in a car. No, they would set things straight right now so that Jane could slot the whole Alex Warner experience in its rightful place in her mind. She needed to stop worrying and wondering about Alex and what might have been and get back to what was real. Her campaign depended on it.

"Can I come in before some photographer pops out of a bush or something?"

Alex again peered over Jane, then swung the door wide open and stepped aside. They fleetingly grazed shoulders as Jane passed, and the infinitesimal touch sent a small shiver of unwanted pleasure through Jane. That Alex could even do that to her without trying deeply concerned her. *God, I've got to stop this.*

"Nice place," Jane said above the opera music booming from hidden speakers. "Do you listen to opera music often?"

Alex made a dash for the stereo to turn down the volume, almost tripping over an ottoman in her haste. CD containers of Bocelli, Maria Callas and Josh Groban cluttered the floor, and Jane smiled at this side of Alex she never knew. Alex shrugged impatiently, her tone veiled. "Just when I'm in the mood."

"And what sort of mood would that be?" Jane asked, feigning indifference, but wondering like crazy if Alex had been as unhappy these last ten days as she had been. Waiting for an answer, Jane moved to the soft, leather couch that was the color of butterscotch. It whispered as she sat down. A half-bottle of Australian Merlot sat on the glass coffee table beside an empty goblet.

Wine and depressing music. Alex is as upset about all this as I am. While the thought gave her a small measure of comfort and vindication, it also saddened her to a depth she didn't expect.

Alex stood by the dining room table, her hands jammed into her pockets in that nervous habit she had. "I doubt you've come here to talk about my musical tastes," she said flatly. When Jane didn't reply, Alex turned toward the kitchen and retrieved another wineglass, clearly resigned to the fact that Jane wasn't going anywhere. "Merlot?"

Jane agreed and Alex emptied the bottle, topping off her own glass and filling Jane's. She sat down on the couch a polite distance away and silently sipped her wine, leaning forward on her elbows as if to put more distance between them.

Jane sighed irritably. "Alex, I'm not going to bite, you know."

Alex gave her a sideways glance, but said nothing.

After a few strained moments, Jane sighed again. "I *am* going to give you a hard time, though." She sidled closer, then took a bolstering gulp of wine before setting her glass down. "I need to

142

know why you left so suddenly."

Alex set her own glass down and wearily scrubbed her face with her hands. "I left because I needed to," she replied crisply, still not looking at Jane.

Jane felt a geyser of anger rise up in her. "Just what the hell is that supposed to mean?" She exploded off the couch, staring down at Alex, arms crossed. She'd suddenly had it up to her eyeballs with vague answers and Alex playing the martyr. "Alex, I have no idea what happened between us, and I can't seem to get a straight answer out of you."

Alex looked up at her, her eyes the color of churned up seawater. "*You* can't get a straight answer out of *me*?"

"Look, you're the one who kissed me into the next century, and then you just disappear without a single word. Tell me what I'm supposed to think, or . . ." Jane threw her hands up in the air. " . . . or, do, for God's sake!"

Alex jumped up, her face hard and flushed and just inches from Jane's. "In case you've forgotten, you kissed me back. Or was that just some momentary and forgettable lapse in your heterosexuality?"

Jane smarted from the words and the hurtful tone. "It wasn't like that, Alex." At least, she didn't think it was. "And if I'd forgotten about the kiss, I wouldn't be here right now."

Alex seized Jane's arms in her vise-like hands. "What do you want from me? Do you want me to help you commit political suicide? Is that what you want?"

Jane felt tears gathering, both from the pain of Alex's grip and the sting of her words. And she was not pleased with herself. She had stood up to and triumphed over incredibly formidable foes and insurmountable odds in the political arena, and yet, at this moment, she felt like a little girl—vulnerable and unsure and rejected and just wanting to make things right between them so she could get on with her life.

"I—I don't want anything from you. I just need to know why

you left," Jane stammered. "And why you kissed me the way you did. And why . . . and why you act like this is all my fault."

Alex loosened her grip, only to clasp Jane fiercely to her chest, like a rag doll. "God, I'm so sorry," she mumbled into Jane's hair, her heart thudding hard enough for Jane to feel it through their clothes. "I left because I didn't want to hurt you—or your future. I care for you too much to let that happen. Don't you know that?"

Jane pulled back ever so slightly, her gaze settling unwaveringly on those lips that had the power to make her so weak. "Tell me why you kissed me the way you did."

Alex managed to look both hurt and indignant at once. "I—" She collected herself and started over again. "I kissed you, Jane Kincaid, because you're the most beautiful, incredible, exciting woman I've ever met. And I don't know what's been happening to me—to us. I just know that I want to kiss you and touch every time I'm near you. So badly that it makes me crazy."

Jane gasped in surprise as Alex, with lightning-quick speed, pulled her close again and began savagely kissing her. Jane returned the kiss with the ferocity of weeks of pent-up want and impetuousness, her hands roughly brushing over Alex's muscular back and shoulders. She needed to feel the solidity of Alex right now. Needed to know that this time, Alex wasn't going anywhere.

Their fused bodies gently landed on the creamy couch, and as the kiss grew and persisted, Jane felt herself suspended, as though she were floating above them. Tiny shock waves shot up and down her spine, moist heat abruptly and achingly lodging between her legs. Her desire was so fierce, it pounded in her ears and in her chest and in her very core. God, how she wanted Alex. She'd always wanted Alex, she realized now. She just hadn't quite known what to do with that wanting.

But Alex did. Oh, did she ever. She was sucking the faint taste of wine from Jane's lips, her tongue tracing the outline of her mouth before darting inside for a spirited exploration. Alex moaned and pressed into Jane in a sure sign that things would not be stopping with a kiss this time.

It felt so good, so natural to kiss Alex this way, to want her like this again. Her desire annihilated any thoughts of the campaign. All that mattered was that they were here together, alone and completely shut off from the world.

Oh yes, Jane thought wickedly, knowing exactly what she wanted and hoped for, and it wasn't for Alex to stop this time. Nothing else mattered in her life beyond the next kiss, the next sensual touch.

She pulled her mouth away and looked into eyes that had morphed into the color of sparkling emeralds. "You asked me what I wanted from you," Jane said breathlessly, as Alex looked at her quizzically. Jane swallowed, her throat tight with desire. "Please . . ."

"Please?"

Jane squirmed beneath Alex's hard body, her pelvis finding and latching in perfect symmetry onto Alex's. "I want you to make love to me, Alex." She felt hot and flushed under Alex's penetrating gaze, and knew Alex was silently measuring the veracity of this bold, unequivocal demand. Jane reached up and stroked Alex's cheek tenderly. "I want you on me, Alex. In me. All over me. I want you to taste how much I want you."

The shock of her own huskily spoken words was quickly snuffed out by Alex's voracious mouth. The intensity of the kiss exultantly sealed the mutual agreement and expectation of what was to come. There would be no turning back. *She's going to make love to me right here on this couch!* The excitement of the thought sent hot blood wildly rushing to Jane's lower body. She wanted nothing more than to be consumed by Alex, to give her yearning body up to the desire that had been distracting her for weeks but was now slowly melting her into helpless submission. She could not even fathom the idea of stopping. No. She needed this like she needed to breathe, to eat, to drink.

Jane moaned loudly when Alex's attention moved down her jaw and neck, where she kissed and nipped her throat. In her impatience, Jane's legs opened wider. With a boldness unfamiliar to her, she thrust herself up and into Alex's body in search of the vital friction she craved. The building blocks of an orgasm were already firmly and delectably taking root, but Alex was pinning her with her strong body, effectively halting Jane's self-indulgent surging, letting her soft kisses drive Jane wild.

A tongue darted out and licked Jane's ear playfully. "Good things come to those who wait, darlin'."

Jane growled in mock displeasure. "Waiting isn't one of my attributes, in case you haven't noticed."

"Oh, I notice everything about you, sweetheart," Alex burred, and Jane felt her spirit soar even higher. She nearly stopped breathing altogether when she felt Alex's hand decisively and expertly crawl up inside her top and settle exquisitely on a breast.

"Ohhh!" Jane gasped as Alex squeezed gently. She felt her top slowly being pulled up with Alex's other hand. Her eyes snapped shut as soft wetness found her other breast, Alex's firm tongue skillfully suckling and licking her nipple into rock-hard pleasure that bordered on painful. She arched into Alex, pushing her entire breast into Alex's mouth. "Oh, God, Alex." Jane's breath was coming in short, excruciating bursts, and she knew she was not far from erupting into the most wicked orgasm ever.

"Alex," she demanded in a ragged voice. She was nearly delirious with desire and couldn't fathom how much more her body could take. She was not above begging. "I want you so much. Please."

Alex continued to feverishly and ravenously consume Jane's breasts. Her teeth playfully tugged on a nipple, eliciting a sharp moan from Jane.

Jane's body was in full, numb surrender when Alex finally stopped and looked longingly at her. "You are so incredibly beautiful, Jane. I want to touch every part of you with my mouth. Are you sure you want me to?"

Jane whimpered and her eyelids fluttered closed again. She could only nod her assent, and before she knew it, Alex was mercifully undoing her pants and sliding them down her legs. She arched back into the couch as Alex's lips tenderly and unhurriedly trailed down her stomach, her body so rigid now, she felt like a guitar string about to snap.

She found herself marveling at how Alex's little kisses were so soft, so tender, yet so passionate. She knew her black, cotton briefs were dripping wet, and she wanted nothing more than to be free of them, but Alex appeared to have other ideas. A hand faintly brushed over the panties, and Jane tried to press into Alex's teasing palm.

"You're so *wet*," Alex murmured in awe. "I want you to wait for me, baby." She playfully caressed Jane through the cotton, her fingers tracing tiny circles over Jane's swollen flesh. "I want you to wait until my mouth is on you and my tongue is in you. Then I want you to come all over my face."

"Oh, God! Yes!" Jane croaked. She moaned again as her body shook with eager anticipation. *Alex, Alex, Alex.* Her mind could form no other words but the simple, yearning call for her. Every thought, every feeling coalesced into that one name as Alex continued to play with her.

Jane thought she could not possibly hold off any longer when Alex began to fulfill her promise. Her fingers drew the panties aside just enough to make room for her tongue, and when it found her, Jane felt herself dissolve to a new level of liquid pleasure.

She pushed back hard into the soft couch as Alex's tongue lightly, but in quick, sure strokes, plundered and caressed her to the very edge of diabolically sweet, swirling, delicious orgasm. She yelled out as Alex's tongue suddenly and firmly penetrated her, pushing deeply and rhythmically inside her, filling her. Jane ground herself against Alex's face, and they rocked together in quickening pace until Jane could no longer contain the strands of orgasm emanating from her center. The violence of her explosion stunned her. It was so deep and forceful that it felt as though her very core was hot lava spilling out of her and into Alex's eager mouth. She continued bucking as Alex stayed with each furious convulsion, her tongue pumping and provoking even more from Jane.

She yelled out as the final vestiges of her pleasure ebbed from her. Her body trembled a final time, and she was completely and joyously drained to a level of numbness she had never felt before.

Alex finally disengaged and she licked her lips indulgently, grinning at Jane. "You taste every bit as good as I knew you would. God! You are an *incredible* woman, Jane. You're so beautiful. So responsive." In one swift move, she had crawled up to Jane and began kissing her deeply.

The shock of her own salty sweetness on Alex stole her breath again and she closed her eyes, wishing without hesitation that they could start all over again, only this time she would explore Alex's body with the same sweet vigor. She had never come so thoroughly and passionately before, and she could still feel the faint, electrifying vestiges of Alex's fingers and tongue on her.

"Jane, honey," Alex said. "I love you. I love you so much."

Alex was embracing her tightly, but the declaration did not immediately permeate this new world of pleasure Jane was still immersed in. There was something about . . . *love*.

What? Jane felt herself flinch in panic. *Oh, my God. Jesus. What have I done?* Jane mentally tried to cast off the still-pleasurable sensations coursing through her. She felt as though she were trying to swim to the surface of heavy, swirling water that kept trying to pull her back down again. She did not want to wake from this dream.

You can't love me, Alex. You just can't. Oh, God. Not now.

Alarmed, Alex pulled back to look at Jane, her face showing

her worry. "Jane? Are you okay?"

Jane's smile came tentatively. "Of course. You were absolutely wonderful, Alex. And I . . . I've never . . . nothing that good has ever happened to me before." She felt suddenly awkward and pulled her top protectively over her still-exposed breasts.

Alex grinned and tenderly caressed the stray hair away from Jane's cheek and neck. "Did you hear what I said, Jane? God, I'm so in love with you. Do you know how long I've wanted to say that?"

Jane swallowed past the lump in her throat. Thoughts of her campaign, of her future, that had so easily been banished moments before, now came rocketing back to her. *Oh, God, please don't do this, Alex. Not now.* Trembling, she stared up at Alex and was speechless.

"Jane?" Alex looked more crestfallen by the second. "Tell me what's wrong."

Jane knew she was going to hurt Alex, knew that she'd made a grave mistake by coming here. "I can't tell you what you want to hear, Alex."

Alex scampered off Jane and stood beside the couch, her face visibly paling. "Why not?"

Jane sat up and quickly pulled on her rumpled pants. "I just can't. Not right now."

Alex's voice wavered. "Are you saying you don't feel anything for me?"

"No, Alex, that's not what I'm saying at all."

Alex's face hardened into anger. "Why did you let me fuck you, Jane? Just tell me that much!"

"Oh, please," Jane replied impatiently. It wasn't just about sex. Couldn't Alex see that?

"You can't be honest enough to tell me you love me, but you'll fuck me. That's just great, Jane. How very moral of you."

The rebuke was like a slap as Jane shakily rose from the couch, straightening her clothes. "Alex, you're turning something beautiful into something vulgar and distasteful. Please stop. It's not the way you think."

But Alex wasn't listening. Her voice was like a fist poised to smash. "I suppose you want me back on your detail so I can fuck you senseless every once in awhile, huh? Maybe in the limo, would that turn you on? How about backstage somewhere in a broom closet?" Alex's tone spewed venom, and it was ugly. "Just think of the wonderful stolen moments we could have, Jane. I could get you off in an elevator, or we could join the mile high club, or—"

"Stop it!" Jane quickly turned away, half stumbling, half running to the door. She could not turn to look back at Alex one last time. She did not want to see the cold fury and anguish there. There was so much she longed to say, but she could not. Not right now. Maybe not ever.

Jane drove as far as she could before tears blurred her vision and forced her to pull into a Wal-Mart parking lot. She signaled to the agents following her that she was okay before she sobbed against the steering wheel. She cried for the woman she had just hurt and she cried hardest for her own loneliness, even as her body still pulsed from the extraordinary lovemaking.

Minutes passed before she began trying to make sense of what had just happened.

C'mon, Jane, you know you wanted Alex to fuck your brains out. It was why you didn't wear a bra . . . you wanted your tits to look tantalizing. You wanted Alex to eat you up with her eyes, and she did. And then she ate you the way you wanted her to, and for a few minutes, the world stopped. So don't go acting all shocked that the woman has feelings for you, that she wants more than just a roll in the sack. That she wants all of you. Carter warned you that she was in love with you, but you wouldn't listen. You've been daring her to admit her feelings, and now she has.

Jane knew she was wrong to have let the sex happen, to have given her body to Alex while keeping her heart at a safe distance. She knew that, and it sickened her that no words could undo what had happened. She did care very much for Alex, but her feelings were so deeply mired, so complex, that she couldn't possibly try to make sense of them, let alone make some proclamation of love. There was so little room in her life right now for herself. She needed time to label her feelings, to get used to the idea that her heart's glacial encasement had begun to melt. And perhaps most of all, to accept that it was another woman she wanted.

Jane cried again and felt an overwhelming desire to just quit the race. Not tomorrow. Today. Now. She didn't need this crap—not the race, and certainly not this wretched loneliness and guilt and confusion. She could be on a plane in hours to Mackinac Island, where she could pity herself in solitude and figure out what to do with her life. And maybe even figure out how to love again. She sure as hell couldn't figure it out in this pressure cooker called a campaign.

C'mon Jane, you know you can't quit the race before it's finished. You're not a quitter.

The words resounding in her mind sounded unmistakably like something her father would say to her, if he were alive, and Jane felt herself go very still. There were people depending on her, she knew. There were the abused women and children she had pledged to help; the families of soldiers overseas who had been promised an end to war under her watch; the poor and jobless she had promised better health care to. Without a strong voice—her voice—her "Blueprint for America" would be nothing but a worthless dream, a tiny footnote in history. There were people who believed in that dream—*her* dream.

Even Alex, if she weren't so rightfully angry and hurt right now, would probably urge her to continue, too. Jane felt the crushing weight of sacrifice like she never had before. She had

151

made many tradeoffs in politics with the bigger picture in mind, like trading votes on insignificant issues in order to cash in a favor for something big later on . . . relenting on some of the finer details of a bill in order to see it passed, because small gains were better than no gains.

But it had never felt so personal before, so painful. She had never dreamed her heart could become political currency.

Alex wiped away a final tear with a hand still faintly smelling of Jane's sweet desire, and dialed her friend Kim's number. Sitting in the dark, listening to more opera and drinking a second bottle of wine with her still-unwashed hands and face, Alex grew more despondent. She realized now that making love to Jane had been a mistake. Jane had made that excruciatingly obvious. But when she saw Jane at her door, looking so achingly adorable and vulnerable, she hadn't been able to help herself. Especially not when Jane had looked at her with those smoky dark eyes and demanded Alex make love to her.

She heard her friend answer the phone.

"I'm in deep, Kim," she said shakily into the receiver.

"What's wrong, girlfriend? You sound horrible."

Alex swallowed a sob. "You were right earlier. About Jane. I'm so *fucking* in love with her." *Oh, sweet God. There it is, out loud. Finally.*

"Oh, no." Kim exhaled audibly over the phone. "Shit. I'm sorry. What happened?"

Alex haltingly explained, pausing many times to collect herself and to wipe away tears.

"Yow! You *are* in a bad way, girl. What are you going to do?"

"I don't know, Kim. Dammit. I *know* Jane cares for me. A lot. She wants to be with me, I can feel it in her body language. I can see it in her face, in the way she responds when I touch her, for Christ's sake. She just won't admit it, she won't let herself—"

152

"Now wait a minute, Alex. You gotta let this thing go, as hard as it is."

Alex paused for a long moment. "You're probably right."

"No, I *am* right! Oh, Alex. People like Jane use other people to get what they want, okay? That's what makes them such good politicians. And she's better than most. Remember that."

"No, Kim. I can't believe that about her. I can't! When I touch her, she—"

"Alex, that's just sex talking."

"No, I swear it isn't, Kim."

"Alex, look. Even if she loves you to death, she's not going to throw her future away for you. To really *be* with you. Sure, she'd probably keep you for awhile as her closet kitten, but is that what you want? Sneaking around, waiting for the axe to fall when the Republicans find out her dirty little secret?"

Alex's sigh was more of a groan. "No, I don't want that. Of course I don't."

Kim sounded relieved. "Good. Then you've got to stay away from her, Alex. Don't give her another chance."

Numbly, Alex nodded into the phone. She knew Kim was right.

Chapter 9

Jane threw her cards down on the table. She knew she could not beat the full house Carter was probably holding, and what's more, she didn't care. He could have her ten bucks. What she really wanted was slipping further from her grasp by the hour.

"You want to go downstairs and thank your supporters?" Steph asked in a voice every bit as tired as Jane felt.

Jane nodded and stood up. California had been good to her. Not good enough to make her the nominee, but that was not the fault of the eager supporters and volunteers who were waiting downstairs in the hotel ballroom.

Jane gave them what they wanted—a raucous ten-minute speech that promised her work was not finished and her dream and her drive were as strong as ever. She would not let them down, she said. Nor would she let down the people whose voice she had become. They could count on her to continue to fight, and to win.

They cheered her wildly, then exuberantly shook her hand and hugged her and patted her on the shoulder as she snaked through the crowd. Their passion could almost make her believe she still had a chance in the race. Almost.

In the elevator back up to her room, Jane sagged in exhaustion. "What are the final numbers, Jack?"

Her chief of staff had a sheaf of papers clenched in his fist. He peered at Jane above his half-moon reading glasses as he began reading off the numbers. It was as bad as Jane feared. She'd beat Collins in California, but barely. The other Super Tuesday results, which were now final as well, were worse. She'd been clobbered in Colorado and Texas, same with Minnesota and Missouri. She'd held her own in New Mexico and Hawaii and Washington State, but those were small potatoes.

They strode through the hall to the suite of rooms they'd rented for the night, Secret Service agents following them at a polite distance.

"What's the delegate numbers now, Jack?"

"Collins has you by over two hundred delegates."

"And how many more are left?"

"A dozen smaller primaries. About four hundred delegates still up for grabs."

Jane let a Secret Service agent open the door ahead of her. She flipped off her Givenchy pumps and headed for the couch. Steph wordlessly handed her a shot of brandy.

"I think we need to have a serious talk," Jane said, watching Steph and Jack share a worried glance.

"Jane," Steph urged. "Don't hit the panic button yet."

Jane took a calming sip of brandy and felt the adrenaline from the speech fall away. Exhaustion took its place. "Who said I was?"

Steph smiled. "You're right, sorry. I just don't want you to think—"

"What I think," Jane said quietly, "is that our options are running out and we need a meeting." Jane knew she was feeling low right now and that it wasn't the right time to talk about the future. "We're flying back to Washington in the morning. Steph, can you arrange dinner catered at my house tomorrow night for us all? We'll talk then."

"Sure thing, Jane."

Jane watched the hired caterers take away the remnants of the roast chicken with all the fixings. As good as the meal had been, it hadn't dissolved the gloom that was weighing her down.

Jane and her three closest staff members retreated to the living room with their coffees, Jane closing the French doors behind her to give them privacy. They were looking at her eagerly, expectantly, and she so wanted to give them that fearless, tireless, optimistic leader they'd gotten accustomed to. This time, it wasn't in her. This time, she felt like a general whose troops demanded a final stand she knew she could not condone.

She sat down in a wingback chair flanking the gas fireplace that someone had earlier thought to switch on. She balanced her coffee mug on the chair's arm. "Carter, Steph, Jack. It's been a tremendous pleasure working with all of you these last few years, and especially . . ." Jane steeled herself against her rising emotions. They'd been through so much together. "Especially these last few months."

"Jane, wait," Carter pleaded. "You sound like you're throwing in the towel or something."

Jane sipped the hot coffee, stared at the highly polished wood floor. "Maybe I am."

"No," Steph said adamantly.

"You can't," Carter implored simultaneously. He looked like he might cry.

Jack said nothing, and Jane looked at him now. "Jack? You've been around the political block a few times. Enough times to know when it's time to call it."

"Are you asking me if I think you should?" He was being purposely enigmatic.

Jane knew it was her decision. It wasn't fair to burden anyone else with it. It'd been her decision to run, and it would be her decision to quit. She shook her head at Jack. "No, I'm not. But you know I don't have the numbers. All of you know that."

"You're still in it, Jane," Carter said. "It's only the end of March. We can still make a killing in the primaries left, and if we win those—"

"Carter," Jane said gently, admiring his youthful enthusiasm. "Look at the primaries we have left. Texas, Kentucky, North Carolina, Montana, South Dakota, Arkansas." Her eyes pinned her young aide with brutal honesty. "Do you really think I have a hope in hell of winning those cleanly?"

Chastened, he shook his head.

Jack sighed heavily. "She's right. All those states are conservative, which means they'll all go for Collins. The polls have long ago indicated that."

"Then that's it," Jane said with almost clinical detachment. "The longer I hold out in this race, the worse it is for the Party. Right, Jack?"

The elder statesman of the team nodded sadly. "It hurts the Party if it drags on much longer. Still, Jane." His eyes were brimming with tears. "You're so close and—"

"I know." Jane waved a hand at him. She would not give into the emotions the others were so obviously feeling right now. One spark from her and the room would ignite into a crying fest. It wasn't her style to let emotions dictate strategy. "Being close is a sentence in a history book. It doesn't mean anything."

The doorbell rang in the distance and Jack leapt up like he'd been expecting it.

"What's going on?" Jane asked as he strode to the French

doors.

"There's someone you should talk to before you make up your mind about anything."

When he returned with the tall and ever-elegant African-American woman on his arm, Jane let out a squeal of delight and jumped up from her chair.

"Well, look at you, Jane Kincaid," the woman said, hugging her. "You look fabulous, but you've gotten thinner by the week. Aren't they feeding you?"

Jane kissed her cheek. "Oh, Clara. You've been talking to my mother, haven't you?"

Clara Stevens let out a laugh. "So what if I have? Someone's got to give you hell."

Jane clutched her hand and led her further into the room. Clara greeted Carter and Steph warmly, and Jane shot a knowing wink at Jack. "How did you know I needed Clara?" she whispered.

He winked back and squeezed her hand. "I'm not as dumb as I look, you know."

"Oh, Jack. You and Clara are like surrogate parents to me. You know your opinion and hers matter to me more than anyone's."

"Well, the only opinion that counts for squat right now is yours. We're just your sounding boards." Jack signaled Carter and Steph to follow him out of the room. "Talk to her, Jane," he said. "Then make up your mind. That's all I ask."

Jane kissed him on the cheek and watched the three of them go.

"Jane, honey." Clara motioned her to the sofa. "I'm so proud of you."

"Don't," Jane squeaked, feeling suddenly close to the edge.

Clara Stevens was a legend, a giant. She was the unofficial matriarch of the party, and had been for years. She'd gotten her start in the Civil Rights movement in the 1960s, became a vocal and powerful opponent of the Vietnam War and had risen through the powerful back rooms of Washington. She had the ear and the respect of everyone over the years from congressmen and senators and Supreme Court justices to presidents. Her intelligence was razor sharp, her internal fortitude unshakeable, and her gut instincts were rarely wrong.

Jane sat beside Clara and let her enclose her in her arms.

"Ah, there now, honey." Clara's chunky bracelets clanged with her affectionate pats. "You've set this town on fire, young lady. And the nation, too. There is nothing to hang your head about."

Jane wiped a stray tear from her cheek, but she would not cry. She was stronger than that. Clara had been all for her campaign, even though she had officially kept at arm's length from any of the candidates. She'd given Jane her tacit approval last summer, and now Jane felt like she'd let her down.

"Clara, I'm sorry. I gave it everything."

"I know you did, child." Clara held her hand tightly. "And the Party thanks you for it. You've reminded the stuffed shirts of our roots. And our responsibilities. You've kept everyone a little more honest, Jane. What you've done will go tremendously far in helping us beat the Republicans in November."

Jane nodded grimly. "It just won't be me leading that charge in November."

Clara's eyes were kind, her voice soothing. "I would have given everything if it could have."

Jane knew Clara never let her ideals get in the way of reality. She was a dreamer, just like Jane, but she knew the difference between a dream and a goal, between reality and fantasy, between what was attainable and what was not. When to cut your losses in this business was sometimes most important of all.

"It's over, Clara."

"Now, there's where you're wrong. Your race for the nomination is over, yes. But you still have a role, Jane."

Jane could not fathom anything but her failed bid for the nomination. She hadn't officially failed, of course. She could hang on, stay in the race, knowing that her loss was a foregone conclusion that would become official at July's national convention. But doing that would make it look like her party was split along philosophical lines—between her liberal platform and Collins's more moderate one. It would look like the party was pitting one against the other, and it would leave bitter feelings heading into the presidential election.

"Maybe," Jane said grudgingly. "But where does it leave all those people I pledged to help?" She looked at Clara, feeling stubborn and angry and helpless. "I promised to help them, and I can't do that if I'm not president. That's what's lost in all of this Clara. It was never about *me*."

Clara tenderly stroked Jane's hand. "Let's say it is about you for a moment. What do *you* want, Jane?"

The question hit her like a punch to the gut. She stood up shakily and walked to the large bay window that looked out on her tidy backyard with its blooming magnolias barely visible in the twilight. "What I want I can't have," she said quietly, her back to Clara.

Nothing had been right since Alex's departure. It was like a light in her had gone out. She'd plodded on and tried her damnedest, acted as if everything was okay, as if that dalliance at Alex's house had never happened. She tried to pretend her heart wasn't in tatters, but it was. The loss of Alex was every bit as substantial as the loss of her dream.

"Clara," Jane turned toward the older woman. "The reason you never ran for office. It was because you refused to sacrifice your relationship, wasn't it?"

Clara had never discussed the subject with Jane before. She'd been an old family friend for years and had helped Jane's father get elected. But Clara's preference to stay in the background all these years was a given. Jane always thought it had been too bad, that it was the country's loss. Now she felt a kindred appreciation of what Clara must have gone through many years ago.

Clara smiled at Jane. "Yes, Jane. I wouldn't have been able to live with the loss of that."

Could Jane live with the loss of Alex? She'd thought she could. Now she wasn't so sure. It felt like there was a gaping hole in her soul, and it wasn't just because her bid for the nomination was over.

"Look, child. My situation is completely different than yours. You're single. I haven't been single since I was twenty-five."

"Clara—"

"And my lover is a woman, Jane. You can't even know wh—" Clara's mouth hung open in shock, her eyes penetrating Jane's with sudden realization. "Oh, my Lord, Janey. Are you in love with a woman?"

Jane raised her hand to brush away a fresh tear. Clara was suddenly before her, wrapping her in another of her tender hugs. "How did it happen?" she asked gently.

"I—I don't exactly know." Jane's voice crackled. "I don't even know if I'm in love with her. I just know . . ." *That I need her so badly right now, it hurts.*

"Come here, child." Clara ushered her back to the sofa, her arm still around Jane. "You've given her up for this campaign, is that what's hurting you so?"

Jane bit her bottom lip and nodded. "I made a choice, Clara. I chose for both of us."

"And now you feel the loss of both your campaign and her."

Jane nodded again, feeling stronger now. She was not one to dwell on life's losses. She knew she'd made the choice she *had* to make. "But it's over, Clara. There's no going back. I have to move on." Jane laughed hollowly. "I'm just not sure what I'm moving on to."

"Are you sure? That it's over with this woman?"

Jane remembered the bitter, hurtful way they'd left things the last time they'd seen each other. Oh yeah, it was over all right. Over before it ever really started. "My career has been my life for a long time, Clara. It's who I am. And it's who I will continue to be."

Clara looked at her skeptically, then shrugged. "I was never as strong as you, Jane."

"Yeah, well, at least you don't go home to an empty bed every night."

"Oh, honey."

"Clara, please. I don't want pity. Not from you."

"You're right. I respect you, Jane. So much. And I trust you to do what you think is right."

Jane looked at Clara, full of so many unasked questions. "I don't want to just give up, Clara. I mean, I know I have to quit the race. But . . . it just all can't be for nothing, can it?"

Clara looked at her with unspoken sympathy, but not pity this time. "It doesn't have to all be for nothing, Jane."

"What do you mean?"

"Dennis Collins and I met earlier today. He asked me to feel you out on whether you'd consider being his running mate."

Jane felt her stomach bottom out, and she didn't know whether she was relieved or alarmed. "Are you serious?"

"Do I look like I'm kidding?"

Jane laughed. "No, you don't."

"Well?"

Jane stared at the fire for a long time, feeling conflicted. Playing second fiddle to her adversary—or to anyone, for that matter—certainly wasn't her preference. Going for the vice-presidency was second best, the consolation prize. It meant giving in, compromising. More sacrifices. "I don't know if I could do it, Clara."

"You should consider it, Jane. It means your agenda, or at least some of it, will see the light of day."

"Only if I fight like hell for it."

162

"Are you saying you're not prepared to fight for what you believe in?"

"No, of course not. That's what I've been killing myself for over the past year."

"So, you just keep fighting, and maybe in eight years, the White House will be all yours, Jane. You'd be the anointed one. Our party's future. Think about that."

Jane studied Clara and saw nothing but support and encouragement.

Jane went through the motions of another primary, then conceded the nomination to Dennis Collins. She threw her personal support, as well as the delegates she'd already won, behind her one-time opponent. Earlier in the day they'd made the official announcement that Jane would be Collins's running mate, and it was finally—and firmly—okay with her. Jane had made the best deal she could to salvage the fight for her "Blueprint For America." It would take a backseat to Collins's agenda, but it was better that than a forgotten footnote in some future history book.

They had come together to make the announcement in Chicago, the site of the national convention in less than three months. Jane felt comfortable in the city that had once been her home, and although she did not feel completely comfortable yet with Dennis Collins the man, she was comfortable with her decision. She didn't have to care passionately for the man. She just had to be able to work with him.

Jane felt apprehensive about seeing Alex for the first time since the day that had been both her happiest and her cruelest. But it had to happen. She and Collins would be spending a lot of time campaigning together over the coming months and she would have to get used to Alex's presence again on a regular basis. She didn't quite know what to expect, but she knew it would not be the same between them. It would never be the same again.

As Collins stood on the stage at Grant Park before the city's famous Buckingham Memorial Fountain for his second speech of the day, Jane retreated to the back of the stage and took the empty seat beside Alex, who acknowledged her with a cool quirk of her eyebrows. Alex's mood matched the cool April breeze blowing in off Lake Michigan.

"Hello, Alex," Jane whispered, feeling more nervous than she'd ever felt giving a speech or presiding over a Senate committee hearing.

Alex's eyes never strayed to Jane. She kept careful watch over Dennis Collins, her security subject, and the crowd. "Hello, Jane," she answered evenly, as though they'd only met once or twice before.

A fresh round of pain slammed into Jane. They really were strangers now. She willed the hurt away, determined to play it as cool as Alex. It was probably for the best that way. "Alex, you left something behind awhile ago and I wanted to return it."

Alex still didn't look her way. "You're right. I left a lot behind."

Jane felt her knees weaken. *You and me both, honey.* She dug into her pocket for the familiar smooth black stone she had once given to Alex. She pressed it into Alex's tense hand and felt a small tremble in response. She knew Alex remembered the stone just by the feel of it. She hoped she remembered the feel of her fingers, too. "It's yours, Alex. I want you to keep it."

This time Alex turned to her, but Jane was up and moving toward the front of the stage. Her speech was next.

Jane started out on a stool, holding a cordless mic, a spotlight hotly capturing her like a brilliant, lone star in a clear, darkening sky. She began with a self-deprecating joke, and it wasn't long before she had them hanging on her every word. The crowd was smiling with her, and when her smile faded, so did theirs. As her mood deepened, so did the audience's. It was a unique and powerful example of cause and effect.

Jane launched into a story about a tearful mother of an innocent child killed in a drive-by shooting in L.A. The woman had run beside Jane's convertible in a parade, begging her to do something to stop the violence, until she had run herself to exhaustion and collapsed on the sidewalk.

Jane paused to collect herself, and then her fist came up to pound the air. Her voice shook with anger and incredulity. "Have we exhausted ourselves trying to find solutions to end violence in our streets? Have we tirelessly worked to keep kids in school, to help them discover and achieve dreams? Have we sapped the social programs we have, and wracked our brains to come up with new ones to help struggling parents? Have we really even *tried* to get guns out of the hands of those who would use them for evil purposes?" She paused, her voice thick with disapproval. "No. We have not even broken a sweat, ladies and gentlemen. We have not even left the starting gate."

Jane stalked the stage like a cat, moving fluidly, pausing to look someone in the eye, stretching a hand out to implore her audience. She spoke like an evangelist, pleading passionately, questioning and probing just enough to leave the audience slightly uncomfortable, before calmly pointing out the solution, which, coming from her, sounded so simple and achievable.

"It is right to help the less fortunate, and yet it is much easier to ignore their plight," she continued. "It is right to want clean air to breathe and safe water to drink, and yet it is so easy to use the environment like it is a disposable commodity. It is right to want good health care and fair access to education, and yet we don't *demand* these things of our government. It is right to want happiness . . ." Jane croaked out the last word, sending a jolt through Alex, who sat beside Dennis Collins at the back of the stage.

"It is right to want happiness, ladies and gentlemen, and yet we cannot even begin to know happiness without food in our cupboards, a decent job to go to every day, a safe street to live on. Only *then* can we emerge from the shackles of our basic needs to let our hearts and minds and bodies soar to new and incredible heights." Jane's fist settled over her heart and her voice quivered with emotion. "To where our dreams can take root. To where love and friendship flourish. To where the generosity in our hearts can blossom."

Like the other three thousand or so people in the audience, Alex's attention was completely riveted on Jane, and yet she alone recognized the unspoken pain in Jane's words, in her face, in her gestures.

If only you would just let yourself love me back, Alex thought simplistically. But she knew nothing was simple about any of it. Jane had made her choice, and she, Alex, could never be a part of her life. It was clear Jane could not or would not give herself to Alex. They were practically strangers now. False hope would not change that, Alex reminded herself. She was no longer angry at Jane, just resigned to the bleak reality of their situation.

Jane had returned to her stool, crossing her legs casually, her lanky frame hunched slightly. Her voice had softened but was still heavy with resolve. "Without caring, responsible leaders in government, we cannot have happiness. We cannot be the best we can be, and we cannot achieve the richest fulfillment we can, without a government committed to protecting and insuring that our basic needs are met. Make us, your government leaders, accountable for your happiness, ladies and gentlemen."

The audience stamped and whistled, and Collins joined Jane on stage for the typical pose of joined hands, upraised in victory. Signs bearing Jane's name bobbed and waved frantically in the twilight, and Alex felt her heart melt again for the remarkable woman she had so hopelessly fallen in love with.

Chapter 10

With all the suspense gone from the Democratic National Convention, it was just an excuse for a giant love-in and one hell of a party that went on for days. Alex had never seen anything like it. There were receptions and banquets, pep rallies and feel-good seminars, and, of course, a lively celebration every night.

It was a dramatic change from the two weeks Alex had just spent in training at the base in Quantico the Secret Service shared with the FBI. Training was an ongoing part of a Secret Service Agent's career. Truthfully, Alex had been glad for the break. She'd enjoyed the firearms requalification and the defensive driving course. And the tactics course, where she'd gotten to kick a little butt. The nightlife had been anything but dull, too. She'd shared several nights with a very sexy, blond FBI instructor. She'd been under no illusions that the affair was anything but just a pleasant distraction, a way to pass the time. And that'd been just fine with her. Her heart wasn't capable of anything more. It might never be.

Jane and Collins had already given their final acceptance speech to the delegates. They looked good together, Alex had to admit, as she watched them share an obligatory dance at the closing celebration. The Collins-Kincaid ticket had surprised her a little, once she'd gotten over her disappointment at Jane pulling out of the race. She'd understood it in rational terms, how the combination of a mature, fatherly, conservative Democrat and his smart, sexy, liberal sidekick was sure to blow the Republicans right out of the water. Emotionally though, she didn't quite get these political mergers and backroom deals, this selling yourself to the highest bidder stuff.

But she refused to judge Jane for it, as she watched her move from the dance floor to join in an animated conversation with people Alex didn't recognize. Jane was an intelligent woman with high standards, and if she felt joining the Collins ticket was the right thing to do, then it was. Alex's faith in Jane was still well-rooted and she trusted her judgment implicitly. Well, her political judgment, anyway.

Alex looked at her watch, knowing her shift was just about up. Collins was bidding people goodnight, which would make the handover to the other agents easier. She wanted to call it a night too and crawl into bed, but something held her back.

She could not stop watching Jane across the large ballroom, looking spectacular in her Democrat-blue Vera Wang dress with the drop shoulder. Alex was mesmerized by the delight in Jane's every expression. She was absolutely glowing and had never looked more beautiful to Alex . . . well, there was one *other* time. Alex felt the stirrings of hot arousal in the pit of her stomach before it quickened and shot down her legs. Remembering the look of pure thrill and joy on Jane's face during their lovemaking made her pulse race all over again. She felt sweat tickling her forehead and she rubbed fleetingly at it. *Oh, God.*

"Hey, Alex!" Carter sidled up to Alex, looking delighted and more than a little inebriated. K.C. and the Sunshine Band sang "That's the Way I Like It" from huge ceiling speakers. It was the perfect song for Jane and her staff. Carter put his arm around her shoulders. "You off duty, stud?"

Alex scowled good-naturedly at him. "Yes, and I could use a drink or three."

Carter disappeared and returned within seconds with a tumbler of Scotch for her. They clinked glasses.

"Good God, Alex. Our girl is pretty great, isn't she?"

Alex winced. "Yeah, she is."

"We've missed you, Alex. All of us. Jane hasn't been the same since, you know."

Alex looked at him and didn't bother to hide her surprise. "She hasn't?"

Carter shrugged. "She's been strong out there on the campaign trail. Better than ever." He looked at Alex questioningly. "But . . . I dunno. Something's missing. Something important. She's not happy, Alex. And it concerns me."

Alex took a deep drink and looked again at Jane across the room in animated conversation with someone. She wouldn't have guessed that Jane was lonely and hurting too, and it gave her a fleeting sense of perverse comfort.

She turned to Carter. She knew she had to give Jane her freedom—cut her loose from whatever guilt and desire she still felt for Alex. It was not doing either of them any good. Jane needed to be at her best in the coming months and so, for that matter, did Alex. It was time to clean up those loose pieces, to truly let one another go. "Carter, I need your help."

He leered at Alex, his eyes mischievous. "You want me to help set you up with one of the hot babes here? You are off duty, after all."

"Carter, I'm serious."

"Oh, sorry. Just trying to help."

"I need a few moments alone with Jane."

Carter shook his head. "Oh, no you don't, stud. I don't want you seducing the next Vice President of the United States and sending all our hard work down the drain." He wasn't entirely kidding, Alex knew.

Too late anyway, I've already seduced her.

"Carter, don't worry. I'm not going to do anything stupid." Her eyes pleaded her case. "I never said good-bye, and I think I need to."

He regarded her for a moment before nodding slightly. "You're right. You didn't, and you do. I'll call you on your cell phone when she turns in for the night." He glanced across the room. "It shouldn't be long." He gave Alex a look of warning. "Just don't hurt her, Alex. And don't fuck anything up." He didn't need to add the word *again*.

Alex rapped softly on the door of the hotel suite. Her legs quickly turned to jelly when Jane answered, a look of surprise flickering across her face.

"Alex," Jane said, a little breathless.

Alex looked around quickly, catching the eyes of the two agents stationed in the hallway. She nodded at them. "Can we talk?"

Jane wordlessly opened the door to let Alex pass. The large living room of the suite was cast in the soft light of a solitary lamp. City lights twinkled in the dark like the glow of hundreds of cigarettes outside the expansive windows.

Alex turned around and breathed deeply, happy beyond words just to be with Jane again in such close proximity. *God, you are so beautiful.* Jane's hair hung loosely over a satin, light blue robe, and under Alex's gaze, she nervously cinched it tighter to her body. Her lips were parted in surprise, or nervousness, or perhaps anticipation, Alex couldn't be sure. Jane looked curious but patient. And so unintentionally sexy.

"Congratulations, Jane. I mean that. I think you and Collins are going to make a heck of a team." Alex smiled, opposing emotions fighting for supremacy. She was happy for Jane, wanted to see her get everything she wanted. But she knew that each of Jane's victories was another loss for Alex—for them.

Jane tilted her head in solicitation. "Thank you, Alex. But that's not why you're here, is it?"

Alex felt the worry lines creasing her forehead. "No. I wanted to talk."

"Are you still angry with me?"

Alex expelled a held breath. "No, I—"

"You'd have a right to be," Jane said quietly. "Come, have a seat."

They moved to a richly upholstered couch the color of Champagne, the city lights winking in front of them.

"I'm done being angry, Jane. I'm sad for us." Alex was only a blink or two away from tears. The pain felt so real, it was almost physical. "So fucking sad, it hurts."

Tears began welling in Jane's eyes too, shocking Alex. She'd expected Jane to remain stoic, impassive, cool. She expected another brush-off and not the tear spilling down Jane's cheek.

Alex raked her eyes over the soft silkiness of Jane's robe. She so badly wanted to reach out and touch the cool, smooth fabric, run her fingers down Jane's arm and back up again to her neck. She ached to caress with her lips and her fingers the soft place just below Jane's ear, at the corner of her jaw.

"Jane," Alex managed with effort, her voice husky. "I still want you so much . . . I've never stopped wanting you."

Jane's long fingers brushed the wetness from her cheek. "Alex," she finally said. "You don't have to—"

"Yes, I do, Jane." Alex's fingers darted across the distance and stroked Jane's hand. When she didn't pull back, Alex continued caressing softly. She couldn't be this close to Jane and *not* touch her.

"I know you can't have a relationship with me," Alex choked out.

"Oh, Alex," Jane said tenderly, her free hand closing over Alex's stroking fingers, stilling them. Her touch felt warm, welcoming. "I didn't want it to end the way it did. I never wanted to hurt you. Or me."

"I know. Neither did I." Images of that day at her townhouse flashed in her mind. "I love you, Jane. You're the first woman who's made me feel that way since Julia. I just wish . . . oh, hell, I don't know. I guess I wish things could be different."

Jane's cool demeanor suddenly shattered and she fell into Alex's arms, her body shaking. Alex clutched her tightly, protectively.

"It's okay, baby," Alex murmured, pressing Jane's head against her shoulder. "I understand, I really do."

"No," Jane rasped. "No, Alex. I want to explain." She pulled back just a little, until her watery gaze held Alex's. She labored to steady her breathing. "That day . . . at your place. I—I couldn't resist you, Alex. I wanted so badly to make love with you, I just— I couldn't think. I didn't want to think about anything else. You do that to me."

Alex bit back a smile. "Thinking is sometimes highly over-rated, you know."

Jane hesitated before smiling through her tears. "In my line of work, and I imagine yours too, Alex, thinking is kind of critical, wouldn't you say?"

Alex was about to zing a comeback at Jane when she was overcome with the desire to kiss her. Their faces just inches apart, Alex's mouth closed the distance with lightning quickness and captured the velvety heat of Jane's. Alex ignored the soft cry from Jane—unsure whether it was one of surprise or pleasure or protest—and kissed her soundly. She was elated when Jane's body melted into hers.

172

Alex felt her arousal awakening deep within her, knew that she would soon be twitching for relief. She had come to say good-bye, but now as she kissed Jane and held her in her arms, she knew she was in trouble—knew her will was quickly crumbling. It was so damned hard to be strong in her presence and especially in her arms like this. Whatever Jane wanted from her, she would happily give it. If Jane wanted a closeted and infrequent affair with her, she would do it. *Anything that would mean more moments like these.*

"Alex," Jane said, gently pulling away from the kiss. Her hands framed Alex's face, her fingers soft and tender. "I don't want to hurt you anymore, Alex." Her eyes were equally gentle and tender as they settled on Alex's. "This is so hard for me, Alex. I want you so much. But I just can't. *We* can't."

Alex felt—again—like she'd just been kicked in the stomach. It hurt to breathe. She had half expected this, but it didn't lessen the pain. *God.* She just wanted so much to be near Jane, however infrequently. She realized now how much she'd missed Jane these past months, how empty she felt. She was used to putting her body on the line for Jane, but now it was her heart she was offering up so easily, and she couldn't stop herself. It was like being on the edge of a cliff and letting the momentum push her over.

"Jane," Alex said hoarsely, her body still prickling with unspent desire. "Let me make love to you. Let me touch you." She breathed heavily, her body trembling. "Let me make you come. I want to so badly."

Alex saw the desire rise like a flame in Jane's eyes. She pressed into Alex, slipped her hands around Alex's neck and kissed her with desperation. *Oh, yes, she wants me just as much.* Alex hungrily sucked at the soft, full lips, her energy matching Jane's spirited desire. She circled her hands in small caresses along Jane's back, gently moving them to Jane's waist, and felt the heat of their bodies fuse. Alex felt Jane tense as her fingers slid to the robe's silky belt. *If I could just touch her skin . . .*

Roughly, Jane pulled back and scurried off the couch. "Alex," she said huskily, running her fingers coarsely through her hair. "I can't think when you do that to me."

"I don't want you to think. I want you to just feel. I want you to just *be*."

"Oh, Alex." Jane frowned, sadness darkening her face. "Don't you know that's impossible? If I could be with anyone right now, it would be you."

Alex was exasperated. They'd already parted on poor terms once, and she would not see that happen again. And then she felt her anger relent to pity for Jane, who, she realized, could not find it within to allow herself real happiness and fulfillment. It was a gift Jane could not give herself. Strangely, her vulnerability and inherent loneliness made Alex love her even more.

"Jane, honey, it's all right. I can accept that we can't be together . . . that you can't love me." She looked at Jane imploringly. "At least let me see you once in awhile . . . as friends . . . as . . . as whatever you want."

Jane smiled dolefully and carefully sat down beside Alex, taking her hand in hers. Their fingers found each other's like they'd held hands a thousand times before.

"Alex, you're the sweetest, most wonderful, giving woman I've ever met. I mean that." She bent and kissed Alex's hand. "You are ready to love again, Alex. And I'm so happy that you are." She looked heavenward before closing her eyes tightly, and Alex could see the agony and disappointment in her face. "It just can't be with me, Alex." When she looked back at Alex, her resolve was firm. "And I won't have secret, fleeting trysts with you. You're too special for that. You deserve so much more."

Reluctantly, Alex stood up to go. She appraised Jane speculatively. "You deserve more than that too, you know."

"Maybe one day I will."

Chapter 11

The rest of the summer came and went in a blur for Jane. And while the season was changing, her hectic pace was not. The cities and faces had become indistinct and merged into one another, like the lines on the many highways she traveled. Though the end of the campaign was nearing, she could no longer fathom what it would be like not to hit the trail day after day: the speeches, the walkabouts, the interviews, ribbon cuttings, even christening a new freighter in Detroit named after her father. She wouldn't miss the exhaustion, but a part of her would miss the adventure and the ever-changing landscape.

"Three weeks to go, and things couldn't look better," Jack Wilson gushed at their morning briefing. Usually dour and serious, the chief of staff's mood had seemed to lighten with each passing week of the campaign.

"Howard's been a lame duck for awhile, but now he's basically a dead duck," Jack said triumphantly. "Especially after tonight," he grinned from behind the rim of his coffee cup.

Jane sipped her own coffee contemplatively. She was confident about the television debate tonight between herself and the incumbent vice president, Ben Palmer. She and her staff had been spending part of every day for the last couple of weeks practicing, and an expert from Collins's team had already prepped both she and Collins, who would debate President Charles Howard tomorrow night in the same studio.

"Let's not get too cocky," Jane cautioned. They all knew that Howard and Palmer were proving to be poor opponents so far. In fact, Jane and Dennis had been feasting on them and their poor records, and the polls reflected the unevenness of the contest. But overconfidence could turn voters off, she knew. So could attacks that appeared too vicious. She would have to walk a fine line between confidence and humility, decisiveness and thoughtfulness.

Steph Cameron clattered into Jane's hotel suite, her bulging leather briefcase in hand. She was grinning. "Top of the morning to you both. Nervous?" She winked at Jane before heading for the carafe of coffee at the breakfast bar.

Jane reclined on a loveseat with her coffee cup, her feet on the coffee table. "What do you think?" She smiled back at her aide and old college friend.

Steph took a seat beside Jack on a facing sofa. "I'd say you look like you've got the cat by the tail, which, by the way, you do."

Jane sipped her coffee, luxuriating in the Colombian aroma and knowing it was probably among her few quiet moments of the day and evening ahead. "Nervous, no. Not yet. But I'm not ready to say I've got the cat by the tail, as you put it."

"Well, you're wise to be a little cautious," Steph replied. "At least let the rest of us indulge in a little arrogance."

Jane laughed shortly. "Too much work to do yet before we

celebrate. And besides, something unexpected could happen to turn things on a dime. Howard *does* have the advantage of being the President of the United States right now, which means it's his to lose and not ours to win."

Steph pouted.

"What time do I need to be at the studio?"

"Six. That's two hours before the debate starts."

"Lord, don't tell me I need *that* much time in makeup and wardrobe. I know the campaign has taken a toll on me, but do I look that bad?"

Steph and Jack laughed in unison.

"You look that *good*," Jack said through a smile. "Collins was told to be at the studio three hours before his debate starts!"

Jane smiled, not at all concerned about her looks, but at least the topic was a momentary distraction. "Okay, well, that makes me feel better. And I'll feel even better than that if you tell me my opponent is pulling into the studio . . . oh, about now," she said, glancing at her watch.

Steph grinned. "Well, I'm not sure about that. But you've got nothing to worry about, Jane. You're going to look gorgeous and you're going to knock them dead."

Jane frowned. "Gorgeous, I don't care about. I want to look . . . I don't know, big-sisterly and CEO-ish all at once. And then I want to sound like the next Vice President of the United States."

"Don't worry," Steph said. "You'll be in a nice Versace suit, and I promise they won't go too nuts on the hair and makeup. And you *are* the next Vice President of the United States."

Jane shrugged, her mind drifting. "When does my mother arrive?"

"She'll be coming in sometime before the debate starts," Jack said.

"Damn," Jane muttered. "You couldn't talk her out of it, huh?"

"You know her. She wants to be there, and once she's made up her mind . . ."

"Yeah, yeah, I know. I'm just afraid I'll get nervous knowing she's in the audience. She'll probably start giving me hand signals or something."

"Is that legal?" Steph asked, only half joking. "Anyway, once you get going, girl, nothing's going to make you nervous out there."

Jane swallowed a mouthful of coffee, hoping Steph was right. Between her mother's presence and Collins watching from the wings, which also meant Alex would be there . . . The cameras and the millions of people watching wouldn't be so bad after all.

"Where are you going?" Jack asked her as she stood up.

"I think I need a long, hot bath."

Jane was quietly going over her notes in her expansive dressing room at CBS Studios at 524 West 57th Street. The hair and makeup people had finally left her alone, and her dark blue jacket and skirt hung from a nearby hanger, ready for her. She wanted to prolong her peace and quiet and the wearing of her old jeans and denim shirt for as long as she could before she had to be on stage under the hot glare of the lights and the cruel scrutiny of the cameras.

A light knock on her door preceded a rush of energy into the room.

"Mom!"

Maria Kincaid looked striking in a bright green dress and a short, cream-colored jacket cut neatly around her trim waist. She gave Jane an animated hug. "Darling, it's so good to see you. Let me look at you."

Maria stood back appraisingly.

"Mom, I know what you're going to say. I haven't been eating or sleeping enough."

"I see you've developed the ability to read minds now. That

will serve you well as vice president, you know." Maria smiled proudly. "You look . . . wonderful."

Jane frowned, detecting a trace of reproach in her mother's voice. "What?" she said, hands on her hips.

"Nothing, dear."

"Mother. What's bothering you?"

"I just wish there was someone taking care of you, since you're not the best at taking care of yourself. That's all."

"Mom, I'm fine. Really. Just tired. You know what it's like."

Maria sighed dramatically. "I wish Alex Warner were back on your detail. I'd feel so much better knowing she's there. Why can't you get Collins to give her back to you?"

It had actually been days since Jane had thought about Alex, which was very unusual. She saw her almost weekly, whenever she and Collins campaigned together. They were cordial, almost friendly. But they'd never again discussed their last intimate conversation—Alex's declaration of love and her very tempting offer of sex, and Jane's gentle and somewhat tenuous rejection. Spending too much time with Alex, especially any alone time, was lethal, because Jane had still not gotten her out of her system. But if she were at least beginning to think about Alex less frequently, it was a start.

"Mom." Jane grew impatient and snapped, "I have more to worry about right now than who my agents are. And I haven't exactly seen Alex busting down my door demanding to come back."

"I know, dear. It's just that she promised me she'd take care of you. I don't understand."

Jane felt her heart lurch at her mother's revelation. When had Alex promised to take care of her? She couldn't allow herself the luxury to imagine what it would feel like to have someone "take care" of her. To come home to at the end of the day, to share a laugh with and a hug. "I don't need taking care of," Jane answered pointedly. "I'm doing fine."

Maria quirked a skeptical eyebrow. "I hope so. Still, I miss Alex. She's a good woman."

Jane blinked at the simple statement. *Yes. She is a good woman.*

The door thudded open and Will Carter barged through, looking both nervous and excited. "They're ready for you, Jane."

Jane's first and, she hoped, last moment of distress came in Vice President Palmer's on-air greeting.

"My. You're even prettier in person." He smirked as he looked from Jane to the camera. "She really is, you know," he said coyly to the TV audience.

Jane was stunned, totally unprepared for his comment. She had not expected her looks to come up in the campaign, but she should have, she realized. Her opponents might try to imply that she was too pretty to be taken seriously on the world stage. And anyone who didn't know Jane or who hadn't been paying attention to her campaign might believe it. She was not naïve about her looks. She knew they had opened doors for her. But opening a door and staying there were two different things.

Palmer took her silence as his cue to keep at it. "Your beauty, Ms. Kincaid, could almost make one forget the issues."

The live audience laughed, but Jane only gave a perfunctory smile. "Lucky for you, Mr. Palmer, I'll remind you pretty quickly."

The audience laughed again, and Jane relaxed, though she was still not done with her opponent. Humor and wit would make her point much better than ruthless aggression. "I'll even give you a nice, glossy eight by ten if you'll let me get on to the real issues this country wants to talk about."

The audience guffawed and she knew she had struck a point. She caught a nod of approval from her mother off in the shadows.

The moderator jumped in with his first question. "Ms.

Kincaid. Are you ready for the second most powerful job in this nation?"

Jane smiled warmly, in contrast to her words. "If I wasn't, I wouldn't be wasting everyone's time." She looked directly at the camera. "I've never been more ready for anything in my life. But it's not just about whether I'm ready. I think it's about whether this country is ready for a change, and I believe it is. Our economy is in worse shape than it was four years ago, and that means we have people who aren't eating as well and who aren't getting proper medical care. We have people losing their houses, their jobs. We've also lost another couple of thousand soldiers who have been toiling without the progress they need to justify their being there. We're all ready for a change."

"Mr. Palmer?"

The vice president's face had reddened a shade. "I agree with some of Ms. Kincaid's points about the last four years. But that's what is key here—four years. One term is not enough to do everything we want to do. We have the foundation now. We need another term to watch our programs and policies really flourish and result in positive changes."

Jane was shaking her head. She couldn't resist interrupting, even though she knew it was forbidden. "A house built on a weak foundation is sure to fall down, Mr. Palmer."

The moderator held up a hand. "You'll get time for a rebuttal later, Ms. Kincaid. Mr. Palmer, the question was, are you the better choice here?"

Palmer smiled cockily, his fleshy neck bulging over his collar. "Of course I am. I have had many years in government. And experience is no match for a fat bank account and a well-known family name." He shot a look of disgust at Jane.

"Ms. Kincaid?" the moderator prompted.

Jane quietly seethed, but she would not be drawn into a personal attack. She steadied herself before she answered. "There's an old quote that says, if you want your place in the sun, you have to get out of the shade of the family tree. I think I've done that. Helping people and trying to make a better world can't happen if you don't venture off the family farm, Mr. Palmer. And it doesn't happen if you never leave your ivory tower, either."

The audience clapped their approval, and Palmer gave a small scowl. Jane smiled sweetly.

"Ms. Kincaid. The billionaire Warren Buffet recently said he thinks the wealthy aren't paying enough taxes. That he's taxed at a lower rate than some of his employees. Do you agree with his point of view?"

"I think we all want an America where everyone has an equal chance. Where your family background or the color of your skin don't predetermine your future. I think those who are better off have a responsibility to the community and to those around them. So, yes, I do think the rich aren't taxed enough. And I think President Howard's tax cuts have decimated our social system, and that is something I would work to change." Jane stared into the camera, her fist clenching the lectern. "It all comes down to what kind of a society we want to live in."

"Mr. Palmer?"

"A welfare society is what you're talking about, Ms. Kincaid." Palmer was condescending now. "I don't think that's the society anyone wants us to live in."

Jane smiled knowingly. "I'm not talking about charity, Mr. Palmer. I'm talking about equality. I'm talking about an equal playing field. I'm talking about honoring hard work and not just rewarding wealth. *That's* the kind of society we want."

The audience applauded, and it wasn't just out of politeness. Jane knew her verbal punches were landing.

"What would you do to seal the Mexican border to illegal immigration?" the moderator asked Palmer.

"Enforcement first, that's my policy," he answered breezily. "I would double the border patrol."

"I don't know how you're going to find room in that budget

to double the border patrol with all the tax cuts you're proposing," Jane fired back. "What are you going to do, pile more on the backs of single mothers and the elderly?"

"Of course not," the vice president snapped. "There's enough for everyone, including more border patrol."

"Sure," Jane replied testily. "Tell that to the poor people of Lowndes County in Mississippi and the displaced victims of Hurricane Katrina. Or the disabled living on six hundred dollars a month. Tell them there's enough for everyone."

The moderator was about to interrupt with another question, when Vice President Palmer glowered, and said, "I suppose you have all the answers, little lady."

Jane simply smiled, her anger on a simmering boil, her tone curt. "If I claimed to have all the answers, I'd be a Republican. And another thing." Her jaw tightened. "I'm nobody's little lady."

A collective gasp from the small audience, followed by ensuing murmurs of delight, buoyed Jane. Oh, yes. She had him now. And she did. The rest of the debate continued with Palmer on the defensive and Jane scoring obvious points. Palmer revealed no fresh ideas and Jane easily made hamburger meat out of his administration's current policies.

Dennis Collins greeted her with a warm handshake and a congratulatory pat on the back offstage. "You're going to be a tough act to follow tomorrow, Jane."

"That won't be a problem for you, Dennis. Howard is every bit as much out of his league as Palmer."

Her mother hugged her and told her how proud she was.

"I wasn't too much of a bitch, was I?" Jane whispered to Alex, standing near a wall just a few feet away.

Alex smiled glowingly and Jane felt her breath catch in her throat. Alex looked as good as ever, and she still looked at Jane like she wanted to throw her over her shoulder and cart her off to the nearest motel. The fleeting fantasy nearly made Jane trip.

"I thought you were perfect," Alex said, blushing a little.

Jane forced herself to move along and wondered if there would always be that chemistry between them. She both cherished it and cursed it.

Jane had planned to watch her running mate's debate from backstage, just as he had watched hers. It was important to show solid support for one another, even if it was off-camera. The newspapers were sure to notice her presence.

She dined at the hotel with her mother and her closest aides, glad her turn in front of the camera was over. Jack pointed at his watch. It was time to head to the studio.

"I just need to go to my room for my coat." The late October evening was chilly, foreshadowing another season changing.

Jane opened the closet of her suite and selected a black overcoat. It would go nicely with her black pantsuit and cobalt blue blouse. She almost always wore something blue these days to fly the colors of the party, just as Collins usually wore a blue tie or a blue shirt. It was superstition more than anything.

The door to her suite suddenly burst open and Carter thundered in, startling Jane. Far more alarming was his face, which, even for his coloring, was nearly white.

"What is it?" Jane knew something was wrong, and even as she asked the question, she mentally braced herself.

The hand clutching his cell phone shook uncontrollably. "Dennis's motorcade has been hit."

"What?" Jane felt the blood drain from her own face. "Dammit, what are you talking about, Carter? Hit . . . like shot or blown up or what?"

Maria Kincaid was hot on the heels of Carter, having followed him in. She looked as stunned as they did.

"It . . . they . . . It was a car accident. A—another car crashed into his limo at an intersection about twenty minutes ago. They were on their way to the studio."

"Was he hurt?" Jane needed the facts as quickly as she could get them.

"A broken leg, I think."

Carter still wasn't calming down, and Jane didn't understand. "Is it life-threatening?"

"I don't think so. They're being taken to Bellevue Hospital."

The hair on the back of Jane's neck stood up. She caught the look in her mother's eyes and knew immediately her worse fear had come true. Alex had been hurt.

"How badly is Alex hurt?" she asked in a voice she didn't recognize.

"I don't know."

Jane rushed for the bathroom, holding her stomach, hoping to hold back her nausea long enough to make it to the toilet. She did—barely. Her mother followed her in after a moment and rubbed her back reassuringly. Jane couldn't speak. She could only shake her head over and over.

"When you're ready, we'll get some more information, Jane."

Jane finally stood up on shaky legs and splashed cold water on her face.

"I'm sure Alex will be fine, dear. She's a strong woman."

Jane turned to her mother. "We don't know that she'll be fine, Mother," she ground out, her voice thin with anger. "We don't know a goddamn thing. Alex could be dead for all we know."

She saw the hurt in her mother's eyes, but now was not the time to be worried about her feelings. "You know better than to minimize something like this with me, Mother." The Kincaid family had been through more than their share of heartache and tragedy. She thought of her brother, Joe Junior, dying so young, then her husband Dan, taken so soon from her in a plane crash. Then it was her father. It hurt that her mother would try to diminish the possibility of Alex being hurt.

"Jane, I—"

"Let's go, Mother." Jane led the way out of the bathroom. Her suite had quickly filled with Secret Service agents and staff members. She was so used to having people around her anymore, she barely noticed.

"Collins is down with a broken leg," Jack reported. "He's going into surgery soon."

"What about Alex Warner?"

Jack looked at her like she'd just asked about the theory of relativity. "What?"

"I want you to find out how Alex Warner is," she answered in a tone that meant she expected an answer yesterday.

"Jane, we need to talk about—"

"I'll check," Carter intervened before Jane blew a gasket. She blinked her thanks at him before he left the room.

Jane retreated to the sofa and collapsed into it. She didn't know what she would do if Alex were really hurt . . . or worse. *Oh, God, no. She can't be. Please.* Jane knew without a doubt that she would give it all up if Alex could be all right. But she also knew it wasn't her decision to make right now. She felt more helpless than she'd felt in years.

"All right, Jack," she said quietly. There was work to be done, no matter what news of Alex awaited her. "What do we need to do?"

He sat down, oblivious to the anxiety that threatened to make her ill all over again. "The debate tonight is cancelled, of course. The press are going crazy right now. They're asking for statements from everyone, including my cat."

Jane raised a tired hand to her throbbing temple. She'd have to get out there and perform. Tell everyone that the ticket was strong, that the campaign would go on, that she could take the wheel for awhile. And then win the election practically by herself. She didn't know if she could do it, especially if Alex . . .

"I need to hear from Carter first."

Jack gave her that look again. "Hear from him about what?"

"About Alex," Jane snapped. She leveled a piercing glare at her chief of staff that could have peeled paint off a wall. "I can't go out there and pretend everything's okay if it's not. I have to know if Alex is going to be all right first." She saw her mother nod in silent agreement.

"Christ, Jane. You need to reassure—"

Carter reappeared, his mouth a thin line of worry.

"What?" Jane barked impatiently.

"Alex has a head injury. They're running tests. She's . . . I don't think she's conscious."

Jane felt suddenly dizzy. "Fuck. What the hell happened, Carter?"

He shrugged helplessly. "Apparently some drunk ran a barricade at an intersection and they were broadsided. So far it doesn't sound like anything more than that."

Jane's thoughts were still on Alex. "Tell me she's going to be okay, Carter. She *has* to be okay." They were all staring at her and she felt like wringing each of their necks until she got an answer.

"I don't think we'll know any more for awhile," he answered lamely.

Jane stood and began to pace, running a hand nervously through her hair. She knew everyone was waiting for her to make a decision, to act like a leader, to be strong. And she was strong. She'd pushed herself through tragedies before, was familiar with pressure and knew how it galvanized her and sharpened her senses. This time was different, though. It felt like, finally, this was one tragedy she might not be able to withstand. She appealed to her mother with a look.

Maria moved to her, took her hand, and gave it a squeeze. "Janey, you can do this. You are the strongest person I've ever known, and it's time for the country to see that, too. That's the one quality that has propelled you here."

Jane knew that was true. She'd sometimes been too strong for her own good. Like with Alex. *Dear Alex.*

"We can go to the hospital right after you give a speech," Maria added.

"The studio is holding everything," Jack interjected. "You can do a live speech to the country and then a short scrum to the press afterward."

Jane stood up. She swallowed hard and found the strength she would need in the coming hours. "All right, Jack. Let's get working on the speech on the way over. But I'm going to the hospital right afterward."

"Of course. It wouldn't look right for you not to."

"I'm not talking about going there for Collins," she hissed, then marched out of the room, her coat slung over her arm.

Chapter 12

You could almost forget you were in a hospital, Jane marveled as she took in her surroundings in Bellevue's well-appointed VIP lounge. The hospital, as well as being a world-class trauma unit, served as the medical facility for dignitaries visiting New York City. That part was obvious. The huge top floor lounge with the expansive windows was richly carpeted and furnished with expensive, dark leather sofas and a large screen television. It even had its own kitchenette with top end stainless steel appliances, including a coffeemaker that was working nonstop.

The room was filling by the minute with Secret Service agents and a scattering of aides belonging to both Jane and Dennis Collins. Jane was thankful the media were being kept well away in a separate area off the hospital's main floor lobby. Her live speech and the media throng afterward had gone well, but she didn't need any more harassment right now. The energy for holding herself together had just about vanished.

Flanked on a couch by her mother and Will Carter, Jane drummed her fingers on her lap. "Maybe someone should page that doctor again. "Christ. Doesn't she know I want to talk to her?"

"She knows, dear," Maria supplied gently.

"Are you sure they know Alex doesn't have any family and that we're the ones they should talk to?"

"Yes, Jane," Carter answered smoothly. "They've been briefed on the situation. They know they're not to give any information on Alex's condition to anyone but us and Alex's superiors."

Jane could barely contain herself. For two hours, she'd been the picture of cool and collected, but now she felt as though she might explode if she didn't soon hear news of Alex. A lanky figure in dark blue scrubs and surgical cap entered the room. Carter, who seemed to recognize the doctor, stood up and briskly motioned her over.

Jane rose and forced herself to stay calm. "How is Agent Warner, doctor?"

Dr. Wong, who had introduced herself as Alex's neurologist, told Jane in a neutral voice that her patient's condition was guarded. Alex had suffered a linear skull fracture in the crash.

"No real damage shows on the CT scan, but we're keeping her in an induced coma for another day or two to try to keep any brain swelling down. We'll do another scan tomorrow for a closer look."

"No surgery at this point, then?"

"If we need to do a craniotomy at any point, we will. But there's no hematoma that we can see . . . nothing to repair."

Maria clutched Jane's forearm comfortingly. "Then she should come out of this okay?"

The doctor set weary brown eyes on Maria. "She should, yes, but I always hesitate with head injuries to forecast the future with any precision. She could have months of headaches, some memory loss even."

Jane's heart sank. She was relieved beyond belief that Alex was going to make it, but there was no guarantee she would recover fully. "Can we see her now?"

Dr. Wong nodded. "But please keep it short."

Jane knew what the ICU would look like. She knew what to expect. During her medical training, she had seen inert patients connected to the machines that took care of all their necessary bodily functions, including breathing, while they recovered from grave illnesses or trauma. It was an antiseptic, impersonal environment full of medical hardware. Even the patients took on an artificial look.

What Jane was not prepared for was the icy fear and shock she felt when she walked into the small, glassed-in room. Alex lay unconscious, her head heavily bandaged, her eyes tightly closed, her left cheek bruised. A tube snaked into her mouth, connected to a ventilator. An intravenous line ran into her left hand. Electrodes monitored her heart rate and blood pressure, the steady numbers on a nearby screen offering only a small measure of comfort to Jane. Machines whirred.

Oh, Alex! Jane grabbed the chrome bedrail to steady herself. She felt her mother's presence just inches behind her, but her attention remained riveted on Alex. She looked so vulnerable, so weak, her form so still and almost lifeless . . . it was not the Alex she knew—so strong and athletic and capable. No, this was some one-dimensional imitation of the woman Jane had come to care so deeply about, to need on such a deep level. The thought that Alex may never be that person again lanced Jane with razor sharpness.

Jane sucked in a ragged breath as she felt her fear morph into anger, then fear again, and finally into a deep sadness that made her whole body slump in weariness. She touched Alex's arm, then caressed it lightly. Her skin was warm but unresponsive.

191

Jane's spirits sank to a new level as she watched Alex's chest rise and fall with the timed precision of the ventilator.

"Alex," Jane said quietly, bending low to her ear. "I need you to get better. I need you to do it for me." She felt tears coalesce and she tried to swallow them back, but failed. "If you do that for me . . ." Jane couldn't finish. She felt only despair and could not fathom the future without Alex. The realization hit her with brutal force.

"Darling," Maria offered soothingly. "I think we need to get you out of here. Let me take you back to the hotel."

Jane let her mother gently guide her away from Alex's bed.

Numb with pain and a loneliness she couldn't put words to, Jane sought solace in a large tumbler of bourbon and drank it like it were healing nectar. She curled her legs beneath her on the sofa in a protective pose, letting the alcohol warm where she felt chilled and anesthetize senses that were already dulled.

"Honey, I don't think alcohol's going to—"

"Mother, don't," Jane answered dryly, taking another sip.

The room was illuminated only by the soft light of a Tiffany lamp on an end table, and Jane was glad for the shadows and the obscurity she found in them. She knew her agony must be all over her face. She didn't want her mother's—or anyone's—company, but Maria Kincaid had refused to leave her alone. In defiance, Jane decided she would sit and drink and let her sorrow swirl recklessly and silently inside her. She was good at seeking out privacy, walling herself off, even in a room full of people.

"She's going to be all right, you know." Maria poured herself a drink from the bottle of Jack Daniels on the coffee table.

"Don't give me that bullshit, Mother. We don't know that."

If Maria was shocked by Jane's tone and language, she didn't show it. She sat down at the opposite end of the sofa and sipped her drink. "You're right. We don't know that. But we can hope,

Jane." She stared until Jane turned to face her. "Sometimes that's all there is. Sometimes . . ." Maria's voice faltered. "Sometimes hope is the only thing that keeps you sane."

Jane blinked back tears. She reached across the space for her mother's hand and held it. "I'm sorry, Mother. We've both lost a lot, haven't we?"

Maria Kincaid nodded, stoic again. "Alex means a lot to you, doesn't she?"

Jane squeezed her mother's hand harder than she intended. "I can't lose anyone else." The words came out strangled.

Maria slid over and put her arm around Jane's shoulders, gently pulling her close. "I know, Janey. I don't want you to lose anyone else, either."

Jane felt a sob thunder through her and she gave into it, letting her emotions reign over her in a way she had not allowed since last summer, in the car after leaving Alex's townhouse. She knew her mother's arms were around her, but she felt almost disconnected to her body as it rocked and trembled and erupted in tears and racking sobs.

After several long moments, Maria wiped Jane's face with a tissue, disengaging enough to look at her. She cupped Jane's chin tenderly. "You've always kept too much to yourself, Jane. You've always been so good at sweeping your feelings aside and plodding on, no matter what the cost. You can't always do that with love."

Jane blinked hard to cast off the last of her tears. When she opened her eyes again, she saw that her mother knew exactly what Alex meant to her. There was no judgment, only recognition.

"I love her, Mom."

"I can see that, dear."

"You're not upset?"

Maria shook her head and smiled faintly. "I only want you to be happy, Jane. That's all I've ever wanted."

"Oh, Mom." Jane let her mother hold her again. She felt the weight of so many fears and worries lift. Years worth. She hardly recognized the weightless feeling.

"God," Jane said. "I can't believe I'm just now finally realizing how much I love her. How much I need her in my life." Saying the words finally made it much more real.

Maria extricated herself from the embrace and stroked Jane's damp cheek. "I think you realized it awhile ago. I think you're now just admitting it. Accepting it."

"Did you know?"

Maria shrugged lightly. "I could tell on the island last spring that there was something between the two of you. Alex must be a very special woman to capture your heart."

Jane nodded, reaching for her drink. "She is." She smiled and sipped her bourbon. "She's really wonderful." Jane remembered Alex's touch, the feel of her body against her. And the way she kissed . . . so soft and firm and demanding and relenting, all at once. She wanted more touches and more kisses . . . so much more of Alex. It couldn't all end before it had even really started. *Could it?*

"Are you okay, dear?"

"Even if Alex is okay, I don't know that there's a chance for us."

"Does she love you?"

"God, yes. But I . . ." She let her voice trail off, feeling hopeless again.

Maria smiled patiently. "Let me guess. You resisted her love."

Her mother was rarely wrong in her perceptions. "Yes, I did. And I hurt her in the process."

"If she loves you, she'll forgive you," Maria answered calmly. "Without forgiveness, love really isn't worth much, you know."

Jane thought back to her parents' long marriage. They had been true companions, true partners, but there had been rough patches too. And they'd always managed to emerge from them, stronger than ever. She'd always wanted that for herself. Maybe now she was finally ready to make the sacrifices love required. She had not been before, not even with her husband in their all-too-brief marriage. Oh, she thought she'd loved him, but they'd loved each other only when it was convenient to . . . only when it didn't interfere with their jobs and their goals and their too-separate lives.

Jane took a deep, purging breath. "I just hope I have the chance to show her my love."

Maria smiled. "You will."

"I want a life. With her."

"My God. I never thought I'd hear you say that. It's about time you wanted that for yourself. That you wanted it all."

Jane wished it were that easy. "The problem is, I can't have it all. I can't have both Alex and my career."

Maria's eyebrows rose sharply. "Why not?"

Jane sighed irritably. "C'mon, Mother. No one's going to vote for a lesbian to hold the second most powerful office in this country."

"Wait a minute. You just told me how much you love Alex, and already you're going to—"

"Whoa," Jane said emphatically, holding her palms up. "I didn't say I was giving Alex up."

Maria looked stunned. "You mean you're quitting the ticket?"

"If Alex comes out of this, I won't give her up again." She felt her throat constrict. "That's what I was about to promise her in the hospital."

Maria nodded, clearly pleased. "I didn't think you had it in you."

"What?"

"The ability to put love before everything else, especially your career."

"Well, I guess I'm one up on Daddy," Jane said sarcastically.

Maria's gaze turned steely. "That's not true. Your father

always put me and you kids first."

Jane made a face. "He was never home, Mother. His career was everything to him."

Maria shook her head emphatically. "You didn't know your father as well as you think you did."

"I don't get it."

"Why do you think he never ran for president or vice president? Why do you think he turned down a cabinet post in Jimmy Carter's administration?"

Jane was dumbfounded. "I thought the timing was just never right for him."

"He never did those things because I didn't want him to. And he didn't want to either. He didn't want to be traveling the world all the time, away from all of us. Having so many demands on his time." Maria looked piercingly into Jane's eyes. "He knew what was important. Especially after Joey died. I was so afraid you wouldn't realize those things for yourself."

Jane swallowed fresh tears. "God, I didn't know. I mean, he was always pushing us kids to follow in his footsteps. Me in particular. I thought he wanted me to . . ." Jane couldn't finish. Alex, months ago, had already knocked the ground beneath her away. And now, her father—her compass—was suddenly not what she thought. She was not sure of anything anymore, except for her love for Alex. *And maybe that's the point.*

"Honey," Maria said softly. "He wanted you to succeed, to do some of the things he didn't do. Because he knew you had the talent and the drive. But he never would have wanted you to give up true happiness for it."

Jane dropped her head into her hands, digesting this new information. She had told herself—convinced herself—that she was in politics to effect change. To help people. And it was true, those things were her driving force. But she had also forged ahead because she thought that's what her father would have wanted. Now she suddenly felt unencumbered by the family legacy. She'd felt somewhat free after her father had died—or at least she'd thought she did. But not like this. Now she was no longer shackled by memories and her own misjudgments.

"My God, I'm free," she mumbled quietly, exultantly.

"Yes, you are." Maria smiled. "Do you still want it?"

Jane knew exactly what her mother meant. She laughed foolishly. "I do."

"That's my girl."

"But I'm not sure it's possible."

Maria winked. "Greater minds than mine would surely disagree with you. I think it's time Clara had a visit to New York City, don't you?"

"I won't even consider anything until I know Alex is going to be all right. That's all that matters to me right now."

Jane secluded herself in Alex's room for much of the following two days, watching the sleeping woman she knew without hesitation was the love of her life. She tenderly stroked Alex's hands and arms, her cheek. She tousled her hair, squeezed her fingers. She hoped her touch conveyed the love she felt so fervidly. She forced patience on herself, because she so badly wanted to tell Alex how she felt, what she regretted and to talk of love and the future and forgiveness. But there would be time for all of that. Right now Alex needed to feel her love, her presence.

Jane was astounded at how quickly and easily the decision had come to her, now that she'd made it. And how utterly right it felt. She would not—could not—live without Alex. She would love Alex with every cell in her body, and she would fight for her and for their love, no matter what the cost. She hoped and prayed it wasn't too late with Alex.

Jane smiled at thoughts of what she would do to Alex once she got her alone and out of the hospital. *Oh, my dear.* Jane took a fluttering breath and held it for a long time. *I'm going to start with little kisses right there along your jaw. And then I'm going to kiss your neck and your throat, and of course your mouth. And I'll nibble on your lips, while my hands—*

A low, prolonged groan came from Alex, startling Jane from her sexy thoughts. When Alex's eyelids fluttered and then opened, Jane's heart skipped at least two beats.

"Darling? Alex?" she said urgently. She felt as though she were on a precipice, suspended, and she would either soar or crash to the bottom, depending on how the next few moments went.

Alex stared back, and Jane noticed immediately that the pupils were dilating properly. *Oh, thank God!*

"Alex, honey. Just take it slow, okay?" Jane stroked her cheek, trying hard to sound calm. "I'm here with you."

Alex struggled to speak around the breathing tube.

"Honey, don't talk. You've got a breathing tube in your mouth. I'll go and get the doctor and they'll take it out for you, okay?"

Jane rose, elated and anxious, but Alex pulled hard on her hand, drawing her back.

"It's okay, I'm not leaving you for more than a minute. I promise." She watched as Alex's eyes slid closed again. "You sleep, darling. I'll be here."

An hour later, Jane found her mother in the VIP lounge.

"Good news, I take it." Maria smiled.

Jane nodded. "She's waking up. Now, how about we go find Clara and have that meeting?"

Jane's announcement that she wanted a meeting came as no surprise. In fact, a meeting was long overdue. For two days, both Jane's and Dennis Collins's staff had been begging for a strategy session. The final two weeks of campaigning would fall on Jane's shoulders, and they were anxious to get her out on the road and in the media spotlight, capitalizing on the public's sympathy over the car crash. Her refusal to get back on the campaign trail had caused endless hand-wringing and temper tantrums, and little in the way of understanding.

Jane looked around the spacious VIP hospital room, leveling her gaze at each person assembled at her behest. There was Collins, lying in the hospital bed with his leg in traction, looking irritable and impatient. His chief of staff, a middle-aged man whose girth showed he'd eaten too many rubber chicken dinners and drank from too many courtesy bars, looked equally testy. Jack Wilson stood with his arms crossed over his chest, looking implacable. Steph Cameron looked more nervous than anything as she anxiously returned Jane's gaze, while Will Carter gave Jane a lopsided grin of encouragement. She almost felt like a lamb in a den of wolves, until she remembered the reason they were all here. This was her show now, and she would not be derailed.

"Everyone," Jane said evenly, ignoring her racing heart. "I've called this meeting because there's something I need to tell you all. It's something that might mean the end of . . . all of this." She held out her arms, knowing everyone was hanging on her every word now. It was exactly where she wanted them. "Something has happened in my personal life that may jeopardize my future in politics."

Jack's face fell. Steph gasped loudly enough to attract everyone's attention. Carter watched his boss, slack-jawed.

Jane ignored the quiet curses from Collins and his chief of staff, Tony Anstett. She knew they were expecting the worst—tax fraud, accepting bribes, a drunk driving conviction. Jane suppressed the urge to giggle. Paid sex. *Like that would be so unique in Washington.*

"It's not something scandalous. Not to me. Not ever. And that's something you all need to remember."

"Christ, Jane," Jack said. "You're killing us. Just tell us what you're talking about."

Jane would not be rushed. "I'm telling you all straight up that I want nothing more than to be the next Vice President of the United States." She looked squarely at Dennis Collins. "This campaign *will* go ahead. And I still feel that we will win. But the challenge will be greater now."

"Aw, shit, Jane," Collins ground out. "What the hell have you done?" He glanced sideways at his chief of staff with an I-told-you-so look.

Jane felt anger rushing through her. "I haven't *done* anything wrong." She looked at Carter for support and instantly saw it. "I've fallen in love with someone. And it changes everything."

"When did you have time to do *that*?" Steph blurted out in astonishment.

Jane laughed softly, then shared an indulgent smile with Carter. She loved her staff. They'd been through so much together. Jack was an old and dear friend, a father figure. Steph her college roommate. And Carter had rejuvenated her staff since he joined them two years ago. They had all been incredibly loyal and dedicated—she couldn't have asked any more of them. They were family, and yet, when it came to what mattered most to her now, they were strangers. And she regretted that.

"This is hard for me," she said, looking at each of her staffers. "But you need to know the truth." Anxious faces waited on her, and Jane felt like a professor presiding over a class, about to divulge some great and secret theory. "Over the course of the campaign," she continued in a voice more composed than she felt, "Alex Warner fell in love with me. And I with her."

The room was eerily silent for an instant. It was like anyone getting bad news—it took a moment for the words and their meaning to register, and then it was like the air being let out of a balloon. Their stunned disbelief exploded all at once into a chorus of curses and questions and exclamations.

"I know I've just thrown a grenade into the middle of the

room," Jane said. She was at peace with her decision, but she knew the others would not be, not yet. Maybe not ever.

"Holy fuck," Collins yelled. "No, Jane, no. Anything but that. For Christ's sake!"

"Anything but that?" Jane gave him a castigating stare. "So you would prefer that I just told you I ran someone over last night after a few too many cocktails?"

"For Christ's sake, Jane." Tony Anstett held his hands up in supplication. "Let's everyone just calm down for a goddamned minute. You're in love with another woman. What does that mean exactly?"

"What do you think it means?"

Anstett shrugged stubbornly. "Have you slept with this . . . with Alex Warner?"

Jane stole a quick glance at her staff. "Yes."

Anstett shrugged beefy shoulders again. "Okay. So what? It's just your sex life. It has nothing to do with politics. Shit like that happens all the time. It'll be easy to bury."

Jane's mouth flew open. "Shit like what, Tony? Shit like finding the love of your life? Shit like putting your fucking heart, and your ass, and your whole goddamned future on the line like I am right now? Because tomorrow when I call a press conference, it's all gonna be out there."

"What?" Collins and Anstett exclaimed in unison. "You can't do that!" Collins shouted. "It'll ruin us!"

Jane shook her head forcefully. "No, it won't. In fact, it's our only option. And if you don't believe me, perhaps you'll believe Clara Stevens."

As if on cue, the door flew open and Clara, with the air and carriage of a goddess, marched through.

"Ladies and gentlemen," she said in her rich, contralto voice, nodding crisply all around. Her presence was very powerful, like a storm sucking all the air out of the atmosphere. Jane was pleased. No one could command a room or an audience like the inestimable Clara Stevens.

"Everyone. Good day. As of today, I've joined Jane's staff as an advisor." She winked at Jane, a smile softening her serious features for just a moment. "And it is my pleasure to help out an old friend." Her jaw stiffened as she turned her attention to Collins and Anstett. "What I'm really here for is to advise all of you on how the rest of this campaign is going to go."

Collins grumbled loudly. "Shit. I need more pain medication."

Sleek, gray eyebrows rose in amusement. "Glad to see I'm already being a pain in the ass, Dennis." She smiled wickedly. "And I'm just getting started."

Clara pulled up a chair and sat down, crossing her long legs. Long red fingernails tapped her knee. "Let's talk about how we're going to handle Jane's newfound happiness."

Collins rolled his eyes. "Look, Clara. I can save you all a lot of time. Jane's off the ticket. It's as simple as that."

Clara remained remarkably calm. "No, she's not. It would be political suicide to remove her now, and you know it."

"We're poised to win by a landslide," Collins snarled. "With two weeks left, I could probably put my dog on the ticket and we'd still win."

Jack leapt to Collins's bedside. "Now just wait a goddamned minute. You and President Howard are two sides of the same coin. It's only the party affiliation card in your wallet that makes you any different from him. Jane's the one everyone knows is bringing real change. She's the heart and soul of this campaign."

Anstett stepped up to Jack, just inches from his face. "Fuck you, Jack. The kind of change she's bringing to the table now would kill us."

"Hold on, boys," Clara interrupted. "Listen to yourselves. What's going to kill us is the way the three of you are acting. Tony and Jack, sit down and listen. Dennis." The nails had stopped tapping. "Jane is an asset to the ticket, with or without this new revelation. She wouldn't be on the ticket if you'd thought otherwise."

The presidential candidate sighed grumpily. "I still think she should resign."

Jane held her tongue, hating the way she was being talked about in the third person, but Clara was running the show now. And she trusted Clara with her life.

"It didn't work when McGovern switched horses in seventy-two and it won't work for you, either," Clara said matter-of-factly.

"Fuck me." Collins looked resigned, but he was still smoldering. He looked sharply at Jane. "Why didn't you tell me about this sooner?"

"I didn't realize it sooner."

Anstett cast her a disbelieving look. "You mean you didn't realize you were a dyke when you slept with her? Shouldn't that have been a clue?"

Jane bristled. It wasn't any of their business, and yet it was. There was no such thing as a personal life in politics. "When I slept with Alex, I thought it was a one-time thing. I made sure it was. Now . . ." Jane looked at her aides and felt reassured. "Now I realize that I want to spend my life with Alex. If she'll still have me."

"You mean we might be doing all of this for nothing?" Collins asked in astonishment.

Clara leaned forward in her chair. "You're splitting hairs, Dennis. The important thing is that Jane realizes she prefers to spend her life with a woman, and that she cannot 'bury' that, as Tony suggested earlier. Jane's integrity, and yours by extension, is at stake here."

Jane's aides grunted their agreement.

"So here's what's going to happen," Clara continued, rising from her seat. "Jane is going to come out in a press conference. She'll answer as many questions as there are, even if it takes all day. She will be completely forthright. And you, Dennis, will be happily sitting right there beside her in your wheelchair with your leg attached to the ceiling, if that's what it takes."

Carter chuckled audibly, drawing a scowl from Collins.

"You'll be like the supportive father figure who will give anyone a black eye who tries to mess with her," Clara added, stalking the room like a cougar. "Jane will be an example of how inclusive this party is. An example of its diversity and its unification. It will be a winning formula, no question about it."

"If you're so keen on all this, Clara, how come you've never run for office?" Anstett asked gruffly.

Clara gave him a withering look. "You don't ask the head coach of a football team why he's not out there knocking heads or throwing eighty-yard passes, Tony. And that's what I am here, a head coach." She looked fondly at Jane. "Besides, times are different now. We've come a long way. Look at the growing number of states allowing gay marriage."

Jane smiled back. "Thank you, Clara."

Jack looked protectively at Jane. "Jane, I am only going to ask you this once, and then never again. Are you *sure* about this?"

Jane squared her shoulders. It was important they all knew there was no equivocation on her part. "I've never been more sure about anything, Jack. This is who I am. This is how I want to live my life. The voters will be made to understand that, and if they don't want me to serve them, then I'll retire from public life."

"Jane," Steph said, her tone quiet but imploring. "It's not that simple. Maybe—"

"No, Steph," Jane shot back. "It really *is* that simple."

"Okay, then," Jack said definitively. "Let's sharpen our pencils. We've got a press conference to do in less than twenty-four hours."

Jane's shoulders sagged in relief. She felt more hopeful than she'd felt in days. She knew her staff would do everything they could to see that her decision didn't keep her from getting elected.

Carter sidled up to Jane, guiding her to a quiet corner of the room as the others began hashing out what would surely be hours of raucous and even acrimonious strategizing.

"Congratulations, Jane. For what it's worth, I think you're doing a real gutsy, wonderful thing. And I think you're a very lucky woman. Alex is crazy about you."

"Thank you, Carter. And I hope I'm still a lucky woman." Her smile slid away. "I haven't exactly been reciprocating Alex's love. I'm not sure she'll forgive me."

Carter was still beaming. "She will."

"You think so?"

"Oh, yeah. But I'm not sure she'll be thrilled with the public part of it. You know how she hates the spotlight. Those stories in the paper about her this summer really threw her."

Jane winced. "I know. God, she's not used to it, is she?"

Carter chuckled. "Not knowingly, anyway."

"Okay, Carter. All this talk is starting to scare me."

"Relax, boss. And if she gives you any grief over your decision, you can blame her unreasonableness on her head injury."

"Good point." It was going to be a lot to ask of Alex. Maybe too much.

"When are you going to talk to her?"

"She's just coming out of the coma. I thought I'd wait until tomorrow morning when she's more lucid."

Carter grimaced. "Ouch. Doesn't give you much time if she doesn't agree with your plan."

Jane nodded bleakly. "I know."

Chapter 13

Alex tried to swallow but her throat felt like it'd been trampled by a herd of buffaloes. Only her head rivaled it in the pain department. It felt as though a nuclear bomb had gone off in it. *Gawwwd!* Her body hurt in places she didn't even know had nerve endings. *That must have been some car crash!*

Her doctor told her what had happened two-and-a-half days ago. She was lucky, she said. *Could have been much worse.* The doctor's words rolled around in her mind like a pinball. It sure didn't feel like it could have been worse. She told Alex she was lucky her brain hadn't bled or swelled much. She could have died, or at the very least, suffered brain damage. Instead, she had escaped with a hairline fracture and a concussion.

Okay, so she was lucky. Lucky to be alive. Lucky to be going back to her life, such as it was. *God.* It was so empty without Jane. These last few months, she had just been going through the motions—doing her job, eating, sleeping, breathing.

Jane had been very sweet, sitting in her hospital room while Alex drifted in and out of consciousness. But surely it was out of pity or guilt, and once Alex was out of the hospital—maybe even sooner—Jane would probably make a fast break for the campaign trail and back to a busy life that didn't include her.

The door to her room whooshed opened and Jane stepped in, looking a little harried but as beautiful as Alex's foggy brain remembered. Jane's smile was subdued, as though too much enthusiasm might send Alex back into a coma.

"Hi," Jane said softly, pulling a chair up to the bedside and kissing Alex's cheek.

Alex blinked as if the lights had been switched on suddenly. She found it hard to speak for a moment or two. Her head swam a little. Her thoughts were thick and bunched up, like cotton.

"Hi," she finally managed.

"How are you feeling, sweetheart?"

The endearing term felt wonderful. She smiled delicately—it hurt too much to grin. "Better. Now that you're here." *Don't go. Please don't go.*

Jane reached for her hand and gave it a squeeze. "Do you feel well enough to have a talk?"

Alex closed her eyes for a moment, trying to clear her head. She wanted nothing more than for Jane to stay and talk . . . and talk and talk. Anything to keep her here.

"Sure," Alex said.

"You had us all pretty scared, you know."

"S'okay. Doctor says I'll be fine."

Jane smiled reassuringly and kissed Alex's hand. "Yes. That's wonderful news. All your scans are good. You don't know how happy that makes me."

Alex had no memory of the actual crash. She remembered being in the backseat of the limo, across from Dennis Collins. Remembered screeching tires, then nothing.

"How is everyone else?" she asked weakly.

"You were the worst off. Collins has a broken leg. The agent driving the limo has a separated shoulder. The driver of the SUV that T-boned you is still in critical but stable condition." Jane's brow furrowed. "He was drunk. Drove right around a cop and through a barricade."

Alex squeezed her eyes shut. How heroic was that? Almost done in by a drunk driver. Her eyelids flew open. "Kind of an inglorious way to almost die."

"Alex," Jane said severely. "Your job scares the crap out of me as it is. What scares me even more is that hero mentality of yours. It drives me crazy that you make a living by putting yourself in harm's way."

Alex was confused. The crash wasn't *her* fault.

"Never mind," Jane mumbled. "That's not what I wanted to talk about."

Alex felt her heartbeat quicken, heard the resulting beeps speed up on the monitor. What could Jane be here to tell her? Was she about to give her some devastating news the doctor had held back? Or that she had to go back right away to campaigning?

"Alex, I've learned something about myself the last few days."

Alex swallowed thickly and forced a smile. "Guess you'll have to do those campaign brochures over again then, huh?"

Jane's eyes widened at Alex's attempt at humor.

"Sorry," Alex said.

Jane was looking at her doubtfully. "Maybe this isn't the right—"

"No." Alex raised her hand weakly off the bed. "Please." She studied the rough texture of the white institutional ceiling tiles and quietly despaired. Whatever Jane was about to tell her, it really didn't change anything. Her life was shit anyway. "Go ahead."

Jane smiled nervously. "Alex, I know this might sound a little unbelievable to you. And I'll certainly understand if you need time to think about things . . . or time to, well, hopefully not to reconsider. But if you—"

"Jane, you're babbling. That's not like you."

"Sorry, you're right." Jane took a deep breath. "Alex. What I've found out about myself is that I really can't live without you. I *want* you in my life. More than anything." She squeezed Alex's hand, her eyes liquid with longing and fear.

Alex knew she should feel supremely happy, but all she felt was doubt. Maybe it was her fuzzy brain. Brain damage, that was it. Maybe there had been some brain damage, because what Jane said couldn't be right. It couldn't be.

"I don't understand."

Jane smiled nervously. "I know this is a lot to throw at you right now. But it couldn't wait."

"What couldn't wait?"

Jane's smile warmed. "The fact that I love you. The fact that I don't want to live without you in my life, Alex. The fact that I've never needed anyone the way I need you." The rush of words stopped only when Jane paused to breathe. She leaned close, her light perfume tickling Alex's senses, and she kissed Alex's cheek—a kiss soft and tender that promised much more. "I love you, Alex Warner. And you will never know how sorry I am it took me this long to accept that. I just hope . . . I hope it's not too late."

Alex was sure she had stopped breathing altogether, except that the heart monitor still beeped steadily. This couldn't be happening. Jane confessing her love? Saying the words Alex had longed to hear for so long? Had Jane been in the crash too and suffered brain damage?

"Jane . . ." Alex's voice trailed off as she tried to gather her thoughts like so many scattered leaves. Then she nearly laughed. "Are you . . . are you crawling back to me on your hands and knees asking for another chance?"

Jane beamed and kissed Alex's palm over and over. "Yes! God! I'm so sorry it has to be in this stupid hospital room." Her eyes shone with love, and it was the most perfect, beautiful thing Alex had ever seen. "But when you're better, I have a romantic evening all planned."

Alex bit back a smile and tried to look stern. "Tell me your plans and then I'll tell you whether I forgive you."

"Hmm, let's see. There'll be roses. A whole room full of them. White ones." Jane pressed their interlocked hands to her chest and laughed. "And lots of wine, of course. Champagne. And a lovely dinner."

"Music?"

Jane's eyes danced. "Oh, yes. Some Ella, of course. Sinatra. Mel Torme. Rosemary Clooney. Diana Krall."

Alex laughed feebly and tried to ignore the excruciating headache it ignited. "You really are a romantic. Okay, I'll forgive you."

Jane leaned over and kissed Alex sweetly. Alex felt almost as though she could levitate off the bed out of pure joy. She had never dreamed of Jane coming back to her this way, but now that the moment was here, she didn't know if she could truly accept it. Oh, she wanted to. Wanted to pretend they could ride off happily into the sunset together . . . that nothing would ever come between their love. But she'd been through too many disappointments before to fully believe it could happen, and now she struggled with the purest joy she had ever felt and the worst gloom.

Alex knew she had to bring them both back down to reality. She hated having to say the words she knew needed saying. "Jane, have you really thought this over?"

Jane smiled blissfully. "Didn't you once say that thinking is highly overrated?"

"I'm serious." Alex felt shaky. Felt afraid she might actually talk Jane out of all this. But for both their sakes, they couldn't just blindly leap into it as if they were two regular people with-out a care in the world. They had to talk about it, debate it, examine it, be sure about it. She didn't want to be responsible for any future regrets Jane might have.

"I'm serious, too. And there is nothing more to think about. It's time for my heart, Alex. It's time. I won't put aside my feel-ings anymore. Not for anything."

"Oh, God. You really do want this." *Okay, now it's time to really be scared.*

"Yes, I do. I want you, Alex. No matter what else happens."

"What about the election?"

Jane's smile radiated confidence. She winked. "I have people working on that."

Alex smiled mischievously. "What, buying you the election? Because I think that's what you're going to have to do now to win."

Jane laughed. "I see your sense of humor didn't get knocked out of you."

"Sorry."

"Don't be. I love your sense of humor. And no, I do not have to buy the election. I'm going to come out in a press conference in a couple of hours." Jane smiled nervously. "With or without your permission."

Alex stiffened. "What if I said I didn't want you to do that?"

Jane's jaw was set in that way Alex knew so well. *Yep, she's going to do it.*

"I'm sorry, Alex. I'm a public person. There is no private little corner of my life where I can hide. I want the public to know who I really am, Alex. To do my job well, I cannot be two differ-ent people—one private and one public. Can you understand that?"

Alex nodded slowly. "Yes, I think so."

"Do you want to be with me, Alex?"

Alex felt her stomach bottom out. "Yes. God. More than anything, Jane."

Jane's face collapsed in relief and joy. "It's going to be difficult for awhile."

Alex smiled. "I'm no stranger to difficulty, you know."

Jane scrutinized her lover. "You're the best thing that's ever happened to me, Alex."

Alex laughed. "Or the worst. You can decide which one after election day."

"Oh, God, Alex. Do you never stop?" But Jane was grinning.

"Are you sure you want to jeopardize the election because of me?"

"Don't even question that for a minute, darling. If I lose because of who I love, it is *not* our fault. And I will do everything in my power to make sure I don't lose in two weeks." Jane squeezed Alex's hand. "I don't do anything in half measures. And I'm certainly not going to start now."

"I know. I've slept with you, remember?"

Jane pinched Alex lightly on the shoulder. "Just you wait until you're better."

"Believe me, waiting won't be easy."

Jane kissed Alex on the lips again. "I love you." She rose and dropped Alex's hand. "I'm sorry, sweetie, but I've got a big meeting before this press conference. You can watch it on closed circuit television if you want. It's going to be happening downstairs in the conference room, but I think you need to stay well clear of the zoo."

"God, I'll be nervous for you, Jane. Are you sure you're going to be okay?"

Jane smiled reassuringly and hesitated at the door. "I will be knowing that I have you waiting for me at the end of it all."

"You know I will be. You'll come see me afterward?"

"Yes, darling. I love you. Get some sleep."

Alex felt her body sag. She hadn't realized she'd been so tense throughout Jane's visit. She'd had no idea hearing the words

212

she'd longed to hear from Jane would be so stressful. "I love you, too, Jane."

It was like a strategy session for a battle. Jane was the general. Her aides—Jack, Steph, Carter, Clara, and even her mother—pitched suggestions and took turns critiquing them. Jane mostly listened, confident they were all clear on the mission—that Jane was unshaken in her determination to come out to the public at the first opportunity, that she was doing this foremost for herself, but also to be fair to the voters, and that she was well aware of the stakes involved. In her gut, she knew she was doing the right thing. And for that, she felt she would be rewarded.

Like a mathematician, Carter outlined in detail for Jane how much public support she had at the moment. The car crash, the debate she won all on her own . . . it was like a bank account, and right now the account was full. Except that Jane was about to make a huge withdrawal.

"Give us your best guess, Carter," Jack said pointedly. "How is she going to score at the end of all this?"

Carter shrugged lightly. "I think she's going to get hammered for the first few days. But then I think people will come around."

"The question is," Clara said, "is there enough time to get the voters back?"

Jack rubbed his hands together. "We'll just have to work extra hard. If we put in double the effort, everyone, we can make it seem like we've got five weeks instead of two."

Jane looked around the room, surveying her troops. She knew they were already run ragged, bone weary from months of campaigning. But they were so close now.

"Look," she said slowly. "I know I have asked more from all of you than anyone has a right to ask. And you've always done it with everything you have and without complaint." Jane felt her emotions bubbling to the surface. So much had happened the last few days. "This hasn't been easy on any of us." She made eye contact with each one. "I can't promise you we're going to be rewarded at the polls," she said roughly.

"You don't have to," Steph answered with a smile. "We all love you, Jane. And it's promise enough knowing all of us are part of something big . . . bigger than anything any of us could do singularly."

Jane nodded her thanks and gave Steph a special smile. "It's been a helluva ride, hasn't it?"

Jack stood up, signaling an end to the meeting. His craggy face was split with a huge grin. "It's going to be a helluva finish."

Jane stood in the small anteroom, alone, gathering her thoughts and her courage, for the biggest public statement of her life. She'd already done the hard part, she reminded herself. She had opened herself to Alex. Had already taken that step that would forever change her life. But even with a lover by her side, it was one hell of a lonely journey.

A soft knock at the door announced Carter's presence. "Hey," he said quietly, closing the door behind him. "Just wanted to wish you luck and all that." He smiled awkwardly.

"Thank you, Carter." Jane gave him a quick hug. "And thank you for your friendship. It means a lot."

"Oh, hell, woman. Now's not the time to get all sappy on me. Where's that fighting spirit?"

Jane shook her head lightly. It seemed like all she'd done lately is fight. Fight to be taken seriously as a contender, fight to get her social agenda on the front pages, fight for Alex, and now, fight for her political future. "Oh, Christ, Carter."

Carter gripped her shoulder tightly. "You're doing the right thing, you know. And it's your courage that makes you so strong. It's made you who you are."

Jane looked at him skeptically. "C'mon. I'm no braver than

most. I'm just stupid enough to ignore good sense."

"Look. I knew a long time ago that Alex was in love with you, that something was happening between the two of you. And I discouraged it because I was scared for you. Scared it would ruin everything." Carter's expression was one of wonder and admiration. "But you. You're ready to risk it all. And that means you've got bigger—ahem—balls than anyone I know."

"Carter—"

"No, seriously. You give the rest of us more strength than you could ever imagine. We're there with you, Jane, no matter what."

"Hey, I thought we weren't going to get all sappy?" Jane laughed at Carter's sheepish look.

"Sorry. You're right. I'm supposed to be giving you a pep talk. I think."

"It's okay, Carter. I'm fine. Other than feeling like I'm ready to go to the gallows. Although, a quick, painful death might be easier than the skewering I'm going to get for days on end."

Carter waved away her cynicism. "They love you, Jane. They'll forgive you."

Jane felt her nerves harden. "But why should I have to be forgiven for anything? That's the part that burns me."

"Hey. You're preaching to the converted. It's just the way it is. You know that."

Jane nodded grimly. "People like you and I need to change all that, Carter."

Carter grinned, his eyes alight. "That's why you're going to win this damned election, Jane. That's why you *need* to win this thing." He winked playfully. "I'm looking at the new poster dyke of the Western world."

Jane laughed, oddly thrilled and scared at the same time. "Let's not get carried away, kid."

"Yeah, well, if anyone can handle it, Jane, you can."

"Thanks for the vote of confidence." Jane moved to the small window in the room, absently scanned the gray skyline and felt a shiver in her veins. "I can't help but feel like I'm about to fall off a cliff."

Carter walked up behind her and touched her shoulder lightly. "You are. But you'll be falling into those big strong arms of Alex's, don't forget."

Jane smiled, remembering what was really important. "Yeah. I will."

Alex watched Jane's news conference on her small television, stunned at Jane's composure and courage. She felt more than saw the shock of Jane's announcement when the camera panned the tightly packed room, and yet Jane acted oblivious. She delivered without an ounce of ambivalence or apology, yet neither was she cocky or cavalier. Alex marveled at how Jane always seemed to strike just the right chord, always seemed as though she were completely in control of the situation. She was calm and unequivocal, forthright and yet congenial. There was real joy beneath Jane's words. She looked far from sad or unsure, and that, Alex knew, would go a long way in how the public would perceive her in the coming days and weeks. Even Dennis Collins managed to make it look like it was news worthy of celebrating.

Life with Jane would never be easy, Alex knew. If she were to lose the election, she would simply go on to something else equally challenging and demanding. She was too smart and too talented and too driven to sit around the house and take up knitting. That part of Jane was so much of what made her irresistible. And if she were to go on to become the vice president, well, life would be one heck of a merry-go-round for both of them.

All I can do is jump on and hang on for dear life. Alex smiled. She did not want to go back to her meaningless life, where her job had become everything and the idea of loving again seemed impossible, if not repulsive. No. That was no way to live. Being around Jane these last few months, being a part of her life, coming to believe in and be inspired by her vision, her purpose, by the woman herself—*that* was living. She could be swept up or swept away. Take a chance or be at its whim.

Jane stepped into the room, grinning widely. Alex grinned back with the relief and satisfaction of having made her own silent commitment.

"Well?" Jane prodded. "Did you watch?" She ran to Alex's bed with the springy energy of a kid. She kissed Alex spiritedly.

"You were spectacular," Alex said. "God, I love you." She raked her eyes appreciatively over Jane. "I can't wait to ravage you."

Jane moaned quietly. "Wow. Remind me to hold regular press conferences."

Alex smiled, wanting always to remember Jane this way—happy, excited with just a hint of nervous energy, confident and a little impatient for the future.

"I'm so proud of you," Alex said. "You really did it. You really went for it."

Jane kissed her again, long and slow this time. "For better or worse, it's all out there now. And you know what, Alex? I've never felt so frigging good in my life. It makes me feel like anything's possible, you know?"

Alex reached for Jane's hand. "Coming out is the most liberating thing you can do for yourself."

"I can see that. Was it difficult for you?"

Alex shrugged. "Sure. It's never entirely easy, not for anyone. There were some recriminations in the early days of my career, but you get through it. Friends help. Love helps even more."

"Well, if that's true, I should have an easy road ahead."

"I hope so, darlin'. I'll try to be a good partner to you, Jane."

Jane squeezed Alex's hand, her face tightening, her bottom lip quivering ever so slightly. "Oh, God, Alex. I really want to be a good partner to you, too. But I . . . with my career . . . with . . ."

Alex's heart was breaking at Jane's anguish, but she let her continue.

"I just don't know how good a partner I'll be, Alex. I want to give you so much. I want to be there for you."

"Shh," Alex soothed, caressing the smooth skin of Jane's forearm. "I know you love me, and I know you'll find a way to make it work for us. We'll both find a way to make it work. There's too much to lose if we don't."

They kissed again and Alex knew she must be feeling better, because she wanted much more.

"Thank you for believing in me," Jane said in a quavering voice.

"I'll always believe in you, Jane. That will never change."

There was a soft knock on the door and Jane's mother tentatively stepped in.

"C'mon in, Mother," Jane called out, then whispered to Alex, "she's going to ask you to come to the island to recuperate."

"No need to try to warn her off, dear. Hello, Alex."

Alex smiled at Maria Kincaid. She was thrilled to have a glimpse of what Jane would be like in thirty years and wondered fleetingly what their life would be like then. Whether Jane would begin to slow down by then. God, she hoped so. "Hello, Maria."

"It's sure good to see you sitting up and talking, Alex." She glanced at Jane, smiling and shaking her head at the two of them.

"What?" Jane asked.

"I've just never seen you this happy, dear. I'm trying to get used to the sight of it."

"Well, you don't have to try to get used to it all at once. You've got many years to get used to it."

"I look forward to it. Alex? When you get well, you'd better put your best running shoes on."

Alex raised her eyebrows in question.

"That is, if you want to keep up with my daughter."

Alex laughed. "I can't promise I'll be able to keep up. But I'll certainly try."

Maria laughed. "I look forward to *that*, too. Listen, Jane's right. I'd like you to come to the island house with me and recuperate until the election."

"But . . ." Alex looked from one to the other. "I want to be with Jane."

Maria smiled patiently. "I know that. But you'll be in the hospital another week and my dear daughter will barely have time to eat or brush her teeth, let alone spend any time with you. Am I right, Janey?"

Jane grudgingly agreed. "She's right, Alex. And I'd feel better knowing you were resting and being looked after."

Alex tried to conceal her disappointment. They were probably right. She would only be a drag on Jane right now. "When will I see you?"

"Election day. If you're up to it. I'll vote in my constituency. We'll meet in Detroit and fly to Miami to wait out the results with Collins." She shrugged. "It's his day and we have to go to his city. And after that, we'll fly right back to the island for our own celebration—or pity party."

Alex leaned closer to whisper to Jane. "Is that when we get to have the romantic evening you promised?"

Jane laughed. "I love a woman with priorities." Her eyes grazed over Alex with a sexual hunger that was staggering. "We'll need to have a party, but we'll spend a few days together on our own." She wiggled her eyebrows suggestively at Alex, then tossed a look at her mother. "Right, Mother?"

Maria laughed. "Yes, dear. Anything you want."

Oh, yes, Alex thought happily, feeling suddenly drowsy. *Anything I want. And I know exactly what that is.*

She drifted off to fantasies of Jane, wrapped naked in her arms.

Chapter 14

The last two weeks of the campaign were the most grueling yet. Jane had never worked harder in her life, and she hadn't exactly been a slacker before.

There was little time to think of Alex or even to call her, but Jane missed her more than ever. Now that they had committed to a future together, it was torture to be apart. Jane wanted to get on with their life together, with loving each other, and it took all her determination and powers of concentration to focus on the campaign—to see through what she had started so long ago.

Jane's public announcement about her sexuality had sparked a predictable firestorm in the media. The journalists and photographers were like frenzied sharks, relentless in their hunger for more. If she'd thought her press conference would adequately address the issue, she was badly mistaken. They would not let it die, asking her endless questions about her love life, her sex life, her views on homosexuality, her and Alex's plans for the future. Would they get married? Have children? Would Alex be a stay-at-home wife? Would she accompany Jane in public? Would they ever kiss in public? Be seen holding hands? Did she worry about her credibility as a potential world leader, particularly in countries where homosexuality was outlawed? What would she say to people who were religiously or morally opposed to her way of life?

Jane would not be broken or worn down. She answered every question as best she could, even using humor sometimes to alleviate the tension. Her sexuality had become the dominant issue of the campaign, and while the fact that it overshadowed everything disappointed her, she was resigned to it. There was no other way. For many voters, she knew her revelation was shocking, but the sooner they dealt with the shock of it, the sooner everyone could just get *over* it and get *on* with it. At least, that's what she told herself. And one day, her sexuality would not be the first thing people talked about. She could hardly wait for that day.

Gradually, more and more support began to coalesce. It came from newspaper columnists, liberal blog sites on the Internet, women's groups, gay and lesbian groups, labor unions and professional organizations. Jane was the mule on which they could heap all their social complaints, and she went with it, promising to be their voice and their muscle where she could. If anything, her public declaration had strengthened her integrity and respect within many communities and organizations. Those who did not support her never had and probably never would, and their disapproval had only grown more vociferous. Jane took more heat than usual from her adversaries, but she took much more joy from her allies, who seemed to be multiplying by the day.

Jane quickly found herself becoming a cultural hero to many. She'd been astonished when, just the other day, a woman tried to thrust a phone number in her hand. There'd been other sudden propositions from women, too, including a very brazen one from a governor's assistant. She was definitely not used to this kind of attention and she didn't find it particularly flattering because she couldn't imagine going to bed with anyone but Alex.

Alex. Jane cast a sly glance at Steph Cameron, who was trying to make small talk with the good-looking press secretary to the governor of North Carolina. She'll kill me for interrupting, Jane thought wickedly, then motioned for her aide.

Steph dutifully appeared at her side. "Yes, boss?"

"Can you ring up Alex for me on your cell phone?"

"Sure thing." She looked curiously at Jane. "It's your shot next, though."

Jane surveyed the sand bunker off in the distance, where she knew her golf ball lay mired. Her mood darkened. She was an adequate golfer, but sand shots were positively not in her repertoire.

"Don't worry, it'll probably be another five minutes before we even get up there."

"Will that give you enough time with Alex?"

Jane laughed. "We're not having phone sex, Steph. I just wanna say hi. Hear her voice."

Steph winked and disappeared, phone in hand.

Jane cast a sweeping glance over the hordes of Secret Service agents, aides, journalists and photographers following her and the governor around the golf course. She wasn't thrilled to be here, and neither was the governor, she knew. He was a conservative Democrat, and Clara had used all her persuasiveness to arrange the public outing, which was intended to convey that Jane was relaxed with the election just days away, and that a southern, conservative, high-profile Democrat still supported the Collins-Kincaid ticket. They were supposed to walk and golf nine holes, but Jane knew they'd be lucky to get in four or five holes. Which suited her just fine. The weather was a little too warm and she was tripping over people. She could barely swing her club without hitting a camera.

Steph's phone was pressed into her hand.

"Alex? Honey?"

"Hey, sweetheart. Where are you?"

Jane frowned. She wasn't even sure anymore. "Some golf course in North Carolina. We must be on the coast because I can see the water."

Alex laughed. "Maybe you'd better get a geography tutor. Wouldn't want you showing up for the inauguration in Boston or something."

Jane stepped away to give herself more privacy. "After all this traveling over the past year, *I* should be giving the geography lessons."

Alex paused. "Do you think you can find your way back to Michigan?"

Jane smiled into the phone and lowered her voice. "You don't have to worry about that, even if I have to crawl my way there. I can't wait to see you, darling."

She could hear Alex take a deep breath. "I'm going out of my mind missing you."

Jane sighed out of exhaustion and frustration. "Three more days. God, I'm almost down to counting the hours."

"You sound so tired, sweetheart. I'd like nothing more right now than to hold you and let you fall asleep in my arms."

Jane became wobbly at the thought. She'd like nothing more right now than to be in Alex's arms, letting the woman she loved take care of her. "Oh, God, Alex. How did you know the exact thing I needed to hear?"

"Lucky guess."

"Yeah, right. Hey, how are *you* feeling?"

"Fine."

"Liar."

"I would never lie to you, sweetheart. Well, unless I was just trying to make you feel better."

"Like right now?"

Alex laughed. "Actually, I'm feeling a little better every day. And your mom is taking wonderful care of me. I think I've gained back the five pounds I lost on the coma diet."

"Yup, that sounds like my mother. I'm glad she's fattening you up." Jane's assigned caddie was waving her on toward the dreaded sand bunker. "Listen, honey. You know how to golf, right?"

"Mmmm, maybe," Alex answered cryptically. "Why?"

"Because I have to make a sand shot and I have no idea how to."

Alex laughed teasingly. "A candidate's job is never done."

"Shut up," Jane teased back. "Are you going to help me, or not?"

"I'm at your service, my love."

"Ooh, now you're talking," Jane purred.

"You don't exactly sound like you're concentrating on your next shot."

"Oh, I'm concentrating on something, all right. And it's not golf."

Alex laughed. *God, it was so good to hear her laugh.* "I thought you wanted my help with your golf game?" Alex growled in her ear. "Unfortunately, that's all I can help you with right now."

"All right, all right. Golf it is. So, how do I do this shot?"

"Open the face of your club, hit behind the ball and take lots of sand on the follow-through."

"Just like that?" Jane asked in astonishment. "You make it sound like following a recipe or something."

"It won't be anything you can't handle if you follow those three steps. And if you still can't get out of the trap after a few tries, just hand the club to Steph and make her do it. Isn't that what the hired help's for?"

Jane laughed harder than she had in days. "I love you, Alex

Warner."

"And I love you, Jane Kincaid."

Jane handed the phone back to Steph and marched toward the sand bunker.

It had to be an agonizing day for Jane. She was trying so hard not to show Alex her worry and anxiety, but her eyes were giving her away. They burned with intensity and darted in some kind of synchronization to her private thoughts. She visibly flinched whenever a voice called to her, as though it had physically wrenched her from her inner world. Alex's heart clenched for her.

The rented penthouse suite at the Setai Hotel in South Beach, Miami, was a cauldron of voices and moving bodies, ringing phones and blaring television sets. It was election day, and it was surely one of the most emotionally wracking days of Jane's life, Alex knew. And though they'd not seen each other over the last two weeks while Alex recuperated on the island and Jane campaigned, Alex tried now not to intrude. No one but Jane could know what she was going through, and Alex would not even try to guess. She could only offer a needed distraction when it looked like Jane needed one, though getting her alone had been pretty much impossible. The few hours they'd been together since meeting in Detroit this morning had been anything but intimate. Journalists, staff members and Secret Service agents had been within arm's reach of them all day. You couldn't turn around without bumping into someone. Even a kiss had been merely a peck on the cheek for them.

Alex had missed Jane so much, and even though she knew today was not about them, she was restless with need.

Alex watched Jane unhappily huff her way through a CNN update and decided it was time for another interruption. Only this time, it would not be a card game or a quiet conversation on the terrace. She wanted Jane all to herself, no matter what.

"Hey, good looking," she whispered provocatively in Jane's ear. "I have an offer I know you won't want to refuse."

"Mmmm," Jane mumbled distractedly, her attention riveted on the large television set and the latest forecast of numbers. A long night stretched out ahead and the outlook was still murky. Jane and her aides were obsessing over every exit poll and analysis on the television and the Internet.

"You didn't hear a word I said, did you?" Alex began kneading the muscle knots in Jane's back.

"Huh?" Jane leveled bleary eyes on Alex. Her mouth was a hard line of exhaustion and tension.

Alex sighed deeply, summoning her patience. She loved Jane, was prepared to make the sacrifices of a lover and companion, but she would not idly watch Jane wreck herself or their relationship. She smiled indulgently. "I need you to come with me for a minute."

"Is something wrong?" Jane had turned back to the television again, acknowledging Alex's healing hands with a quiet moan.

"Yeah," Alex answered firmly. "There is. And I need you to come with me a minute to fix it."

Jane frowned, but finally looked more interested in her lover than the TV. "Are you okay, Alex?"

Silently, Alex clasped Jane's hand and began leading her out of the crowded living room, maneuvering them through the obstacle course of furniture and bodies, then through a second living room and past more people who kept trying to grab Jane for a minute of her time. It was like stick handling the puck from one end of the ice to the other, past five defenders, until you had a clear breakaway to the goalie. After several minutes of pure determination on Alex's part, she managed to tug Jane into one of the bedrooms.

Alex authoritatively closed the door, switched on the lock, spun Jane around and kissed her without warning. Jane's eyes widened at first, then slammed shut as their bodies moved closer, touching, joining, pressing together as the kiss deepened. Patiently, their mouths explored one another's. Teeth lightly tugged at moist skin, tongues played vigorously. Jane was moaning softly, and Alex acted on the compulsion to slide her hands beneath Jane's cotton blouse and delicately up her ribcage. She needed to feel her lover's skin more than she needed to breathe right now.

Breathless, Jane pulled back to look at her. Her eyes were smoky with desire. "Oh, God, Alex. I've missed you so much. I'm so sor—"

Alex smothered her words with a ravenous kiss. She purposely backed Jane up against the door and pressed her body into Jane's, as though she might take her right there, up against the door like that—completely reckless and impatient. Alex's body throbbed with arousal, and she ached to touch the woman she loved in all the places that mattered. Jane's neck arched in response to Alex's urgency. Alex suckled the soft skin there, her hands roaming beyond Jane's ribcage and to the soft underside of her breasts.

Alex caught her breath at the feel of Jane's naked flesh in her hands, so warm and smooth and welcoming. Her fingers, hot and tingly, danced lightly over Jane's swollen flesh, tracing the curves, lingering over the small shudders Jane emitted. She had only intended to fool around a little, give Jane some affection, indulge in a few needed moments together. But now. *Jesus*! She didn't know if she could hold back. Didn't know if she could stop herself from the salacious need to unzip Jane's slacks and thrust her hand in there, where she knew it would be welcomed by a warm, wet, embrace. She was so wet and tight herself, it hurt.

"Wait. Alex. Honey." With effort, Jane tried to extract herself from Alex's insistent kisses.

Alex wanted so badly to ignore Jane's quiet pleas. Her fingers found taut nipples and skillfully brushed over them. She marveled at yet a deeper stiffening of sensitive flesh. *Oh, yes.* It was obvious Jane wanted her just as much, and Alex smiled inwardly at the thought of a quick but ardent session of lovemaking.

"Oh, God, Alex." Jane pulled back more assertively. "Baby. Please," she said between breaths, her voice thick with disappointment and frustration.

Alex exhaled in defeat, slowly withdrawing her lusty explorations. She pressed her sweaty forehead to Jane's.

Jane touched Alex's face tenderly and kissed her chin lightly.

"I want you so much, Jane," Alex said huskily. "Let me make love to you. Right now."

"I want to make love to you too, Alex. But I want it to be perfect. I want us to have a nice evening together . . . tomorrow night. We're flying back to the island in the morning, and we'll have our romantic evening. I promise. No matter what happens with the election outcome, we'll have our night."

Alex swallowed, fighting the ebb of her desire. She was tired of waiting. A quickie wasn't the most romantic liaison in the world, but it was better than nothing. "It doesn't have to be perfect, sweetheart. It doesn't have to wait."

Jane kissed her softly. "Yes, it does. Alex, my whole world has been so rushed and crazy over the past year. So much of it is just a blur. I don't want it to be like that with us."

Alex nodded reluctantly. Jane was right. Their first time together as a couple shouldn't be some hurried, fumbling interlude, especially during the tumult of election day. Hell, no. They would wait and it would be damn well worth it.

Alex smiled, rubbed noses playfully with Jane. "Damn right we're going to wait."

An eyebrow rose in response. "We are? I mean . . . you didn't have to agree so quickly."

Alex laughed. "You want me to fight it?" She playfully thrust her hands back under Jane's shirt, eliciting a squeal.

"All right, all right. Stop teasing me, or I'm the one who's going to throw you on the bed and have my way with you."

A new round of desire pulsed through Alex as she toyed with the fantasy of Jane shoving her to the bed, straddling her, her pelvis grinding against her, breasts dipping over her face, brushing against her, rising again. *Oh, God. This is driving me crazy.*

Jane seemed to sense the resurging fire in Alex and pulled away to put some distance between them.

"I'm making it worse, aren't I?"

Alex growled in frustration. "It's okay, darlin'. We'll wait." She moved closer, her finger tracing an invisible line down Jane's jaw and throat. "I want you rested. And I want you all to myself for the entire night tomorrow." With a leer, she added, "Because that's how long it's going to take."

Jane gave a little shiver, her nostrils flaring. She winked slowly, seductively, then licked her lips. "You've got yourself a date."

Alex could not stay up any longer. Her head throbbed and she felt like crap—the lingering effects of her concussion made worse by exhaustion and stress. She looked across the room at Jane, who sat slouched in deep conversation with Dennis Collins. Her heart sank at the dark circles beneath her eyes and the obvious fatigue in her body. Aides strolled by with their laptops and cell phones as the activity showed no signs of abating.

"Alex, you look exhausted." Maria Kincaid crouched down beside Alex's seat. She had accompanied them on the flight to Miami and would return to Michigan with them. "You really should go to bed, dear." Her voice was soothing, her eyes full of concern.

Alex smiled limply. "I don't want to leave Jane. The election is still too close to call, and I know she must be going crazy inside."

Maria smiled. "You're right. She will be going crazy. And she should probably be going to bed with you and getting some rest."

"But she won't," Alex said grimly, watching as Clara bent and said something in Jane's ear.

"Right again. She won't. The West Coast numbers won't be in for a couple more hours. You know this is something she has to do, Alex. She has to see this through, right to the end. They all do."

Alex felt her heart swell. She loved Jane so incredibly much, it felt like that love might swallow her whole, make her disappear inside it. She respected Jane so much, admired all the hard work and commitment she had put into this, her dream. She didn't want to see it end any more than Jane and every other person in this room did. She felt the prick of tears sting her eyes. "God. I hope this works out. I don't know what we'll do if—"

"We can't worry about that right now, Alex." Maria looked across the room at Jane, then back at Alex. "If I promise to look out for my daughter, will you go to bed?"

Alex smiled. "Deal." She rose slowly, waiting for the dizziness to subside. She didn't know if she'd be able to sleep, but she'd at least try. And while she hoped Jane would join her at some point for a few hours of sleep, she knew it was not likely.

Alex awoke to quiet movement in the dawn light, felt the bedcovers being pulled back. A lithe body clothed in thin cotton slid in next to her.

"It's me, honey," Jane whispered.

"Good," Alex replied groggily. "Only sexy women are allowed in my bed. Lucky for you, you qualify."

Jane kissed her softly, then broke away, giggling.

Alex felt her nerves prickle and grew instantly alert. "You're in a good mood. Does that mean . . . ?"

She felt Jane smile against her throat, then trail a line of soft kisses beneath her jaw. "Yes," she said. "It does."

"Oh, my God." With both hands, Alex pulled Jane's face level with hers. She could barely see Jane's eyes in the murky light, but she sensed the joy in them, felt the grin on her face. Alex's throat tightened and she could barely speak. She wanted to cry. "You did it, honey." She kissed the corners of Jane's mouth around her lover's elation.

"Yeah. *We* did it. All of us." Jane's throat was raw with exhaustion and exuberance. "It was close, but California threw us over the top."

"Thank God for the State of California!" Alex kissed Jane, softly at first, then harder. "You can fill me in later. And I want to hear every detail. But not right now. Right now I just want to feel you."

Jane moved closer to Alex, nestling into her. "I could take this nightshirt off and you could show me how happy you are for me," she burred seductively, but there was no mistaking the weariness beneath her words.

Alex licked Jane's throat. "I'll bet you've used that line before."

Jane gasped in mock surprise. "Not in at least six months!"

Alex laughed. "God, I love you Jane Kincaid. I mean, Madam Vice President."

Jane sniggered. "It's just Jane. Just like I told you the first time we met, remember?"

Alex moved on top of Jane, her arms lightly pinning her. "Oh, I remember. You looked so crabby that first time, even though you were beautiful as hell. I thought you were going to bite my head off."

"I was crabby because I thought you were some hardass who was going to make my life miserable."

Alex kissed Jane's forehead, then each cheek. Her mouth hovered over Jane's. "I did have some moments of making you miserable. And don't tell anyone I'm not really a hardass."

Jane's mouth rose to claim Alex's. "You never made me miserable, Agent Warner. I did a fine job of doing that to myself. And to you. I'm just glad you waited for me."

They kissed again, tenderly, and Alex felt her body stirring against the soft, pliant woman beneath her. She couldn't be in the same room as Jane and not want to make love to her. Even in a roomful of people, never mind in the same bed together. It was like some kind of cruel test, all this waiting.

The kiss intensified, and Alex felt the blood rushing hotly through her, igniting her skin, sharpening her desire. Their mouths parted and Alex flicked her tongue against Jane's, daring her to reciprocate. Jane answered spiritedly, pushing into Alex's mouth, her body beginning to pulse rhythmically against Alex.

"Jane. Honey." Alex spoke softly in defiance of the screaming urgency of her body. She knew she was a heartbeat away from pushing Jane's nightshirt up, ripping down her own boxer shorts, and thrusting herself against her lover's rigid desire.

"Don't stop," Jane said breathlessly. "I mean it this time."

"I have to." Alex swallowed painfully. "We're supposed to wait. Remember your promise?"

"Fuck my promise." Jane wrestled an arm free and reached for Alex's waistband.

Alex playfully ran her fingertips across Jane's throat. "I thought politicians never break their promises."

Jane moaned, pressing her pelvis against Alex again. "So I'll be the first."

Alex grabbed Jane's wrist and pulled it firmly away from her shorts, then rolled onto her side and faced her. She smiled, enjoying seeing Jane this way—bossy and insatiable. "I love how you look all hot and pissed off at the same time."

Even in the dim light, Alex could make out Jane's deep frown and the grimace on her mouth. She leaned closer and kissed the tip of Jane's nose. "All right. I know I'm being evil. But I want you to get some rest. I told you, our first time, I'm going to keep you awake *all* night."

Jane rolled onto her back and stared up at the ceiling. "Tell me again why you are going to need me awake the entire night?"

Alex chuckled. That was more like it. "Because that's how long it's going to take me to fuck you every which way I can, and for you to come more times than you can count."

Jane laughed, but Alex noticed her breath quicken. "My, you are such a romantic."

"Okay, okay. I'm not exactly a poet. I prefer to be more direct."

Jane moaned a little. "Direct is good."

Alex reached over and caressed Jane's cheek, brushing her hair away. "Tonight was the biggest night of your life. Tomorrow night is going to be the second biggest night of your life, and I don't want you getting the two of them mixed up."

Jane clasped Alex's hand, gently pulling it away from her cheek and to her lips. "I love you so much, Alex. How did I get so lucky this year?"

Alex watched as Jane kissed each of her fingers. "Somebody once said you make your own luck."

"I don't know if I entirely agree with that. But I'd like to think we weren't an accident."

"We weren't," Alex said with certainty. "I think I've been waiting for you all my life."

"Mmmm. I know I have."

"Can you sleep for awhile my darling?"

Jane yawned. "Only an hour. Two at the most. Then we have breakfast with Collins and all our staff."

Alex smiled in anticipation. "Then we fly to Mackinac Island, right?"

"Right," Jane answered faintly. She was out before Alex could say anything more.

Chapter 15

Jane happily watched Alex take a sip of Chianti, hold it in her mouth to taste it, then swallow luxuriously. She looked like a condemned woman taking her last drink, delighting in every drop of the ruby red liquid.

"My. You seem to be enjoying that wine." Jane took a pleasurable drink from her own glass and gazed over the candlelight, feeling the most content she'd felt in . . . she couldn't remember when, actually. Her soul was at ease, her heart burst with a serene, limitless joy. And even though her body was still tired, it felt at peace. She could not imagine anything being more perfect . . . except perhaps if she were the president-elect instead of the vice president-elect. But she would only look forward now, not back.

Alex grinned. "My first drink of alcohol since that stupid crash."

"Are you okay?"

"More than okay, my darlin'. But I don't think my head will be able to handle more than a glass or two."

Jane smiled slyly. "Perfect. I don't want you inebriated tonight."

Alex raised her eyebrows teasingly and dropped her voice. "Are you planning to take advantage of me?"

Jane laughed, impatient for sex but enjoying the anticipation of it, too. "I just might." She rested her elbows on the table and leaned toward Alex. "You promised something about keeping me up the whole night, remember? I think you're going to be a busy woman."

Alex made a face and pretended to search her memory. "Hmm, I don't remember that. They said there might be some short-term memory loss with this concussion." She raised playful eyes to Jane. "Are you sure I wasn't talking about a marathon game of Scrabble or something?"

"Just for that, that's exactly what I should make you to do!"

Alex's bottom lip sank into a pout. "I promise I'll be good the rest of the night. Scout's honor."

Jane took her napkin from her lap and tossed it on the table, then rose and extended her upturned hand to Alex. She flashed her most inviting smile. "Let's see how good you can be."

Alex swallowed visibly, her eyes widening in unveiled surprise. They danced with nervous excitement. "You're taking me to bed now?"

Jane laughed. She loved those sweet, unguarded moments of Alex's. As a Secret Service agent, Jane knew Alex was well practiced at being cautious and reticent. But in her down time, her feelings, thoughts and expectations infused her voice and her body language so plainly to Jane . . . even if it was just in that softening of her eyes when she was feeling happy, or the way she rubbed her chin pensively between her thumb and forefinger. And there was that mischievous grin that could instantly light up

Jane's world. There was something so inherently forthright about Alex—brutally honest and unapologetically vulnerable, but there was a quiet, hidden strength too.

"God, I hope you never change, Alex."

"Huh?"

Jane took Alex's hand and led her away from the dining room. "Never mind. And no, I'm not taking you to bed yet."

Alex halted abruptly. "You're not?" Disappointment was evident on her face.

Jane laughed and tugged Alex along. "I promised you a romantic evening."

"We just had a romantic dinner. Isn't that enough?"

"Hardly. Especially since my mother cooked it."

Alex's draw dropped in mock surprise. "You're romancing me under fraudulent circumstances?"

Jane stopped and pulled Alex close to her. She threw her arms around her lover's neck. "I'll romance you any which way I can, my dear. Even if it means begging for my mother's help."

They kissed tenderly, unhurriedly, holding each other tightly.

"We really do have all night, don't we?" Alex said, touching her forehead to Jane's.

"Yes. And I intend to use up every minute of it."

"Are you sure you're not too exhausted? Because if you are . . ."

Jane smiled. She was still bone weary. She had gotten perhaps a total of five hours of sleep in the last twenty-four hours. She knew the hiatus from the campaign would be short, because there was much to do in the coming weeks, but not tonight. Tonight was about her and Alex. Everything else could wait another day. Or two.

"Giving in to exhaustion is for the uninspired. And you, my darling, inspire the hell out of me."

Alex kissed her fiercely. "You really are smooth with words, aren't you?"

Jane laughed, took Alex's hand again and led her into the

living room. Fire roared from the grate, casting a warm, dancing glow that melded with candlelight from almost every corner and surface of the room. Rosemary Clooney crooned "Tenderly" from the hidden speakers.

"Wow," Alex enthused. "You really are giving me the full treatment. This is wonderful."

They moved to the couch and sat down, the length of their bodies touching. Jane's long fingers fleetingly traced a line along Alex's denimed thigh. "I may be out of practice, but I know how to do romance."

"You sure your mother didn't mind vacating the house for the night?"

"Ha! Mother loves you. She was happy to do it. Besides, she was thrilled to join the rest of the group at the Grand Hotel. They're probably partying their heads off." Their chartered plane back from Miami had been full of staffers and supporters who were bent on continuing the celebrations.

Alex clasped Jane's hand and held it in her lap. "Your mother's an angel. She's been nothing but awesome while I stayed here. I can't believe everything she's done for me . . . for us."

Jane looked at Alex, surprised to see tears shimmering in the corners of her eyes. She pried her hand from Alex's, reached up and stroked her cheek lovingly. There was so much she still didn't know about this woman who had become such a big part of her—so many little nooks and corners to explore. They had a lifetime for that, but Jane desperately wanted to start now.

"You've never talked about your family life. Your childhood."

Alex turned to face her. She tried to smile, but faltered. "I don't want to talk about it. Not tonight. Not when everything is so perfect." This time, her smile was strong. "Besides, you're all I need, Jane. You're my family now."

Jane caressed Alex's cheek and felt her heart swell as Alex leaned into her touch. She loved Alex so much, the responsibility of it frightened her. "I just don't ever want you to be hurt,

Alex. Or disappointed."

"You can't always stop that from happening," Alex whispered, emotion like sandpaper to her voice. "But you can love me with everything you have. That much you can do."

Jane leaned in and kissed Alex's cheek. "That I will. Always."

Alex smiled through her tears and touched Jane's face in return. "Will you dance with me?"

Ella Fitzgerald was singing "Trav'lin' Light" and they wordlessly rose from the sofa, fingers intertwined.

Completely attuned to the music and each other, they joined in a full body embrace, Alex's arms encircling Jane's waist, Jane's arms curled lightly around Alex's neck. They swayed together against each other, like trees in a gentle breeze. They nuzzled one another's necks, ran fingers through hair, breathed in the scent of skin and hair and soap. There was no need to speak, only a yearning for their bodies to touch in time to the music. It felt magical.

Songs came and went—Diana Krall, Mel Torme, Michael Bublé—and still, they glided across the floor, circled together fluidly as though they'd danced together a hundred times before.

Alex's fingers began to delicately trace the outline of Jane's mouth, and Jane felt herself stumble a step. She quivered at Alex's touch.

"You have the sexiest mouth," Alex said, her breath ruffling Jane's hair. "You have the sexiest *everything*."

"Kiss me, Alex Warner."

Alex devoured her mouth, pushing hard against it, sucking on Jane's lips, nibbling them, licking them, then pressing hard again. Hands, big and strong and warm, began to glide up and down Jane's back, hovering over the lines of her bra. Jane felt her body slowly numbing, her legs weakening, her blood beginning to pump furiously. The tickling sensation began deep in her belly, then blossomed further south as she felt herself beginning to moisten the bright red silk panties she had picked out especially for tonight.

Her throat tightened and her voice came out raspy and halting. "Oh, Alex. I want to make love with you. Now. Please," she said, feeling she would burst if Alex's hands didn't soon find their way inside her wool slacks. *God, why did I choose pants! I should have worn a skirt to save some precious seconds.*

"I thought you'd never ask." Alex's voice was thick and warm, like honey. "Here?"

Jane shook her head, weak and distracted. Her voice came out thin, reedy. "No. In case some of the agents are patrolling out by the windows."

Alex wrenched herself away from Jane, looking determined. "Wait for me upstairs. I'll take care of the fire and the candles and the music."

Alex could be very commanding, and Jane didn't need to be told twice. She took the stairs two at a time, stripped off her pants and blouse and left them in a heap on the bedroom floor. Fleetingly, she wondered whether she should run a bubble bath, but she was too turned on. The bath could wait. She lit a candle on the night stand, then climbed into the queen-sized bed. She'd left her bra and underwear on, deciding to let Alex have some fun removing them.

Faintly, she could hear Alex bustling around downstairs, then heard her bounding quickly up the stairs. Nervous thoughts edged into her mind, eclipsing her elation. She didn't want to disappoint Alex, especially after so much time apart. Jane wanted Alex to be satisfied. She didn't want her lack of skill to ruin an otherwise perfect evening. She wished for years of sexual experience to suddenly inspire her and spare her from the embarrassment of being an obvious novice with a woman.

Alex appeared, slightly breathless and rosy faced, and leaned lazily against the door frame. Her arms were crossed in a display of casual confidence, but she was grinning slyly, as though Jane were her cornered prey. You're mine, her look said—mine to do what I want with.

Jane was envious of Alex's self-assuredness. She forced herself to smile, told herself to breathe calmly and felt the nervous flutters in her stomach slowly subside.

Alex finally slipped into the room, never taking her eyes off Jane. She methodically unzipped her jeans and pulled them down over her form-fitting boxer shorts, then stepped out of them. She was brisk and nimble, but not too hasty to undress. Jane gasped in appreciation at the thick, ropey muscles of Alex's legs. Then again as Alex pulled her shirt over her head, revealing a plain white tank top that starkly showed off muscled shoulders and well-defined biceps and triceps. Jane held Alex's unblinking stare, as if to signal her readiness for more, and Alex stripped completely.

"Oh, Alex. You are so beautiful." And she was. All muscle and softness at the same time—lines and curves juxtaposed perfectly. Jane ached inside at the knowledge that Alex would soon be touching her, kissing her, doing those exquisite things to her body that she remembered so vividly from last summer. She could feel the moisture of her arousal spreading between her legs, her blood pounding out a new beat of desire. It was almost too much.

Silently, Alex pulled back the sheet and gently lay on top of Jane, her strong arms holding most of her weight back. Both moaned softly as their bodies came into contact. With one hand, Alex touched Jane's hair, then her face, and smiled into her eyes.

"Have I told you lately how much I love you?" Alex said.

"No," Jane murmured, then thrust her jaw forward to capture Alex's lips in a bold, fiery kiss. She felt her body stirring beneath Alex as the kiss went on. She couldn't stop the tiny pelvic thrusts that reached up to her lover of their own accord, seeking friction and release, silk against skin.

Alex's warm, wet mouth had migrated to the hollow of Jane's throat, and Jane wanted to scream out at the scorching sensation against her hot, sensitive skin. Hands cupped her breasts through the lacy bra, and she felt Alex's breath quicken against her.

"You don't know how many times since last summer I've thought about doing this," Alex said huskily. "I've remembered everything about your body—how you taste, how soft your skin feels, how you quiver when I touch you."

Jane still could not quite believe they were finally alone and about to make love. It would be the first, true consummating of their love for one another, and the thought excited her beyond reason. "Oh, God, Alex. I've thought about making love with you about a million times. I think I'm going to come the second you touch me there."

Alex's laugh was a low rumble. "Oh, no you don't. You're not going to cheat me out of this."

Jane swallowed thickly, pushed harder against Alex. "I just— I'm so turned on, Alex. Oh, God. I need you to make me come."

Alex snickered, slowly working her fingers just inside Jane's bra. "Oh, you'll come all right. You're going to be coming all night long, my dear."

Jane groaned loudly, squeezed her eyes shut as the throbbing in her center grew more persistent, painful even. Fingers circled around her nipples, eliciting a cry from deep in her throat. She felt herself stiffen at Alex's light caresses, and again at the feel of Alex's tongue on her sensitive flesh, the bra pushed aside. Fingers danced and stroked, teasing her nipples to a painful sharpness. Alex coaxed a breast almost entirely into her mouth and suckled it expertly. A free hand roamed lightly along Jane's stomach, which quivered at the touch, and she wished for Alex's hand to continue its journey south, and quickly. Release was her urgent goal now, and it beckoned like a distant train thundering closer and closer.

Jane's breathing had accelerated along with her pounding heartbeat. With every cell, her body screamed out for the stimulation she needed to climax. As if sensing her growing impatience, Alex's fingers played at the waistband of the skimpy, silk panties, and Jane thrust herself up against the touch. She certainly wasn't any good at playing coy. She knew exactly what she wanted Alex to do.

"Please," Jane whimpered urgently, nearly begging. "Touch me, Alex. I'm going to die if you don't." She had thought how romantic it would be to take their time delighting in each other's bodies, but now that the moment was here, Jane couldn't wait. She was greedy for Alex's proficient hands, for the magnificent things she could do with her mouth.

Alex's hand mercifully dipped beneath the thin material of her skimpy underwear, gliding quickly and lightly over Jane's hard, pulsing clitoris. Jane's thrusting pelvis tried to trap the roaming fingers, but to no avail. Finally, Alex's palm settled over her, cupping her, letting Jane thrust hard against it.

"You feel so good," Alex said, her mouth finding Jane's stomach, her tongue drawing tight circles on her skin. "I want you to wait until I can taste you."

Jane moaned loudly and thrashed her head from side to side. "I don't know if I can—"Her words died in the air as Alex roughly pulled the panties aside, nearly tearing them in her haste, and greedily took Jane in her mouth. Jane cried out sharply, the pleasure so acute and swift, and Alex moaned too. Jane felt as though her body were floating as Alex expertly stimulated her with brisk, flicking strokes that brought her to a throbbing rigidity. Jane selfishly pushed herself into Alex, enveloping her tongue and swallowing it up inside of her, smearing Alex's face with her hot, slick desire. She rode Alex enthusiastically and unapologetically, taking all she needed, moaning encouragement for Alex to push herself further and harder and faster into her. Alex's fingers stroked her clitoris in time with the thrusts and Jane felt her orgasm root itself in her legs. She wanted to enjoy Alex's oral ministrations much longer—oh, God, did she ever. But release crept closer and closer, working its way up her tingling body.

Vaguely, Jane wondered why she had taken no for an answer at dawn this morning, when they'd shared the same bed and some sexless affection. Oh, yes. No matter what Alex said, she should have just pulled up that nightshirt, climbed on top of Alex and straddled her face with abandon. The vision of herself riding Alex that way pushed her over the edge. Orgasm charitably claimed her, rocking her body with wave after powerful wave of pleasure.

She screamed her release, squeezing herself against Alex, letting her ravenously consume the remainder of her desire. But Alex was not stopping. Her mouth and tongue smothered Jane with a new round of enthusiasm.

Jane propped herself up on her elbows, marveling at the sight of her Alex between her legs, pleasuring her with an insatiable energy that seemed boundless. Jane was helpless as a new surge of longing rose in her like a geyser, shockingly fierce and powerful. It was uncontrollable. Her arousal owned her. She could not stop it if she wanted to. And . . . *oh, God* . . . she did not want to stop. Alex was flicking her tongue lightning quick over her center, and she was blinded by the voracious rapture that crested and finally spilled through her like hot lava. Her chest heaved and her strangled voice cried out, weaker this time, and she felt more spent and fulfilled than she'd ever felt before.

"Oh, God, Alex. My love."

Alex crawled fully onto her this time, letting Jane rock slowly against her in the last quiet thrusts of orgasm. She covered Jane with little kisses that were meant to convey her love rather than elicit another round of desire.

"My darling, you were wonderful," Alex said. "You are so responsive, so . . . God!" Alex's eyes took on a warm glow in the flickering candlelight. "You are the sexiest woman I've ever known." She kissed Jane endearingly, almost reverently. She smiled playfully. "And a woman like you needs to be well-sexed."

Jane chuckled, feeling both deliciously evil and deliriously happy. "How will I ever get any work done if—"

"If I'm fucking you five times a day?"

"Exactly." Jane laughed again, wishing they could stay in bed forever with not a single obligation, other than to pleasure one another and bask in their love. The timing of their togetherness wasn't great, Jane knew, and the thought of how busy she would be over the coming weeks already made her feel guilty. There was more staff to hire, four years worth of policy to review, endless meetings with Collins and his staff to map out their direction, the inauguration . . .

"What are you thinking about?" Alex's fingers softly caressed Jane's cheek.

Jane closed her eyes for a moment to jettison thoughts of work. "Nothing and everything." When she looked at Alex, she felt the beginning of tears. She knew Alex had not missed a thing.

"Are you sad?" Alex asked worriedly.

Jane kissed the lips hovering so closely over hers. "I'm stupidly happy."

"But you look a little sad. Have I—"

"Oh, Alex. You are nothing but wonderful." Jane wrapped her arms around her in a bear hug, squeezing tightly the muscles in Alex's back. "The only thing that makes me sad is that we're not going to have hours every day to spend like this."

Alex scrutinized Jane, looking tender and wistful. Her hand casually caressed the hair away from Jane's face. "Then we'll just have to make the most of our moments together, won't we?"

Jane's spirits began to soar again. "Are you sure they'll be enough?"

Alex grinned cockily. "I'm pretty sure I just need about five minutes to rock your world."

Jane pinched her teasingly. "You *always* rock my world. Just don't get into the habit of rush jobs."

Alex deftly rolled them over so that Jane was on top, and she smiled up at her. "I wouldn't dream of it." She gently tugged at Jane's bottom lip with her teeth, pulling Jane closer, kissing her with increasing fervor. Alex's hands had crept between their bodies to cup Jane's breasts.

"Alex," Jane said tensely between kisses. "I'm afraid."

Alex's roaming hands and demanding lips halted. "What are you afraid of, honey?"

Jane felt the heat of embarrassment rush up her neck. She tried to smile reassuringly, but the attempt dissolved into a grimace. "I'm not sure I'll . . ." She was so afraid of this moment of truth, that Alex would discover she was a lousy lover, a fraud, and that the wait had been anything but worth it. She didn't like this feeling of ineptness. It was so incredibly foreign to her. "I don't know if I'll be able to make you, you know, come."

Alex buried her face in the pillow and laughed into it, her whole body shaking. She could not seem to stop and it stunned Jane, who didn't think it was funny at all.

Perturbed, Jane took a deep breath, Alex's laughter showing no signs of diminishing. "I expected my confession to horrify you, not amuse you."

Alex finally stilled her laughter, though her body still spasmed a little. She looked at Jane, her eyes moist and still dancing mischievously. "Honey." She took a deep breath to collect herself. "I can assure you, you won't have any trouble making me come."

Jane moved to straddle Alex. She was starting to feel a little roguish and a grin surfaced. "How can you be so sure?"

Alex's eyes, unblinking, had grown serious. Arousal was coloring her cheeks; her chest rose and fell a little faster. "I just . . . have a feeling. But we'll never know for sure until we try."

Jane began to grind into Alex in a circular motion, letting her breasts sway in rhythm with her hips, and she delighted in watching Alex's eyes follow them intently. Her nipples hardened at the eagerness there and at her lover's accelerated breathing. Alex began to answer Jane's movements with tiny thrusts that grew faster and deeper and more insistent. Together they were thrusting and grinding, their bodies pushing and pulling, giving and taking, their timing perfectly matched in an intimate pelvic dance, the wetness of their mutual desire slicking them both.

Alex moaned softly. Warm fingers reached up and lightly traced the hardness of Jane's achingly taut nipples. Jane answered with her own quiet moans, desire shooting scalding flames up her legs and into her hot center. Just seconds ago, she had been marveling at her raw, sexual power over Alex, but now she, too, was again helpless against that urgent, uncontrollable wanting. It began to consume them both, like an oxygen-fed, raging fire. Immersed in satiating their own, painfully advancing need for release, their friction escalated until orgasm irrevocably freed them. With a final thrust, Jane collapsed into her and they trembled in one another's arms, both savoring the dying embers of their excitement.

"See," Alex said between breaths. "I told you, you wouldn't have any trouble making me come."

Jane smiled and was grateful her momentary sexual shyness had evaporated so quickly. She was grateful for other things, too. "I think that's a new record, you stud, you."

"What?" Alex asked innocently.

"Three orgasms in twenty minutes." Jane grinned, then showed her appreciation with a quick kiss. "I've never known such pleasure before."

"Maybe we can go for four in twenty-two minutes. What do you say?"

"Oh, no. Not until you catch up to me." Jane eagerly kissed Alex, anxious to explore her lover's body with her hands, and especially her mouth.

"Whoa," Alex said, pulling Jane into an embrace. "We've got all night for that, darling."

"Yeah. We do." Jane snuggled in closer, exhaustion suddenly overcoming her. This time she welcomed it and was fast asleep within seconds.

Chapter 16

Guiltily, Alex took another sip of brandy. She knew she'd pay for it later with a pounding head, thanks to the remnants of her concussion. But she needed the alcohol's soothing effects— needed it to help drown out the noise inside the Kincaid house, now full of people, each one monopolizing her. She also needed the alcohol to help flatten the landscape of her thoughts, which dipped and peaked with the sheer magnitude and awe of what her—and Jane's—life would be like from now on.

Jane Kincaid was the vice president-elect. It was an incredible thought that made Alex's chest swell with pride. She was so happy and excited for Jane. She wanted her to have everything she wanted—that was without question. But as much as she wanted her lover to be happy, that same all-encompassing love also meant Alex wanted Jane to herself. Just the two of them, enshrouded in their own blissful world. *I found her, I made her fall in love with me, she's mine.* It was selfish, Alex knew. Selfish to wish for a mundane life for them, to want to cleave to Jane, to want to shut everything and everyone else out. Even just for a little while.

Fleetingly, Alex couldn't help but fantasize about a romantic, banal life together—cooking dinner together, planting flowers in their backyard, reading quietly by the fire, making love every night . . . maybe even talk of raising a family some day. *Yeah, wouldn't that be something?* There were so many things Alex wanted to do with Jane—things so dull and mundane compared with their life now. But it was useless. This was Jane's time. Jane was at her best and her brightest. The president needed her. The country needed her, and she was far too talented and ambitious to waste it on a life of playing house with Alex. No. The woman Alex had fallen in love with was capable of conquering the world.

Alex allowed her own private war to rage on. She blinked slowly from her corner of the living room and swallowed another mouthful of brandy, hazily recounting Jack Wilson's efficient and unemotional advice to her just moments earlier. Jane's chief of staff had bluntly told her that the vice president would have to work long hours and that there would be days, even weeks, where they wouldn't see each other. Jane would be appointed to several committees, would have to preside over the Senate at times, would be required to represent the administration on many occasions, both at home and abroad. Jane would not do well to be encumbered by a demanding relationship. She would need Alex's strength and understanding, and could not afford to take on Alex's problems or weaknesses. Jane *must* be unencumbered at home, he warned Alex in his unequivocal, no-nonsense way. Happy and unencumbered, Alex repeated in her mind, like remembering a shopping list. If Jane were unhappy, it would negatively affect her performance, Jack said. And if she were to take her political career one step further someday, then her performance meant everything.

Alex felt solemn and a little adrift. If she were to be nothing more than a favorite little teddy bear of Jane's to stay on its shelf until it was playtime, well, she didn't know if she could do that. Surely Jane wouldn't want her to—

"Hello, Alex." Clara Stevens smiled carefully at Alex, her eyes quietly probing hers.

"Hello," Alex responded without much enthusiasm. She didn't know Clara very well, though Jane certainly had the utmost respect and affection for her. Alex knew she was not being particularly welcoming to a woman who was both a friend and colleague of Jane's, but she was not in the mood for another lecture—well-intentioned or not.

"Come for a walk with me." Clara's voice was light and assured. She slipped her arm tightly through Alex's with the confidence that her wish would not be denied.

They picked their way around small clusters of people, some in loud, alcohol-fueled conversations, others in hushed tones as they plotted the future. Clara led them to the small, heated sunroom at the back of the house, where tall glass windows adorned with plants allowed them a view of the distant lake that was vast and gray under the matching November skies. They sat down on facing rattan chairs.

"I saw Jack Wilson talking to you earlier." Clara smiled empathetically. "Let me guess. He was warning you not to be a pain in the ass. To be the perfect wife. To keep everything smooth at home while staying out of the way."

Alex nodded soberly, still clutching the drink in her hand like a lifeline. "Something like that."

"And how does that sit with you?"

Alex bristled a little at the woman's directness. She didn't owe this stranger her deepest thoughts and feelings, nor did she feel like another round of expert advice, no matter how sweetly it came out. She shrugged noncommittally. "It's to be expected, I guess."

Clara looked at her quizzically. "Funny, I hadn't taken you for a pushover."

Alex's annoyance amplified. "Pardon me?"

"You're not just going to take that, are you?"

Alex was perplexed. Her jaw tightened as she thought how to answer. "I'm not sure I understand."

Clara laughed a little, rolling her eyes, then leaned forward and clasped Alex's free hand in both of hers. "Listen, child. I like you. I don't know you very well, but I like you."

Alex remained guarded, her hand stiff and cool in Clara's.

Clara's smile broadened. Her eyes twinkled. "I know Jane wouldn't have fallen in love with you if you weren't a real treasure. She's a good woman. And she's very smart. She would not for one minute throw her love away on someone undeserving."

Alex suddenly felt her body flag in relief, like a bent twig snapping back to its rightful, reposing position. *Thank you, Lord. Someone finally remembered that I love Jane.* Clara's words were like a gift, and Alex accepted them with appreciation. She smiled and felt suddenly giddy. "I love Jane very much. I would do anything for her."

"Including fading into the wallpaper?"

Alex's smile quickly dissolved. The woman was nothing if not direct. "What exactly are you saying?"

Clara's hands were very warm and reassuring, and her touch softened her frankness. "Look, child. It's true Jane needs your support more than anyone else's over the next four years. It means you need to listen to her, and be there for her, but it also means you must speak your mind. Your support for her must not come at the expense of your own sense of purpose. Do you understand?"

Alex still felt slightly disoriented, her confidence shaky. She eagerly accepted the lifeline Clara seemed to be throwing her. "I think so."

"A strong woman needs another strong woman . . . and not behind her, but beside her, Alex. Jane needs a partner. Not a child.

Not an escort. Not a fan. And not just a friend. Jane needs the woman she fell in love with." Clara squeezed Alex's hand tighter. "Love her with everything you have. And forgive her for not giving as much back to you right now as you will be giving to her."

Alex nodded slowly, Clara's words like an epiphany. Yes, she told herself resolutely. She could do this. "Well, that's the best advice I've heard in a long time."

Clara winked again, followed by a slow grin. "Don't forget to give Jane a kick in the ass when she needs it. And give her some good old-fashioned lovin' when she needs that, too."

Alex grinned back, remembering last night's hours of fabulous lovemaking. They'd slept in between, resuming their lusty activity first thing in the morning. They had not wanted to get out of bed, had not wanted to stop touching each other. "That part won't be a problem."

Clara laughed. "I didn't think so."

"Aha. There you are, my love." A petite, middle-aged blond woman swept in and stood behind Clara, her hand resting possessively on her shoulder. She leaned down for a quick kiss, and Alex smiled, pleased that Clara was a dyke—that she knew exactly what she and Jane were going through. There was no question she would be their loyal ally.

"Hi. I'm Sophie." The woman reached a hand out to shake Alex's, her smile warm, her touch an unpretentious invitation to friendship. There was a spark in her kind, blue eyes when she needlessly added, "I'm Clara's other half. And you must be Jane's?"

Alex nodded, pleased and proud. "I am."

Sophie squeezed in beside her lover. "She's a handsome devil," she whispered animatedly to Clara, as though Alex were not even there.

"Yes. And smart, too," Clara replied. "And totally in love with our new vice president."

They both turned boldly appraising gazes to Alex.

"Jane could do a lot worse," Sophie acknowledged with a slow nod, then broke into a grin. "You don't mind us giving you the once-over, do you?"

Alex laughed good-naturedly. "Good practice, I'm betting."

Sophie nodded enthusiastically. "Oh, yeah. You haven't seen anything yet, woman. You'll be on the lips of every political wag and every gossiping old hag in Washington for . . . oh, at least three months."

"Great." Alex sighed. "I can hardly wait for my fifteen minutes."

Clara chuckled. "Don't worry. They'll get bored with you soon enough."

"Just ride it out," Sophie advised. "We've all had to do that at one time or another."

"I'll remember that," Alex said dryly, finding solace in her brandy again.

"You'll be fine, child," Clara said. "Just remember what I told you."

"I certainly will. Thank you very much."

Sophie glanced sidelong at her lover. "Just what sage advice were you imparting, my dear?"

Clara laughed. "Why, the secret to keeping your woman happy, of course."

"Ahh." Sophie looked knowingly at Alex and smiled. "Well, Clara *is* an expert at that."

The couple kissed, and Alex immediately felt Jane's absence. She had long ago been swallowed up by the throng of family, friends and colleagues, and while Alex knew she must get used to this instant loneliness, for now she welcomed a little self pity.

"So, Alex," Sophie said. "With Jane off helping to save the world, what are you going to do?"

The question might have been unkind, coming from a stranger bent on judging her, but Alex felt only a sense of relief at the honesty of the question. Since she and Jane had announced their relationship to the world, no one had asked Alex about her future plans, and it annoyed her. Did they think it didn't matter to her, now that she'd caught the most eligible woman in the world? Was that to be her life's crowning moment, "capturing" Jane? Becoming her "wife"? Was she to melt into the background, except to be trotted out on Jane's arm now and again?

Alex shook her head and felt the gathering of tears just beneath the surface. She hadn't even discussed her future yet with Jane. There hadn't really been time, and with the car crash so fresh, Alex feared Jane's reaction. But she was clear in what she wanted. She wanted to go back to work.

Alex blinked to clear her eyes. She didn't want to be rude, but she didn't want to talk about her plans with strangers just now.

"Now, dear," Clara gently prodded. "Always getting straight to the point, hmm? Alex has had a lot to digest over the last couple of weeks. Perhaps her plans are the furthest thing from her mind right now."

Alex cleared her throat. "Actually, I just haven't had a chance to talk to Jane yet."

"Did I just hear my name?"

Jane entered the room and Alex's heart skipped a beat, as it always did, at the sight of her.

Alex beamed as Jane approached. Setting her drink down, she reached out for her hand and was pleasantly surprised when Jane threw her arms around her neck and flung herself on Alex's lap.

"Well," Alex gushed. "Hello."

"Hi," Jane answered breathily. She pressed her lips to Alex's and kissed her hard, her mouth pushing greedily against Alex's, before she softened the kiss. The tip of her tongue flicked against Alex's lips and she kissed her again before pulling back.

"Woo-eee!" Clara and Sophie chimed together.

"That's some kiss," Sophie added admiringly.

Jane smiled at Alex, her eyes smoldering with unspent desire. "I miss you, honey." She touched her forehead to Alex's.

"I'm right here," Alex replied softly.

"I know. But I *miss* you when it's not just you and me."

Alex chuckled. Her hand moved to Jane's knee, then her thigh, and began caressing in small, soft circles. "How quickly can we get rid of everyone?"

Jane flashed an evil smile. "In a flash. I'm the vice president-elect, remember?"

Clara and Sophie stood up.

"Guess that's our cue," Sophie mumbled good-naturedly.

"C'mon, darling," Clara said. "It's a little hot in here, don't you think?"

Sophie took Clara's hand and began leading her out of the room. "Let's find a little corner somewhere and create our own heat."

The couple melted away and Jane, whose eyes hadn't left Alex's, kissed her gently.

"Are you okay, Alex?"

"Yeah." Alex nodded. "Especially now that you're here."

"I'm sorry I'm not always *here* when I'm here, you know?"

Alex nodded again. "It's all right, Jane. Honest. I'm not a child. And I'm not a needy, insecure lover."

"I know that. But all couples need time together. Even if it's just a few moments here and there in a busy day."

Alex smiled lustily. "And then there's always bedtime."

Jane threw her head back and laughed, her throat never looking more luscious and inviting than it did now. Alex planted a lingering kiss on the soft flesh near Jane's collarbone and felt her give a little shiver of enjoyment.

"Mmmm," Jane answered. "Yes. There's definitely always bedtime."

Alex began gently nibbling her earlobe. Her breath ruffled Jane's silky hair. "I want us to go to bed together every night."

Jane sighed heavily. "God. I want that too, Alex. More than anything. But there'll be times when I'm away, and—"

"I know, sweetheart. I want to be with you. Even during those times you're away."

"But—"

Alex's fingers stilled Jane's lips. "Do you want me with you, Jane?" Alex searched for any signs of hesitation or rejection in Jane's expression and saw none. "Be honest with me."

Jane's smile was reassuring. "I will always be honest with you, Alex. And yes, I want you with me. You're my rock, my inspiration. My *love*. I will not lose you, Alex. Not for anything."

Alex hesitated, then squeezed Jane a little tighter to prepare her for what she was about to say. "I want to be your protector again."

Jane's eyebrows quirked in confusion, but she said nothing.

"Honey. I want to be with you as your lover, your partner. But I also want to be on your security detail."

Jane's mouth opened and her chin began to quiver a little. Her eyes darkened ominously. "Alex, please." Her voice was raw with emotion. "When I first heard you were in that car crash, I . . ." She closed her eyes tightly, her forehead creased with worry.

"It's okay, honey. *I'm* okay."

"I know. But I can't go through that again. I can't stand the thought of you getting hurt."

Alex drew a deep, steadying breath and thought quickly of how she could persuade Jane. "And I can't go through the next four years having you gone half the time, and not knowing how you are, and what you're doing, and whether you're safe. *I'm* in the best position to keep you safe, Jane. I really believe that."

For a long moment, Jane was silent, pensive, her face devoid of emotion as she thought. When she finally spoke, her voice was even and matter-of-fact. "There's only one condition for me to accept that."

Alex looked eagerly at her, both excited and fearful.

"I want us to be able to keep each other safe, Alex. And that means we work as a team. Side by side. And no secrets."

Alex smiled in spite of herself, thrilled by Jane's answer. "Secrets? I wouldn't keep secrets from you, darlin'."

But Jane wasn't smiling. "I mean it. Any threats or safety concerns you have, I need to know about them, too. And then we decide what to do as a team."

Alex bit back her sarcasm. "You're right, Jane. We'll work together . . . if it's not too much togetherness for you."

Jane smiled. "There's no such thing, from my point of view." She sighed heavily, her eyes taking full stock of Alex. "I don't want to lose you, Alex. And the best way of ensuring that is to keep you next to me."

Alex laughed. "I feel the same way about you. Why do you think I suggested it?"

Concern etched its way onto Jane's forehead again. "When will you be ready for work?"

"Hopefully by the inauguration."

"No. I want you by my side at the inauguration. As my partner."

"All right. How about the day after the inauguration."

Jane looked contemplative. "It'll take some hoops to jump through, you know. To get you on my detail when we've told the world that you're my girlfriend."

Alex kissed Jane tenderly on the lips, then the forehead, wanting to smooth out those frown lines. "I know you can do anything you set your mind to."

Jane laughed. "You're pretty sure of that, aren't you?"

"Of course. What do you think made me fall in love with you?"

Jane gasped teasingly. "I thought it was my big brown eyes."

Alex laughed and kissed Jane again. "That, too. And your smile. And your sexy ass. And your soft lips, and your superb tits, and your delicious—"

"All right, all right. I get the picture." Jane playfully slapped Alex on the shoulder. "God, Alex. I love you so much."

"And I love you, Madam Vice President."

WHISKEY AND OAK LEAVES by Jaime Clevenger. Meg meets June, a single woman running a horse ranch in the California Sierra foothills. The two become quick friends and it isn't long before Meg is looking for more than just a friendship. But June has no interest in developing a deeper relationship with Meg. She is, after all, not the least bit interested in women . . . or is she? Neither of these two women is prepared for what lies ahead . . .   978-1-59493-093-5 $13.95

SUMTER POINT by KG MacGregor. As Audie surrenders her heart to Beth, she begins to distance herself from the reckless habits of her youth. Just as they're ready to meet in the middle, their future is thrown into doubt by a duty Beth can't ignore. It all comes to a head on the river at Sumter Point.   978-1-59493-089-8 $13.95

THE TARGET by Gerri Hill. Sara Michaels is the daughter of a prominent senator who has been receiving death threats against his family. In an effort to protect Sara, the FBI recruits homicide detective Jaime Hutchinson to secretly provide the protection they are so certain Sara will need. Will Sara finally figure out who is behind the death threats? And will Jaime realize the truth—and be able to save Sara before it's too late?
978-1-59493-082-9 $13.95

REALITY BYTES by Jane Frances. In this sequel to *Reunion*, follow the lives of four friends in a romantic tale that spans the globe and proves that you can cross the whole of cyberspace only to find love a few suburbs away . . .   978-1-59493-079-9 $13.95

MURDER CAME SECOND by Jessica Thomas. Broadway's bad-boy genius, Paul Carlucci, has chosen *Hamlet* for his latest production and, to the delight of some and despair of others, he has selected Provincetown's amphitheatre for his opening gala. But Alex Peres realizes the wrong people are falling down, and the moaning is all too realistic. Someone must not be shooting blanks . . .   978-1-59493-081-2 $13.95

SKIN DEEP by Kenna White. Jordan Griffin has been given a new assignment: Track down and interview one-time nationally renowned broadcast journalist Reece McAllister. Much to her surprise, Jordan comes away with far more than just a story . . .
978-1-59493-78-2 $13.95

FINDERS KEEPERS by Karin Kallmaker. *Finders Keepers*, the quest for the perfect mate in the 21st century, joins Karin Kallmaker's *Just Like That* and her other incomparable novels about lesbian love, lust and laughter.   1-59493-072-4 $13.95

OUT OF THE FIRE by Beth Moore. Author Ann Covington feels at the top of the world when told her book is being made into a movie. Then in walks Casey Duncan the actress who is playing the lead in her movie. Will Casey turn Ann's world upside down?
1-59493-088-0 $13.95

STAKE THROUGH THE HEART: NEW EXPLOITS OF TWILIGHT LESBIANS by Karin Kallmaker, Julia Watts, Barbara Johnson and Therese Szymanski. The playful quartet that penned the acclaimed *Once Upon A Dyke* are dimming the lights for journeys into worlds of breathless seduction.   1-59493-071-6 $15.95

THE HOUSE ON SANDSTONE by KG MacGregor. Carly Griffin returns home to Leland and finds that her old high school friend Justine is awakening more than just old memories.   1-59493-076-7 $13.95

WILD NIGHTS: MOSTLY TRUE STORIES OF WOMEN LOVING WOMEN edited by Therese Szymanski. 264 pp. 23 new stories from today's hottest erotic writers are sure to give you your wildest night ever!   1-59493-069-4 $15.95